THE DOOR TO
BITTERNESS

By the author

Jade Lady Burning
Slicky Boys
Buddha's Money

THE DOOR TO
BITTERNESS

MARTIN LIMÓN

[signature] 9/10/05

SOHO

Published by
Soho Press, Inc.
853 Broadway
New York, NY 10003

Library of Congress Cataloging-in-Publication Data
Limón, Martin, 1948–
The door to bitterness : a novel / by Martin Limón.
p. cm.
ISBN-10: 1-56947-404-4
ISBN-13: 978-1-56947-404-4
1. United States. Army—Military police—Fiction.
2. Military police—Crimes against—Fiction.
3. Americans—Korea—Fiction. 4. Revenge—Fiction.
5. Korea—Fiction. I. Title.

PS3562.I465D66 2005
813'.54—dc22
2005049043

9 8 7 6 5 4 3 2 1

To my son, Aaron

苦生門이 열였다

"You have opened
the door to bitterness."

A KOREAN ADMONITION

1

I stood at the mouth of an alley that bled onto the main drag of Itaewon, the red light district of Seoul. Rows of unlit neon spread down the street, still shrouded in pre-dawn shadow. Acid boiled and bubbled against the lining of my stomach, and I felt the familiar nausea of hangover. All routine, even reassuring. Except for the knot on my head. I fingered it gently. About the size of a hand grenade.

My name is George Sueño. I'm an agent for the 8th United States Army Criminal Investigation Division in Seoul, Republic of Korea. Two minutes ago, I'd awoken face down on the pavement.

After struggling to my feet, I tried to figure out what had happened.

I felt my throbbing head, and my hand came away smeared with blood. Thick and purple. My limbs and fingers were all there. It was early September, 1973. I was in a dark alley. Hundreds of empty brown beer bottles in wooden crates, stacked to the height of a man, clinked softly in the early morning breeze.

How did I get here?

The cold breath of autumn bit into my lungs. It was then I sensed the odd lightness, and the glowering sky sucked the breath out of me.

My .45.

The army-issue pistol I'd been carrying last night. Where was it?

Frantically, I probed beneath my coat and jabbed my fingers into the loose leather of my shoulder holster. Empty. I pulled the inside pocket. Also empty. As empty as a GI's heart.

Weapon, badge, wallet. Gone!

A cold anguish lumped in the pit of my stomach. Losing my .45 and my badge, according to the Uniform Code of Military Justice, was a court-martial offense. Korea has total gun control. Only the military and law enforcement are allowed to carry firearms. If the Korean government took gun control seriously, 8th Army took it even more so.

I searched the alley, peering through the dim light, stopping occasionally to toss garbage out of dented cans. In seconds, piles of filth lay on the ground: broken earthenware jars, smeared with the red juice of fermented cabbage—*kimchee* reeked. Wadded tissue, clumps of toilet paper, smashed green pop bottles, crushed tins that once contained mackerel pickling in brine. The entire mess emitted a cloud of vile fumes. But no .45. And no badge of an agent of the 8th United States Army Criminal Investigation Division.

Whoever attacked me cleaned me out. My money, wallet, pistol, badge.

My head throbbed. I tried to concentrate, piecing together fragments. At first nothing came. Alcoholic blackout. Total. And then, without warning, memory flamed to life. A woman walking toward me. Tall. Statuesque. Winding her way through a crowded, smoke-filled nightclub. Staring right at me. Smiling.

* * *

It was already late, getting on toward the midnight curfew. Without bothering to ask permission, the smiling woman joined me at a small table shoved against the back wall of the King Club, a dive on the strip.

I had decided to sit at a table alone. All the shouting and drinking and smoking along the bar were too much for me. Staff Sergeant Riley and Ernie Bascom, and a couple of the other guys who worked at 8th Army's Criminal Investigation Division, were hollering and hooting for the stripper to perform another number.

A brown bottle of OB Beer sat in front of me, I remember that. And when the smiling woman sat down, I sipped on the beer and it tasted warm. The pungent, grainy flavor of hops and barley and roasted malt rose like a storm cloud through the passages of my nose.

Her face was interesting. The type that puzzles you, trying to figure it out. I took another glance, unable to escape the tired American habit of classifying everyone by race. She was smiling. A girl in a toothpaste commercial. Maybe I was too drunk, but I had yet to figure out which ethnic group she might belong to when she started talking.

"*Byong andei*," she said in Korean, pointing a polished nail at my beer. Bottle no good. "*Kopum i nomu mana.*" Too many bubbles.

Then she raised her narrow shoulders, grabbed her stomach, puffed out her soft cheeks, and mimicked a man trying to burp. It made me laugh. When I did, her eyes brightened and she ran off to the bar. Seconds later, she returned with a clean glass with a red logo pasted on the side: OB on a shield, Oriental Brewery. She pried the bottle from my fingers, lifted it in the air with both hands, and ceremoniously poured the frothing hops into the glass. She was expert. The golden brew formed a perfect cylinder of yellow beneath a white cloud of carbonation that bubbled up to the edge. With two hands, she pushed the glass of beer directly in front of me.

"*Dub-seiyo*," she said. Please partake.

I sipped, allowing a little of the foam to settle on my upper lip. I nodded approval.

"Better," I said.

She stared, still smiling, waiting for me to talk. I didn't. I just studied her. She kept smiling. Gradually, it dawned on my booze-flushed brain that she must be half *Miguk*. The offspring of an American GI and a Korean woman. I figured her to be nineteen at the youngest, twenty-three at the outside.

Twenty years ago, during the Korean War, the Korean Peninsula was crawling with Americans and other foreigners. All under the flag of the United Nations, fighting the communist North Koreans and the Red Chinese Army. Tens of thousands of half-Korean babies had been the predictable by-product. Most were adopted by couples overseas. But some Korean mothers, no matter what the circumstances of their children's birth, couldn't give up their own flesh and blood. Despite poverty, and the scorn heaped on them by Korean society, they kept their children.

Now, two decades later, those kids were adults. Most lived at the lowest levels. The boys as common laborers, the girls often as prostitutes. Even occupations such as cab driver or waitress were too exalted for a half-caste. People thought them unclean. Most Koreans saw them as reminders of the shame and abuse that they'd all suffered during the war.

This smiling woman had grown up tough. There were three faded scars on the side of her head, one next to the ear, another on her chin. Not surprising with a GI for a father who'd probably abandoned her at birth. He might not even know she existed; or worse, didn't care.

Her smile was a wide-open smile. Too broad. The lips too wide, the eyes open almost beyond endurance. It was a practiced smile. A smile that was born not of friendship but of fear. It was a smile that said, I'll do anything you want me to do. Just tell me what you want, but please don't hurt me.

Actually, the more I studied her, the more she repelled me.

It's not that she wasn't attractive. She was very attractive. With soft, light brown, almost blonde hair brushed to one side that fell to her shoulders, and broad, even features. Smooth cheeks and a rounded nose. But the best part about her, the most memorable part, were her eyes. They were startling. Bright blue in a creamy smooth Asian face. She was attractive, all right. But what repelled me was the madness in her forced smile, the madness in her eyes. The history they exposed. The willingness to please. The willingness to do anything for a man with money and power. All engendered by a history of abuse. Abuse that I guessed had lasted for years.

She seemed slightly upset by my gaze, but handled it. She fidgeted, almost imperceptibly, in her chair. Her smile grew broader.

"You like?" she asked.

Like what, she didn't say. But I knew what she meant. Do you like me or anything about me? The question left it all open and the meaning was clear. If you want me, any part of me, it's yours.

The stripper returned to the stage amidst a chorus of hoots and jeers from the drunken CID agents at the bar. Somebody cranked up the volume on the jukebox and somebody else dimmed the lights, and suddenly I felt queasy from all the booze. Without answering her question, I rapped my knuckles on the table, stood up, and staggered toward the *byonso*, the King Club's co-educational bathroom.

When I returned, the smiling woman was still waiting. Sitting at my table, staring at the flat glass of beer in the center of our round table. As I took my seat, she tilted the smooth flesh of her face toward me and her smile was broader, and madder, than ever.

Looking back, I realize that, while I was in the latrine, she'd done what she'd come to do.

As I sipped on the drink, not noticing its altered taste, I thought about her naked. Instead of thinking about how she'd been abandoned by her father and the hunger she must've suffered during the cruel years after the devastation of the Korean War and how her psyche must've been distorted by so much hardship and how I didn't want to contribute further to her debasement, I thought instead of the smooth flesh of her long legs. It didn't take long for desire to make me ignore the essential depravity of taking advantage of a damaged woman, economically desperate. It made me think only of what I wanted. I wanted only her. The physical part of her. Nothing else.

I rose from the table, and when she took my hand I remember being startled at the roughness of her palm. Together we walked outside, through the big double doors of the King Club, out into the cold Korean night.

Despite the blustery wind that enveloped us, I felt warm. Cozy. Close to her. And despite what was about to happen, I think, in my inebriated state I was at that moment happy to be with the smiling woman. Not proud of myself. But happy.

After searching in vain for my .45 and my badge, I gave up and left the dark alley, returning to the main drag. The rows of unlit neon signs still hung listlessly over the barred and shuttered doors of the joints that, by night, teemed with American GIs, optimistic young men on the prowl for new and innovative ways to waste their money.

The dark, early morning street was empty. The King Club, the Seven Club, the Lucky Lady Club, were all closed. Locked. No movement. A lone GI appeared from a narrow alley. He marched bravely to the bottom of the hill, turned left at the

MSR—the Main Supply Route—and began his slow trudge back to 8th Army's Yongsan Compound. About a mile. Most units hold their first morning formation at zero six thirty. I didn't have a watch but I figured it must be past five.

The woman and I had walked down the main drag together. I remember a few glimpses of flashing light, out-of-tune rock bands. I remember staggering, her clutching my waist, shoving her shoulder into me, holding me up. Then darkness. Probably the alley.

If I'd just been drunk, no one would've attacked me. They wouldn't have had the nerve. I'm six-foot-four and in good shape. I know how to fight. If I'd been drunk, I would've heard footsteps behind me. I would've swiveled and faced my attackers and jabbed, or, given enough room, I would've hopped forward and side-kicked someone in the ribs. They wouldn't have taken me down easily. Probably not at all.

From behind me, something scurried. Footsteps? Even then, in my almost comatose state, I tried to turn. I tried to raise my hands. Apparently, I hadn't been fast enough.

I remember the pain. The pain of a heavy clunk slamming into the top of my skull. I remember being upset by it. How had this happened? And then I remember nothing.

Who were these guys? Were they working with the smiling woman? If she'd drugged me, she had to be part of the plan. But why me? Why had they singled me out? Just blind luck, or had they targeted someone—someone alone—carrying a CID badge and a .45?

To have any chance of answering these questions—and to have any chance of recovering my badge and my .45—I had to talk face-to-face, once again, with the smiling woman. But after what she'd done last night, I could count on her to become scarce. To find her, I had first to talk to someone who'd been there in the King Club. Someone who might be able to help me

7

develop a lead. Ernie. He was the logical candidate. He and I had been partners for almost a year and a half. He might seem like a flake to most people—a guy who drinks too much and chases skirts too much—but Agent Ernie Bascom is a good cop. Fearless, first and foremost, and observant. Two excellent traits for someone in his profession. But where could I find him?

A cold autumn breeze blew out of Manchuria and whistled down the main drag of Itaewon. I stepped out onto the street, holding my coat wrapped tightly around my chest, trying now to think like Ernie. What would he have done last night? Where would he have gone? Had he been attacked too? Was he lying in some alleyway nearby, bleeding to death or already dead? No time to worry about that. I had to assume, for the moment, that he was still alive. Ernie had no steady girlfriend out here in the ville. Since his old flame, the Nurse, had been killed, he hadn't shacked up steady with anyone. Not in mourning, mind you, but more as if he were compelled to hop from woman to woman in a mad rush to embrace life.

Or embrace something.

He'd become a regular at 8th Army's VD Clinic. Many days I'd see him hanging around his customized jeep in the CID parking lot, a couple of glass slides behind his ear. When I looked at him quizzically, he said, "In case it starts to drip." I still didn't get it, so in exasperation, he explained. "So I can capture a specimen."

Standing alone on a cold overcast morning in the center of Itaewon, I tried, once again, to think like Ernie. Chances are, last night, he wouldn't have returned to the barracks. We'd been at the King Club. Plenty of Korean business girls there. He'd have grabbed one. Almost certainly. Whenever Ernie saw something he liked, he took it. He never planned anything or put anything off until later so as to savor a particular delight; rather, he always obeyed every physical urge, immediately, no matter how primitive.

A scene from last night flashed before my eyes. Me and Riley hanging onto the edge of the bar, two or three women wrapped around Ernie. One of their faces became clear. Unbidden, her name came to me: Julie. That was the Anglicized version. In Korean it was Pak Chu-li. A waitress, not a business girl, although there's usually not much difference. And I knew she lived somewhere in one of the hooches on a narrow pedestrian pathway behind the King Club. Not off the alley I had been lying in, but farther back amidst the tightly packed jumble of brothels and hovels that house the denizens who work the night.

That's where I had to go.

A cold breeze gathered. I tightened my jacket and began my march into the dark heart of Itaewon.

At the top of Hooker Hill, I entered a cobbled walkway lined by brick walls. Shadow enveloped me.

It took me twenty minutes, pounding on wooden gateways, waiting for someone to emerge from a room and cross the courtyard, and then asking if this was the home of Pak Chu-li, had they seen Ernie Bascom. More often than not I described him: Tall, just over six feet, short blond hair, round-lensed wire-rimmed glasses. Last night he had been wearing a coat and tie, as required on-duty for every agent of 8th Army's CID.

It was the third wooden gateway I banged on that finally opened.

I crouched through and entered a long, rectangular courtyard with a few scrawny chickens behind a wire coop. A row of earthenware *kimchee* jars lined the far wall, and a rusty iron water pump dripped water into a plastic pail hanging beneath its spout. As I approached a row of hooches, the smell of charcoal gas emanating from beneath the *ondol*-heated floor became stronger. A paper-covered door slid open and a sleep-puffed face peered out.

Julie. I recognized her from the King Club. Her eye makeup was smeared and her long black hair was bundled behind her head, held in place by chopsticks puncturing a knot.

I stepped toward the raised wooden porch and said, "Ernie *isso?*" Is Ernie here?

Her eyes widened and she screamed.

In seconds, Ernie's startled face popped out of the door above her, his chest bare. He looked me over and said, "What in the hell happened to you?"

Julie was up now, throwing on her clothes, and soon the electric bulb was switched on and she was dressed in blue jeans and a pullover sweater. She filled a pail of water from the pump in the courtyard and began dabbing at the thick blood that ran down the side of my neck.

"*Apo?*" she asked.

"No," I lied, even though it did.

As Julie worked, clucking away in concern, I questioned her in Korean about the smiling woman.

"She new," she said in English.

"What's her name?"

"I don't know. Mama-san know."

All women in an Itaewon bar, whether waitresses or hostesses or out-and-out business girls, had to register with the owner and show their VD cards to verify they'd been checked by the Yongsan District Health Department and wouldn't be spreading disease to the courageous American allies. If the bar owner failed to enforce this rule, she could be subject to heavy fines. Or even shut down.

"Where's the mama-san live?"

"Why? This woman take your money?"

"Worse than that."

Ernie was out of the hooch, dressed in slacks and white shirt, sitting on the lacquered wooden walkway, slipping on his shoes and tying the laces. He wore his .45 automatic pistol in his shoulder holster beneath his jacket and there was a bulge in the pocket where his badge should've been.

"So who do we have to kill?" he asked.

I opened my jacket, flashing the empty shoulder holster.

"Oh shit," he said.

Julie gasped.

When he'd sufficiently recovered, Ernie asked, "Where'd you wake up?"

"In an alley."

"You searched for the gun?"

"Thoroughly. Not there. Nor badge. Nor wallet."

Ernie kept shaking his head, sadly, as if I were the sorriest piece of maggot-meat in the entire universe.

A .45 caliber automatic pistol is a weapon of massive firepower. My poor judgment, my lack of responsibility, had put that pistol into the wrong hands. Irresponsible hands. Criminal hands. And the misuse of that pistol could cause someone's maiming or death. I was to blame. No one else. Despite what a panel of 8th Army officers might decide in a court-martial, I knew if someone got hurt by that gun, ultimately I'd be judged most harshly by the person who mattered most: me. Unless I recovered that .45, I'd be found guilty. And my punishment would not last for one year or ten years or even thirty years. It would last for the rest of my life.

Julie waved goodbye to the old woman who owned the hooch and the three of us stepped through the wooden gate, back out into the cold alleyway.

The proprietress of the King Club switched on a fluorescent light beneath the long wooden bar and flipped open a thick book with heavy cardboard pages.

"You look," she said.

Each page held three entries, with a black-and-white photograph of a woman, a name, and other identifying information. Their duty position was listed—waitress, hostess, or entertainer—their name, their place of birth, their Korean National Identification Number, their VD card number and the date of their last checkup. All the faces looked lifeless, resigned. Showing none of the spunk I saw in them every night.

It must've been humiliating to travel downtown to a government office and admit you were selling yourself to foreigners, have some bureaucrat fill out paperwork on you and snap your mug shot and then send you down to the VD clinic as the next step in processing your body through the maze of Korean officialdom. All to insure the safety of a bunch of rowdy American GIs.

Julie sat on a stool on the customer side of the bar, sucking silently on a *tambay*, blowing blue smoke rings into the air. Ernie reached into the beer cooler, helped himself to a cold one, and raised his eyebrows in my direction. I shook my head.

Except for the four of us, the King Club was deserted. Cocktail tables sat in front of an empty stage, the straight-backed metal chairs turned upside-down atop them. Earlier, Julie had guided us through the maze of Itaewon's walkways until we reached the home of Mrs. Bei, the owner of the King Club. After I explained the seriousness of the situation, Mrs. Bei consented to take us to her place of business and give us what little information she had on the woman who had been sitting with me last night.

"I felt sorry for her," Mrs. Bei said. "Her skirt and blouse were shabby. She said she had come to Seoul to see her mother and only wanted to work here one night to make some money so she could buy her mother a present before she went home."

It is a Korean custom never to visit anyone, especially one's parents, with "empty hands."

"And Chusok is coming up in a few days," Mrs. Bei said. "She told me she had to save money to properly perform the *seibei* ceremony."

Chusok, the Autumn Moon Festival, was an ancient holiday celebrating a bountiful harvest. It is the most popular holiday in Korea. Families travel many miles to be together and give thanks to their ancestors for providing the precious gift of life. The custom is to pile a table with fruit and other delicacies, wear your best *hanbok*—traditional Korean clothing—and perform the *seibei* ceremony, where you kneel and bow your head before your parents.

"Of course," Mrs. Bei told me, "I had to make sure this woman had a VD card."

She flipped the ledger open to the last page. There, written in ink, with no accompanying photograph, was the entry for the smiling woman. Her name, her Korean Identification Card Number, her VD Card number, her hometown and date of birth. I borrowed a piece of scrap paper and a pen and scribbled it down, copying the *hangul* script verbatim. The name she'd given was Yun Ai-ja. Love Child Yun.

"Did this Miss Yun tell you where she was staying?" I asked.

Mrs. Bei shook her head. "She was staying here. Hoping some GI—some GI with money—would become interested in her and take her somewhere."

That GI, unfortunately, had been me.

Things did not go well back on the compound.

The CID First Sergeant was so angry that every red vein in his pale head popped. Colonel Brace, the newly appointed Provost Marshal, didn't speak to me directly, of course, but word came down that he was livid over having to report to the 8th Army Commanding General that one of his CID agents had been rolled and his badge and .45 stolen. The CG, in turn, had gone ballistic.

Later, Ernie and I talked to every CID agent or MP who'd been in the King Club last night. None of them remembered me at all. Everyone had been drunk and, as expected, paying attention only to their own concerns.

That afternoon, I made my formal report to the Korean National Police concerning the theft of my sidearm and my badge. Captain Kim, the commander of the Itaewon police station surmised, without me telling him, that I must've been drugged. It made sense. Neither Ernie nor Riley nor any of the other guys in the King Club last night had been so inebriated that they'd been unable to walk under their own power. Only me. Captain Kim promised to check with their records division in downtown Seoul, searching for someone known as Miss Yun Ai-ja, and also for any drug-and-mug operations that had been spotted recently.

That night, Ernie and I searched the ville thoroughly, asking everyone if they'd ever heard of a woman who matched the description of Miss Yun Ai-ja. No one had.

The next morning, the KNP records came in and Captain Kim told me that the smiling woman, the woman who called herself Yun Ai-ja, had no police record. Her Korean National ID Card had been a phony. So had her VD card. The smiling woman, at least officially, didn't exist.

Ernie and I kept up our search into the next day and the next. Still no dice. What I was worried about most was that I'd been stalked. I didn't believe that the smiling woman and her confederates, whoever they were, had singled me out of the hundreds of drunken GIs by accident. I believed that they were aware I was a CID agent, carrying a badge and a gun. That's what they were after. And that meant that they had plans for the badge and the gun. Almost certainly. Plans that included using them in the perpetration of another crime.

* * *

It was mid-morning of the third day, when Ernie and I returned to the CID office. Sergeant Riley popped up from his desk.

"Inchon," he said, scribbling on a pad of paper. "The call just came in. You're in a world of hurt now, Sueño."

"What do you mean?"

"Here's the name of the place. The Olympos Hotel and Casino. North of the Port of Inchon on the edge of the Yellow Sea. The KNPs tell me you can't miss it."

I glanced at the paper. "What's some casino in Inchon have to do with me?"

"It's been robbed."

"So?" Ernie said. "That's the KNP's job. Not ours."

"It's your job now," Riley said. "Somebody was shot. Point-blank." He grinned a crooked-toothed grin. "With Sueño's forty-five."

Blood drained from my face.

Ernie leaned across Riley's desk. "How in the hell could they know that? There hasn't been enough time to run ballistics."

"The thieves bluffed their way in using a badge," Riley said. "A CID badge. With Sueño's name on it."

Ernie and I sprinted for the parking lot.

What I feared most had come true. My .45 had been used in the commission of a crime.

I saw the face of the smiling woman, the woman who called herself Yun Ai-ja. I saw her staring at me with her half-mad eyes. She was smiling. Smiling broadly.

And the more she stared at me, the broader her smile became.

2

The City of Inchon sits on the coast of the Yellow Sea thirty kilometers due east of Seoul. It's South Korea's second largest port—after Pusan on the southernmost edge of the peninsula—and, as such, it provides much of the export-import capacity for the bustling capital city of Seoul. Inchon is most famous for the Inchon invasion, General Douglas MacArthur's master stroke during the first few months of the Korean War. An amphibious landing that sliced the North Korean Communist supply lines and forced their army to retreat all the way to the Yalu River on the northern border with China.

Ernie pulled off the two-lane highway, crossed a ridge, and the city spread out before us. A cramped downtown area with a few skyscrapers—none more than five or six stories high—surrounded by a vast sea of tile-roofed homes and shops. The jumble of wood and mortar spread in every direction and jutted into the Bay of Kyongki. On the southern edge of the city sat the port with a few foreign ships, and about a half mile farther out, the huge stone-and-brick breakwater that vainly tried to hold back frothing white seas. If you ventured out into that green expanse and continued east, you'd eventually hit Shanghai and the teeming continent known as China, the Middle Kingdom.

Ernie kept both hands on the jeep's big steering wheel and, chomping on a wad of ginseng gum, wound his way through the busy streets of Inchon. Eventually, we reached the city's central train station. From there it was just a few yards to the Olympos Hotel and Casino. The whitewashed cement edifice sat perched like a conquering hero atop a hill overlooking the Yellow Sea.

We parked the jeep in the small front lot, avoided a few swooping sea gulls, and walked through the glass doors of the lobby's foyer. Yellow-jacketed bellmen bowed as we entered, spouting the requisite "*Oso-oseiyo.*" Please come in. We ignored them and trotted up the red-carpeted stairway with the neon sign pointing upward that said "Casino."

When Ernie and I walked through the front portals of the Olympos Casino, everything stopped.

It wasn't a casino like you think of in the States, with clanging slot machines and flashing neon lights. This place was more like a mausoleum. Our feet sank into plush red carpet as we entered a huge round hall. Chandeliers hung glittering from the ceiling, and unobtrusive classical music was being piped in through speakers.

Korean men in suits, both young and middle-aged, and young women, all wearing the blue dress uniform of an employee of the Olympos Casino—every one of them stopped, immediately, what they were doing. If they were talking, they froze in mid-sentence. If they were about to sit down, they immobilized themselves in mid-squat. If they were drinking tea, they held their cups poised awkwardly at their lips.

Scattered amongst the casino employees were a few men

dressed in the khaki uniform of the Korean National Police, their eyes also riveted on us. Right hands slipped toward the big pistols they wore at their hips.

The only sound was Ernie's gum clicking.

Without turning my head, I told him, "Don't make any quick moves."

Ernie frowned. "What the hell's wrong?"

I didn't answer because I didn't know. Two tall Americans like Ernie and me, wearing coats and ties and visiting places where foreigners seldom tread, attract a lot of attention. I won't say we were used to it, but we were resigned to it. But this was more than the usual reaction to a couple of out-of-place *Miguk*s. This was fear.

The ceiling was two stories high. Across more plush carpeting, in the center of the room, a circle of green felt-covered blackjack tables surrounded a desk and telephone. Most of the employees were huddled there, as if for protection. In the back was a cocktail lounge on raised split-level flooring, and in a corner by themselves were the baccarat tables. A few disgruntled Asians sat there. From the singsong lilt of their conversation, I figured them to be tourists from Hong Kong. The other customers, all Korean, occupied a cocktail table in front of the bar. They were being interviewed by a khaki-clad Korean National Policeman. He hunched over the table, diligently jotting notes.

In back, beyond the baccarat tables, light shone through iron grating. The cashier's cage. Its thick, iron-barred entrance door hung open.

I held my hands out to my sides and walked slowly toward the circle of blackjack tables. "*Na nun, Mi Pal Kun,*" I said. I'm from 8th Army.

A chubby-faced young woman in the uniform of the Olympos Casino began to whimper. Then cry. Two other women threw their arms around her, glaring at Ernie and me.

"I didn't do it," Ernie said softly. "Honest."

One of the uniformed cops stepped forward and frisked me. He seemed surprised at my empty shoulder holster. I'm not even sure why I was still wearing it. Force of habit, I suppose. Or wishful thinking.

Then he frisked Ernie and found his weapon, and Ernie held up his CID badge and offered it to the cop. The cop took it, turned, and carried it over to a wooden table that had been set up near the cashier's cage. Another cop sat behind the table. Ernie and I followed.

All of the casino employees, particularly the young women in their blue dresses, backed off as we walked by, some of them hugging themselves, their eyes wide, as if wary of any sudden movement we might make.

The cop at the table was a thin man whose narrow frame seemed lost in his neatly pressed uniform. He wore rectangular glasses, and a growth of straight white hair shot up from his round skull. His face was weathered, grim, beyond any hope of surprise. His name tag said Won. His rank insignia indicated that he was a lieutenant.

The Korean National Police are a militaristic organization. Uniforms, rank, salutes, basic training—all the things you expect to see in an army. In fact, the Korean government considers the KNPs to be an integral part of national defense. Along with solving day-to-day crime, they are also tasked with being on the lookout for North Korean Communist infiltrators. Infiltrators who routinely slip into the country to commit sabotage, murder, espionage, and various forms of creative mayhem.

Captain Won ran his fingers through his hair.

"*Anjo*," he said roughly, and pointed at two metal chairs in front of his table. He'd used the non-honorific imperative form of the verb "to sit" and, inside the cage, two of the female cashiers tensed slightly. They knew an insult when they heard it.

Ernie sat.

He hadn't noticed the insult. His Korean is rudimentary, and besides, he's not into honorific verbal conjugations. Ernie's a more direct person. If you slap him, he'll punch you right in the nose and proceed from there to kick your butt. More often than not, subtlety escapes him. I, however, considered making a fuss over the way Lieutenant Won had just spoken to us.

Eighth Army offers free Korean language lessons on base. Very few GIs take advantage of them; they're busy chasing women and running the ville. But I go every Tuesday and Thursday night. And during my free time, I continue to study the language on my own, picking up, on the streets of Seoul, words and slang that don't appear in my textbook. Fluency, I hope, will help me in my job. But sometimes it just seems to make it harder. Like in this case, when I realized we'd been insulted.

Given the tension in the room, I decided not to react. There was too much I wanted to find out about what had gone on little more than an hour ago in this casino that was making these employees act so strangely. Nevertheless, to warn Lieutenant Won not to push his luck, I kept my eyes on him as I sat down, moving deliberately.

Lieutenant Won chose to ignore my reaction and continued to speak gruffly. He demanded our identification. Ernie handed him his military ID card and his badge, and I handed him the temporary replacement paperwork for mine. He stared quizzically at mine, probably not even understanding the neatly typed sheets, but he made no comment. He wrote down our names and ID numbers in a notebook. Everyone watched. This was a show for them, to let the employees of the Olympos Casino know that the Korean National Police were not going to take any guff off Americans. Maybe in his own way Lieutenant Won was trying to help us. From the look of the male pit bosses, and even in the eyes of the blue-clad female dealers, violence against a foreigner wasn't completely out of the question.

When he was finished, Lieutenant Won spoke in English.

"Not good."

We waited.

He shook his head and spoke again, "Two bad men. Very bad. They come in casino, they show badge. Your badge." He pointed at me. "You, Sueño. Casino manager he look at badge, say Geogie Sueño. He write down. Here."

Lieutenant Won slid a notepad across the desk. The letterhead of the Olympos Hotel and Casino was emblazoned across the top, and on the clean white sheet were handwritten notes, all in scribbled Korean. One word was written in English. My name: Sueño.

"This guy showed my badge?"

Lieutenant Won nodded.

"To the casino manager?"

He nodded again.

I paused, thinking it over. Until now, I had assumed—I think correctly—that the smiling woman was working with confederates. That she led me into that alley where a man—or two men— were waiting, and they had been the ones who'd knocked me out and stolen my weapon and my badge. Were these the same two guys who'd robbed the Olympos Casino? Or had the smiling woman sold the badge and the .45 to a different set of thieves who'd used them here in Inchon? Somehow I doubted that the badge and the .45 had been sold. Why? Because illegal arms trafficking in Korea is a dangerous proposition. The Korean government believe such a trade is a threat to their national security and, as such, the punishment is death. More likely that the smiling woman and her confederates planned from the beginning to use the .45 and the badge on their own. They were after a big score—a much bigger score than they'd ever find in Itaewon. My badge and my .45 were just a means.

Could I prove any of this? No. Not yet. But it was the theory I was working with for now.

Then I remembered something.

"My photograph," I said. "It's on the badge. Was it switched?"

Lieutenant Won shook his head. "No. Casino manager checked. Not switched."

"If my photograph was on the badge, then how was the casino manager fooled?"

"Man who rob casino," Lieutenant Won said, "he look like you."

Ernie clicked more loudly on his ginseng gum.

"He was an American?" I asked. Or maybe I should've said Chicano. But the distinction between Anglos and people of Latin American descent is not one that Koreans usually draw. To them we're all *wei guk in*. Outside people.

"Maybe American," Lieutenant Won answered. "Seems like. But he wore . . . what you call?"

Lieutenant Won ran pinched fingers across his eyes.

"Sunglasses," I said.

"Yes. Sunglasses." Lieutenant Won turned to Ernie. He flashed a grim smile. "And the man who come with him, he look like you."

Ernie and I gazed around the large room. The casino employees still huddled in small groups, looking for all the world like frightened deer in the middle of a forest.

I turned back to Lieutenant Won. "The casino manager allowed these two men to enter the cashier's cage?"

Captain Won nodded.

"Why?" Ernie asked. "The cashier's cage would've been locked, and there must be an alarm system of some sort. Normally, the cashiers would keep the door locked, sound the alarm, and wait for the police."

Captain Won held up his hands. "Wait. I bring manager. You talk to him."

A thin, nervous Korean man with thick glasses and a toadying manner was introduced to us as Mr. Bok, the manager of the

Olympos. He stood while we questioned him, speaking English and, when his nervousness overtook him, falling back to Korean. He was the type of man who had risen to his current position by ingratiating himself to customers. Never contradicting them, always submissive. A good policy when you're in the process of cleansing people of all their money. Slowly, painfully, Mr. Bok stammered the story of what happened.

While we talked, one of the female employees brought a metal tray with four steaming cups of tea. Mr. Bok didn't drink, Captain Won already had a full cup, but Ernie and I both accepted. The young woman kept her head bowed as she served us, her black hair hanging straight down, hiding her face. She never looked at us. Then she backed away, obviously relieved to be leaving the presence of two foreign louts.

In Korea, serving foreigners is never a savory task. But under these conditions, with the hatred of Americans palpable in the room, it would be particularly objectionable. What sin had this young woman committed to make such an onerous duty fall on her? Probably, she was the newest on the payroll. Sin enough.

When Mr. Bok finished relating his tale, and Ernie and I ran out of questions, we examined the interior of the casino cage. Three frail Korean women, wearing the same uniforms as the dealers, sat quietly on wooden stools in front of empty cash boxes. The two thieves had grabbed the bundles of Japanese *yen*, Korean *won*, and U.S. greenbacks and stuffed them into a single canvas bag before fleeing. The women's hands were still shaking, but Ernie snapped his questions at them anyway. They understood English well enough and answered, glancing at Lieutenant Won occasionally, as if for approval.

There was a back door to the cashier's cage. I twisted the knob and found it open. While Lieutenant Won and Ernie and the three cashiers conversed, I slipped through the doorway.

A long hallway. Not carpeted, but tiled with brown parquet.

I turned left and walked about ten yards to the end of the hallway and opened the door. Another walkway, empty, apparently leading back toward the main building of the Olympos Hotel. In the distance I heard the clanging of pots and the gruff shouts of men toiling in a kitchen. I turned and walked back about twenty yards, passing the door that led to the cashier's cage. At the opposite end of the hallway a narrow passage led up a steep flight of wooden steps. A sign above the entrance said CHULIP KUMJI. Do Not Enter.

So I entered.

Ancient steps creaked.

The walls and the ceiling were made of varnished wood—I'd left the main cement structure of the hotel behind. Puffs of incense wafted past. Jasmine. Pungent, like something from a temple.

At the top of the stairwell, wood slat flooring spread twenty feet toward the open door of what must've been an executive suite. The room was open and spacious. Windows peered out onto the gray clouds hovering above the green of the Yellow Sea.

The incense came from an alcove with a wooden shelf illuminated by a yellow electric bulb. A large photograph had once sat on the shelf, framed in intricately carved wood and backed by black silk. But the glass covering of the photograph lay smashed, the frame broken in two, and the photograph itself had been torn into pieces. Someone, however, had picked up the pieces and arranged them in a neat pile on the shattered glass. Whoever had piled up the shredded pieces had also taken the time to slide two new sticks of incense into a bronze burner. The wicks glowed red near the top: they'd been lit a half hour ago.

I knelt and began to sort the torn photograph. Bits of an eye, a nose, an ear. A neatly cinched tie beneath a starched white collar. A woman's face. Arms covered with intricately embroidered silk. As I shuffled through, I realized that she was an elderly woman with white hair, wearing an expensive *chima-chogori*, the traditional skirt and blouse of Korea. The man, also elderly, wore an ill-fitting Western suit.

Ancestors. Someone's parents or grandparents or great-grandparents.

I set the bits of photograph down and walked into the suite's office.

The view startled me. A vast panorama of Inchon Harbor, suffused with the glow of sunlight. To the south, a row of half-a-dozen merchant vessels, flying the flags of various countries: Greece, Panama, the Philippines. Directly in front, five hundred yards straight out, between the Olympos Hotel and the Yellow Sea, the twelve-foot-high breakwater made of thick wooden pillars and jumbled stone. To the north, a small island surrounded by tiny fishing vessels, most without outboard motors: only bamboo masts and sails hammered from beaten straw, made for plying an ancient way of life. And beyond the island, the churning waters of the Yellow Sea. Above it all, like jealous dragons examining their domain, great storm clouds squatted on thick haunches. A few splats of rain spattered the window pane.

I examined the office.

Couches made of hand-carved mahogany padded with embroidered cushions. Lining the walls, blue-green celadon vases, a porcelain statuette of a fat Buddha, and red plaques slashed with aphorisms written in gold Chinese characters. Sitting in the center of the room, a flat desk made of varnished teak and an expensive-looking leather swivel chair. In front of the desk, a glass-topped coffee table with crystal ashtrays and a mother-of-pearl inlaid serving tray. This had to be the owner's office. Couldn't be otherwise. And those ancestors in the hallway were probably his.

Nothing in the office seemed to be disturbed. Unlike the alcove out front.

Behind the desk, I stepped into blood. I gawked at the puddle of red spreading to the back wall. In spots, the blood was pooled so thickly it looked like jelly on a birthday cake. Deep purple.

I inhaled deeply, trying to fight the dizziness that suddenly overcame me. But the sweet cloying scent of blood made it worse. I held onto the edge of the desk, taking quick shallow breaths until the feeling passed. Then I stood upright.

There was more moisture: a puddle of clear liquid pushed up against the thicker blood. I knelt and dipped my finger in and lifted it to my nose. No odor. Water. Not seawater then, probably regular drinking water. Then a gust of wind blew more splats of rain against the window behind me.

Maybe rainwater. How had it gotten in here? No leaks in the roof. Barely noticeable was a small doorway seated neatly into the wall. Not hidden, but unobtrusive. I grabbed the varnished wooden handle of the short door and pulled. The smell of the sea rushed in, along with rainwater and gusts of wind. Kneeling, I peered outside.

An escape hatch. A fire escape, actually. The outer edge of the stone wall fell straight down, forty feet, to piled boulders lashed by angry surf. Along the wall ran a pathway just wide enough for one man to walk. It was damp and slippery, but in case of fire it would be a means of escape. Where the pathway led I couldn't be sure. Beyond the corner of the hotel, it wound off out of sight. I considered climbing out there to see where it went but thought better of it. What for? Besides, the footing looked treacherous.

Boots stomped angrily up wooden steps.

Quickly, I closed the door, and when I turned, I noticed something under the desk. A strip of embroidered silk tasseled with lengths of string. Without thinking, I grabbed it and stuffed it into my jacket pocket. The footsteps grew louder. When they entered the room, I stood and stared into the eyes of Lieutenant Won.

He was outraged. In angry Korean he asked what I was doing

here. I didn't bother to answer. What good would it do? I was investigating a crime, he knew that. Instead, I asked him why he was so angry.

"This is the office of the owner," he told me in Korean, as if it were obvious why that would make him angry.

"Mr. Bok?" I asked.

"No," Won answered, incredulous. "He's only the manager."

"Who's the owner?"

"Not your business."

I was used to this. Korean cops protecting higher-ups—from the indignity of having to be interviewed by a foreign cop, from the indignity of being associated in any way with crime. The way the KNPs figured it, two Americans had committed the robbery and the shooting, and since they appeared to be GIs, it was the job of Ernie and me to help catch those GIs. It wasn't our job to talk to Korean big shots. And any suggestion otherwise, I knew from previous experience, would be taken by Lieutenant Won as an insult to his competency. We were being spoon fed the little the KNPs wanted us to know, and that's all we would get.

But this case was different.

Sure, it was their country, and according to all law and international treaties, the Korean National Police, and only the Korean National Police, had jurisdiction over this case. Ernie and I were here as invited guests, presumably to help shed some light on the GI angle, and the Korean cops could show us as much as they wanted—or as little as they wanted. But all that was just law. The moment I'd stepped into this puddle of blood, law no longer meant anything to me. It was my weapon that had been stolen, my badge. And it was those two items that had been used in the commission of these crimes. Without my stupidity, without me allowing some smiling blonde tart to drug me and drag me into an alley, this casino would've never been robbed and, more importantly, this puddle of blood wouldn't be on this floor.

I pointed at the blood.

Lieutenant Won and Ernie walked around the desk.

Lieutenant Won's arms were crossed, and his nose was scrunched. He'd known the blood was here, but for some reason he hadn't wanted us to see it.

"Woman shot here," he said, pointing at the ground.

Mr. Bok told us earlier about the young female dealer who had been shot, but he hadn't been specific as to the location of the shooting. Now we knew.

Lieutenant Won pulled a brown pulp envelope out of his pocket. He opened it and let Ernie and me peer inside. It was a bullet from a .45, with its nose scrunched up as if it had hit metal. Then he pointed at a brass hinge attached to the escape hatch. A fresh dent. More than a dent really, an angry scratch.

As if from the claw of a dragon.

"This one, he missed," Lieutenant Won said. "Other one," he turned back to the blood on the floor, "is still in her body."

"And where is she now?" I asked.

"Ambulance take hospital," Lieutenant Won said.

Back in the casino, the three nervous cashiers remained in their cage, perched on wooden stools like exotic birds with fluttering blue wings. The four of us—me, Ernie, the angry Lieutenant Won, and the obsequious Mr. Bok—walked past the cashiers and crossed the carpeted casino floor toward the front entrance.

We had almost reached it when the backdoor of the cashier's cage clanged open. The four of us stopped, turned, and stared back at the cage.

Like leopards, three men glided out. Two were young Koreans, tall, muscular, wearing suits and ties, their black hair slicked back. Between them stood an older man, his gray hair streaked with white. His face was pasty, as if he spent a lot of time indoors, and his cheeks sagged. The three-piece suit he wore was made of finely tailored wool. The way he stood, motionless, made me think that he was a mortician, come to escort a body to the nether realms. He stared at me. Not at Ernie, not at Lieutenant Won, not at Mr. Bok, but at me. For what seemed a long moment, his craggy face remained impassive. Something ugly passed between us. Then, as quickly as the mortician and his entourage had appeared, they turned and slipped back through the doorway.

"Who was that?" Ernie asked.

"The owner."

"Of the entire casino?"

Lieutenant Won nodded.

"We need to talk to him," Ernie said.

"Not possible," Lieutenant Won answered.

I started to protest, but Lieutenant Won held up his open palm to silence me.

"Finish," he said.

Four Korean cops converged on Ernie and me and motioned toward the door. One put his hand on Ernie's elbow, and Ernie shoved him away. Immediately, the three other cops went for their nightsticks, but before they could move, Lieutenant Won shouted an order. They stopped, glaring at us. Ernie and I glared back.

The small pack of Korean cops watched warily while Ernie straightened his coat. Then he turned and the two of us walked out of the casino and trotted down the steps. Under our own power.

"Shangnom-ah!" Ernie shouted.

Another kimchee cab swerved in front of us, horn blaring, and Ernie slammed on his brakes and cursed again. We were winding our way through the heavy midday downtown Inchon traffic, heading for the Huang Hei Medical Center, the hospital where the young female blackjack dealer had been taken. The one who'd been shot.

Korean curse words Ernie had down pat. "Common lout" is what *shangnom* means. Rough talk in the Korean lexicon. He turned to me.

"Why the hell do you want to go to the hospital anyway?"

"I want to see," I said.

"See what? She's a dealer in a casino. Young, female, twenty-two years old. Her name is Han Ok-hi. She was shot with a bullet that appears to be .45 caliber, from a gun that is probably yours. What else do you want to know?"

For a moment I thought I'd punch him. For the first time since I'd met Ernie Bascom, in all the months we'd worked together and arrested bad guys together and run the ville together, I had an overwhelming urge to lean across the gear shift and punch him flush upside his Anglo-Saxon head.

But I didn't. Instead, I held onto my knees and stared straight ahead. It's a trait, part of Mexican-American culture, I'm told, to become very quiet when confronted or angry. To do nothing but think—or better yet, to let your body decide whether to strike or wait and let it pass.

Ernie glanced at me and then glanced again, quickly returning his attention to the swirling traffic, maybe seeing something in me that he hadn't seen before.

For the rest of the ride, he kept his mouth shut.

The nurse at the reception desk, with her straight black bangs and her immaculately white uniform, was surprised that I could speak Korean. But when Ernie flashed his badge and I told her what we wanted, she gave us directions to the room of Han Ok-hi. On the first floor, she said, toward the rear of the hospital. *Chonghuanja Sil*, she said. Critical Care Unit.

We received even more stares as we strode down the long cement corridors of the Huang Hei Medical Center. Nurses and patients swiveled to see; even the doctors looked up from their work. GIs are seldom seen in the City of Inchon. With a total population of about 500,000, only a tiny fraction—maybe two dozen—are GIs assigned to the transportation security unit at the Port of Inchon. Other foreigners, for example the merchant marines who visit the city by the thousands every year, stay mostly near the strip of bars and brothels outside the main gates of the Port of Inchon. Tourists are almost non-existent; except for the Hong Kong and Japanese high-rollers who visit the big Olympos Hotel and Casino overlooking the entrance to the bay.

Two sad-faced Koreans, a man and a woman, sat in a reception area in front of the double-doored entrance to the Critical Care Unit. The nurse at the front desk had already told me they were here: the parents of Han Ok-hi. I was afraid to pause and talk to them. After all, what would I say? I'm the guy who allowed some crazy woman to steal his pistol so your daughter could be shot? Pity welled up in me for this middle-aged couple, but for the moment, I prayed they didn't know who I was or what I had done. Cowardly, yes. But if they dragged me down into their anguish, I might drown before I finished the job I knew I had to do.

Without acknowledging them, Ernie and I pushed through the double doors and into the ward.

The inner chamber of the Critical Care Unit was bathed in a green glow. As we waited for our eyes to adjust to the dim light, a blue-smocked technician, and then a doctor, confronted us.

The doctor's name tag said Oh.

Ernie showed his badge.

"Han Ok-hi," I said. "Where is she?"

Doctor Oh insisted we put on face masks. A pair were found for us, then he ushered us down a corridor. Patients lay on beds

surrounded by paraphernalia: tubes, bottles, air bags, beeping res-
pirator machines. Finally, we stopped. The doctor pointed.

Her feet only reached two-thirds of the way down the bed.
A loose plastic mask covered most of her face; the mask gently
filled, then deflated. Her black hair had been shoved into a
translucent blue cap. Tubes were stuck into her arms and down
her throat and into other strategic spots around her body.

Doctor Oh tried to stop me, but I couldn't help myself. I
reached out and touched the palm of her hand. It was much cold-
er than it should've been.

This was my fault. Sure, I knew rationally that it was the
criminals involved who were responsible. Not me. But that couldn't
change my feelings. That couldn't change the debt I owed to this
small young woman whose fingers lay cold and limp in my palm.
It was a matter of honor now. I had to find the men who did this.
Not for the Korean National Police, nor for the 8th Army
Criminal Investigation Division. Not even for Han Ok-hi herself.
But for me.

Dr. Oh grabbed my elbow. Even through his mask, I could
tell he was frowning.

"Will she live?" I asked.

Doctor Oh shrugged.

On a coat rack near the bed hung a long traditional Korean
silk skirt. I let go of Han Ok-hi's hand and stepped toward it. The
silk was hand-embroidered in red on a pale pink background.
Flowers. *Mugung-hua*. The Rose of Sharon. The national flower of
Korea. Then I remembered. Reaching into my pocket, I pulled
out the strip of silk I'd found under the desk that belonged to the
owner of the Olympos Hotel and Casino. The material hung
loosely in my hands, and I realized it was the short blouse that
matched this long skirt hanging next to the supine body of Miss
Han Ok-Hi. As I hung it on the rack next to the skirt, Dr. Oh
stared at me curiously.

He grabbed my elbow again and walked me down the hallway. Ernie followed. At the entranceway, the doctor motioned for us to step outside.

When I hesitated, he slipped off his mask and said, "It was your gun?" His English was precise, expertly pronounced.

I nodded.

"Would *you* like to see a doctor?"

Before I could answer the double doors burst inward. The middle-aged couple we had seen outside, the parents of Han Ok-hi, stood still for a moment, as if bewildered. Then the woman's eyes focused on me, and her round face contorted in rage. Somehow, she'd found out who I was. Her husband grabbed her arm, trying to pull her back, but she bulled her way across the tiled floor until she stood in front of me.

Her husband looked disheveled, his suit coat wrinkled, his collar loose and his brown tie askew. She wore a traditional Korean *chima-chogori*, the skirt and blouse of white silk with blue embroidery, as if she were on her way to church. Or a Confucian ceremony.

Apparently, hospital gossip had reached her already. She knew that her daughter had been shot by an American gun. One that had been lost in a most irresponsible manner. And she wasn't happy with me. That much was clear.

"*Tangshin!*" she screamed. You!

Then she opened her fingers wide, sharp nails pointing at my face, and charged.

3

━━━
▬

The thieves carrying my .45 and badge walked into the Olympos Casino at eleven hundred hours, the minute it opened. They presented themselves to the security guard—speaking English, flashing my CID badge—and the guard ushered them behind the blackjack tables to the desk of the casino manager, Mr. Bok.

This is another example of the power of Americans in Korea. In the early Seventies, with the United States still in the throes of the Cold War tussle between capitalism and communism, the military junta running Korea receives millions of dollars annually in American military and economic aid. Therefore, representatives of the U.S. Government—even lowly GIs—are not questioned. We're presumed to be legitimate. Questioning a GI would be like questioning cash.

The blond-haired criminal told Mr. Bok that they were from 8th Army CID. They were investigating a case concerning a GI who had been frequenting the casino, attempting to buy American currency with Korean *won*. Mr. Bok denied that there had been any such transaction. Buying American dollars with Korean *won* is a widespread practice on the black market, but it is not legal. Korean casinos allow players to buy chips with U.S. dollars but if you win, the winnings are paid in Korean *won*. Dollars will be replaced only up to the amount for which you bought in. *Won* is a controlled currency and is not internationally traded. Besides, Bok told them, few Americans venture into the Olympos Casino. He would've remembered.

Both of the supposed CID agents wore civilian jackets and ties—just like real 8th Army CID agents—and both wore sunglasses. The man doing all the talking resembled Ernie in that he had light, sandy blond hair and white skin.

The other man, the one who presented my CID badge, didn't speak. He was dark-complected, with brown, wavy hair, and was dressed in the same manner, in coat and tie and shades. He appeared to be American. That is, he was tall, almost six feet, and his shoulders were husky and his arms and legs long, and he had hair on the back of his hands.

Maybe his appearing with an American, and being dressed the same way, had thrown Mr. Bok off. I asked him about this.

He disagreed. He knows a Korean when he sees one. This man wasn't Korean.

I asked Bok if he'd taken a good look at the photograph that accompanied the CID badge. He admitted that he hadn't. The dark man had flashed it at him as if impatient, and after Bok saw the official-looking American document in its impressive leather case, he hadn't mustered the nerve to examine it more closely.

Understandable. Korea is a police state. People aren't in the habit of questioning badges.

Most Korean casinos don't have cameras. The film and the necessary apparatus are seen as being too expensive. What with total gun control, the rate of armed robberies in Korea is less than one-tenth of what it is in the States. Korea is a safe society. Even for a woman walking alone at night through a dark alley. At least, it's usually safe.

Once the two phony CID agents were inside the cashier's cage, the staff stopped paying attention to them. Quietly, so as not to ignite a panic, the Caucasian man pulled a .45 and ordered the security guard to lie face down on the floor. He disarmed the security guard, kept his weapon, and tossed what I presumed to be my .45 to his darker-skinned accomplice. While the Caucasian thief watched Mr. Bok stuff money into a canvas bag, the other thief exited through the back door of the cashier's cage. The Caucasian thief seemed to be surprised and upset by this, Bok said, but he continued collecting the money and making sure that neither Bok nor the supine security guard nor any of the three cashiers alerted other casino personnel.

By Bok's estimate, the Caucasian thief had systematically plundered 2.4 million *won*, about five thousand dollars U.S.

Ten minute later, the taller and darker thief returned, face flushed and out of breath. He was alone, but he looked extremely upset and agitated and, with his .45, he motioned to his partner that it was time for them to leave.

They did. Without further incident. Carrying the canvas bag loaded with loot between them.

After they left, Mr. Bok notified the Korean National Police and soon the entire casino was aware of what had happened. Gaming stopped. Employees and customers alike gathered around the iron-barred cage as the cashiers tearfully told their story. With the now recovered security guard and a couple of the male pit bosses, Mr. Bok entered the hallway behind the cashier's cage and ventured up to the owner's office. There they found the smashed and torn photo of the owner's relatives and, beyond that, the undisturbed office.

Or at least the office seemed at first to be undisturbed. The small fire-escape door was open, and sea air laced with rain blew in. When Mr. Bok went to close the door, he found her. Tearfully, he explained to Ernie and me that Miss Han Ok-hi lay naked and unconscious in a pool of her own blood.

Naked? I questioned him about that, but Lieutenant Won interrupted angrily and claimed that her lack of clothing had nothing to do with this case and nothing to do with Ernie and me finding the GI who shot her. When I asked about the where-abouts of the boss, he grew even more angry.

Apparently, the Inchon KNPs were on the payroll of the owner of the Olympos Casino. No surprise there. In Korea, civil servants supplement their income in creative ways. Technically, it's not legal, but the practice is so widespread that people expect it, so much so that the official salaries of policemen and other government employees are purposely kept low. The public expects them to make as much as their salary, if not more, on the side. Why pay them well if they're going to steal anyway?

I asked again about the owner. I felt it was important that we interview him. Lieutenant Won steadfastly refused. Ernie took over the argument, raising his voice, causing Lieutenant Won to grow red in the face. While Ernie waved his arms and ranted, I pulled Mr. Bok aside. Under further questioning, Bok admitted that occasionally some of the female blackjack dealers perform hostess duties for the casino owner when he entertains guests in his office. Had there been any guests today? No, not that Bok knew of. Then why was Han Ok-hi acting as hostess? Bok blushed at that but wouldn't answer. I asked if Miss Han's hostess duties included taking off her clothes. He flushed and shook his head and refused to answer further questions on the subject.

The Korean National Police arrived only moments after Mr. Bok's telephone call.

A quick search of the surrounding area turned up nothing.

It was thought that the thieves must've had a vehicle waiting nearby. So far, the KNPs had discovered no witnesses who had seen the two men enter the casino or, more importantly, leave. But they were still canvassing the neighborhood and had high hopes that they would convince some courageous citizen to talk to them soon.

Koreans, by the nature of their experience during most of the Twentieth Century, are reluctant to become involved with the police. But they will open up, Lieutenant Won told us, when offered an incentive. The weathered old cop slugged his fist into his leather-clad palm and grinned a crooked-toothed grin.

Before the claws belonging to the mother of Han Ok-hi could rip into my flesh, I threw up my arms. But by then it was too late. She was on me, swinging at my chest, my face, shoving into me with all her strength. I staggered backward and almost tumbled onto one of the patients, but at the last second the technician braced me and kept me from falling. By now, Ernie had stepped past me, and he and the husband and Doctor Oh surrounded the writhing woman and held her. Her face blazed an angry red and she screamed invective at me, most of which I couldn't understand, and then she was spitting and trying to push forward again. The three men held firm. The mother of Han Ok-hi strained against them, and then, as if all her massive strength had left her, she stopped. Her mouth shut and she stared at me, confused. She gazed around the green glow of the Critical Care Unit, as if she had just awoken from a dream.

Her face fell and her palms shot up to cover her open mouth. She crumpled to the ground, crying and screaming and moaning again. Calling out: "Ok-hi, Ok-hi, Ok-hi-ah."

The doctor, the husband, and the technician lifted her back to her feet. Someone rolled in a wheel chair and, after arranging her properly, the husband pushed the mother of Han Ok-hi out of the Critical Care Unit.

Ernie came to stand by me. Doctor Oh talked to me some more but I don't remember what was said. I don't know if I turned down care or promised to see a doctor or anything at all. I don't even remember leaving the hospital.

But we did leave.

And the next thing I knew, I was breathing salt air.

I wasn't surprised that Lieutenant Won hadn't allowed Ernie or me to speak to the owner of the Olympos Hotel and Casino. The Japanese and Hong Kong high rollers brought millions of dollars into the casino every year. With money like that, power had to be close by. The casino owner was probably more influential in the City of Inchon than the mayor. And in Korea, one iron rule I'd learned: important people don't talk to American GIs. Even when those GIs are conducting a murder investigation. Especially when they're conducting a murder investigation.

And without subpoena power, I couldn't do a thing about it. Not without the consent of the Korean National Police, and that wasn't likely. When the owner entered the cashier cage with his henchmen, Lieutenant Won, the tough old cop, had been terrified. Even Ernie had been a little intimidated. I could tell by the way he bristled.

Still, I'm a cop. And like any cop in the middle of a murder investigation, I had questions: Did the casino owner keep money in his office? I hadn't seen a safe but maybe there was one hidden somewhere. Is that why the thief went back there? Did the crook have inside information concerning the whereabouts of a safe? And why had Han Ok-hi been in the office? What was she doing? Serving tea? If so, who to? And why had she taken off her clothes? Where was the casino owner while the thief was wandering around his office? Where were his bodyguards? Had the casino owner seen the thief? Did he think he could identify him and pull him out of a line-up?

I had other questions that maybe had nothing to do with the crime: Who tore up the photograph on the small shrine in the alcove? Who picked up and returned the pieces to their proper place on the pedestal? Who relit the sticks of incense? Who were those two people in the photograph? What did ancestors have to do with all this?

There were too many questions, all swirling madly through my mind. And while I struggled to sort them out, all I could see was the small body of Han Ok-hi, lying unmoving and helpless beneath white sheets. How I wished that she would sit up and tell me, and then her mother, that she was all right.

After leaving the Huang Hei Medical Center, Ernie and I drove to the Inchon Headquarters of the Korean National Police. I sat in the jeep for a few minutes, breathing deeply of the fresh salt air. Ernie waited patiently. When I felt I'd recovered, we went inside. Using the accounts of the casino employees, one of the police artists had already made sketches of the two thieves. After meeting with Lieutenant Won to discuss strategy, Ernie and I returned to the jeep and sat outside the red-brick headquarters building, staring at the sketches.

"Ugly fuckers," Ernie said.

"Yeah," I said, "but now I understand why everyone in the casino was so frightened when we walked in. These two guys look like us."

"Naw, they don't. It's just because of the way they're dressed. Coat and tie. And they're wearing shades. And one of them's Caucasian and a little shorter, and the other one is dark and a little taller. That's the only similarity."

Ernie didn't want to see the resemblance but it was there. Still, he was right that if you took away the Western clothing and set them out on the street standing next to us, no one would mistake them for two stalwart enforcers of the law like Agents George Sueño and Ernie Bascom.

The City of Inchon rises from the sea up to the hills that comprise the downtown business district. From where we sat we could see the big cement block building of the Olympos Hotel and Casino, out to the Port of Inchon, and beyond to the rippling waters of the *Huang Hei*, as the Koreans call it—the Yellow Sea. The sun was low on the horizon.

I thought of Miss Han Ok-hi. Would she pull through? Would she one day be whole and healthy again? Or would she give up the ghost and allow her spirit to rise through this golden glow to join her ancestors?

Ernie broke the spell.

"The KNPs will be looking for more leads all night, talking to cab drivers, checking with the bus companies, seeing if they can locate witnesses and a getaway car."

When a foreigner kills a Korean it makes headlines in the morning papers. The KNPs, although prime players in a highly controlled state, are not completely insensitive to public opinion. Pressure, and a lot of it, would be coming down from on high, and coming down soon. A GI—or someone who appears to be a GI—callously shot a fine young Korean woman. No politician could put up with that. And the sooner the KNPs arrested a suspect, the safer they would be.

I saw where Ernie was going. "So we have to go some place where the KNPs can't."

"The GI angle," Ernie said. "That's why Lieutenant Won let us examine the crime scene. He wants us to figure out who these guys are and where they're stationed so he can collar them."

"We'll make the collar," I said.

"Good," Ernie agreed. "Let's do that. So our first step is to think like these guys. If you had just robbed a casino, shot an innocent girl, and were now on the run with a bag full of money, where would you go?"

"To Seoul," I said.

"Right. To hide amongst the multitudes. But think of how fast the KNPs arrived on the scene, and Lieutenant Won told us the roadblocks on the highways leaving Inchon were set up in a matter of minutes."

"The thieves must've had a vehicle waiting."

"Maybe. Maybe not. Still, it would've been risky to flee Inchon right away."

Ernie was right about that. There was only one superhighway running from here to Seoul, another old meandering country road running roughly parallel, and a third thoroughfare heading south along the coast. Nothing going north or east to the Yellow Sea. KNP traffic units routinely patrolled those three roads, and as soon as they were notified by radio of the bank robbery, they'd have set up roadblocks, checking everyone out, searching bags. They hadn't found any wads of cash or suspicious *Miguks* trying to leave town. If the thieves had tried to escape by sea, they'd be even easier to catch. Korean fishermen talk, and the Korean Navy had been alerted. It was hard to believe that two Americans wouldn't soon have come to the attention of the inquisitive Korean National Police. Fleeing via aircraft was out of the question. Kimpo International, the nearest airport, is located on the road to Seoul, beyond the KNP roadblocks, and all other aircraft was strictly controlled by the Korean military.

"Maybe they beat the roadblocks," Ernie said. "If so, they're gone and there's nothing we can do about it now. But I doubt they would've been able to move that fast. If they didn't beat the roadblocks, if they're still here in Inchon, where would they go?"

"A GI compound?"

"Maybe. That little transportation unit sits right below the Olympos. Unlikely that even a couple of GIs would be stupid enough to conduct such a daring robbery in their own backyard, but stranger things have happened. We'll check it out."

"And the Seaman's Club," I said.

"Yeah. Merchant marines. Who knows?"

Ernie started up the jeep but I motioned for him to stop.

"What?" he said impatiently.

"I just thought of something. Wait here."

Reluctantly, Ernie turned off the jeep's engine, while I climbed out and ran back into the police headquarters building. A half-hour later, when I returned, the sky above the Yellow Sea had turned a dark blue. Ernie was still sitting behind the steering wheel, sleeping, his fingers laced across his stomach. A buzzing yellow street lamp shone down on him. I shook him awake.

He sat up and rubbed his eyes. "What you got?" he asked groggily.

I unrolled a police sketch and held it up to the light of the street lamp.

Ernie whistled. "Who's that?"

"The smiling woman," I said.

He whistled again. "Now I understand why you followed her into a dark alley."

I studied the sketch. The woman was gorgeous. The Korean artist, a talented young man, had captured completely the description I'd given him. He even had her smiling. What he couldn't catch, no matter how many times I tried to explain, was the madness in her eyes. In the sketch she looked beautiful. Radiant. In real life, she'd looked obsessed. Desperate. Crazed.

I rolled the sketch up, walked around and jumped into the front seat next to Ernie. He started the jeep's engine and cruised in first gear down the steep hills. The air began to reek of fish and garlic and the tang of salt-splashed sea.

I hugged the sketch closer, wondering about the smiling woman. Wondering if I'd ever see her again.

First we stopped at the tiny military compound.

The compound was nestled behind the United Seaman's Service Club in the shadow of the huge Olympos Hotel.

It was after regular duty hours for GIs now, and the dark compound seemed deserted. The arch over the main gate bore a replica of the red-and-white 8th U.S. Army cloverleaf patch and said 71st Transportation Company. The entire complex consisted of six Quonset huts, which included the sleeping quarters for the fifteen GIs stationed there.

In the Orderly Room, an irritable corporal assigned the night duty as Charge of Quarters managed to locate an even more irritable First Sergeant. After we identified ourselves and told him the nature of our business, he pointed to a board behind his desk marked "Personnel Roster." There were black-and-white photos of every GI in the unit, arranged in a pyramid from the Captain, who was the Commanding Officer, to the First Sergeant himself, down to the lowliest private. No one was absent without leave, the First Sergeant told us, and everyone had been at their assigned duty stations at eleven hundred hours this morning. We showed him and the Charge of Quarters the sketches of the two thieves the KNPs had provided. Both claimed to have never seen those men before.

On our own, we compared the sketches to the photos on the personnel roster. No obvious matches. But the sketches were nondescript. Almost blurry. As would've been the recollections of a handful of casino employees who probably spent most of their time during the robbery staring at the barrels of the pistols pointed at them. The one sketch was of a generic Caucasian. Pug nose, square face, short hair, eyes unseen behind opaque shades. The other was even less specific. Dark man, dark hair, dark shades. He could be a curly-haired Korean, a Hispanic, a swarthy Caucasian, or even a light-skinned black.

A group of American witnesses might've been able to figure out the man's race. But to Koreans, all GIs are part of one race: foreigners. It was becoming apparent to me that these sketches were not going to be much help.

The Charge of Quarters even decided to be a smartass about the whole thing.

"These guys look more like you two than anybody else," he said.

Ernie and I ignored him. I unrolled the sketch of the smiling woman. Both men leaned forward, mouths open, and for a moment I thought they might drool. When the CQ reached for the sketch, I slapped his hand away.

"Hey!" he said.

"Have you seen her or not?"

They both shook their heads and the CQ said, "I wish I had."

I thanked the First Sergeant for his cooperation. In response, he grunted.

The United Seaman's Service Club was our next stop. All the employees—the cooks, the waitresses, the bartenders—were Koreans, except for the American manager. He was a chubby, bald, middle-aged ex-merchant marine originally from New Jersey, and he definitely did not match the two young faces in the sketches. He claimed the KNPs had already been by and questioned everyone in the club about the robbery. Still, at that time, they didn't have the sketches. We showed the charcoal-limned faces to all the employees, and they all claimed they had never seen them before. The only ships in port currently were one Panamanian vessel manned by Filipinos, one Greek ship manned by Greeks, and a Japanese ship manned by Japanese. None of the crews frequented the United Seaman's Service Club. The Filipinos and the Greeks because they were poor. The Japanese because they didn't appreciate the food.

"Tonight's special is prime rib," the manager told us.

Ernie and I declined. No time for chow.

Then I unrolled the sketch of the smiling woman and showed it around. The Korean men seemed mildly interested, but the women uniformly crinkled their noses. I asked what was wrong. Most of the women wouldn't answer, but one rotund waitress waggled her finger at the sketch and said, "She not Korean."

"What is she?" I asked.

"Maybe . . ." She started to say something but then thought better of it and shook her head. "I don't know."

Everyone denied having seen the smiling woman.

In the cocktail lounge, an elderly Caucasian man lay with his face down on a table near the juke box. The man was red-nosed, unshaven, and snoring.

The Korean bartender stood at attention behind the bar.

"How long has this guy been here?" I asked him.

"We open, most tick he come."

"Most tick" is a GI corruption of the Japanese word *mosukoshi*, which means "in a little while" or "soon" combined with an English expression of time, as in "ticktock." Therefore, "most tick."

"What time did you open?" I asked the bartender.

"Bar open eleven hundred hours."

So this drunk had arrived here shortly after eleven a.m., during or shortly after the robbery of the Olympos Casino.

"Did the KNPs talk to him?" I asked.

The bartender crinkled his nose in disgust. "They no like."

I was seeing a lot of crinkled noses today. Even a dedicated Korean cop is reluctant to talk to Americans. Especially drunk ones. They're trouble. Either they start shouting and throwing their weight around or, if you arrest them, heat comes down from on high, asking why are you ruining the delicate interplay of Korean American relations. I could tell from the reek of the man's breath that he'd probably been drunk since this morning and would've been considered an unreliable witness anyway.

Ernie and I glanced at one another, and he nodded and stepped forward. Using his left hand, Ernie held the back of the man's head down on the cocktail table. With his right, he slipped a wrinkled wallet out of the drunk's hip pocket. He handed it to me.

I rifled through the contents until I found a military ID.

"Retiree," I said. "U.S. Navy Chief Petty Officer. Wallace, Hubert K."

Ernie shook Hubert K. Wallace awake. The startled man stared up at us with red-rimmed eyes. Confused. The bartender handed me a glass of water; I handed it to Ernie. Instead of offering the man a drink, Ernie tossed the contents of the glass flush into the face of retired CPO Hubert K. Wallace.

The man sputtered and sat up, clawing moisture out of his eyes, fully awake now.

"What the . . ."

"Okay, Wally," Ernie said. "Give. What'd you see this morning?"

"See?"

"When you came in for your hair of the dog shortly after eleven hundred hours. You must've seen something. Something unusual going on at the Olympos."

"Oh, yeah," Wallace replied. "You mean those two guys."

Ernie and I tensed. Wallace rubbed more water out of his eye sockets and continued.

"In a hurry," Wallace said, "both of them. A big bag under their arm."

"Under whose arm? The light-skinned guy or the dark one?"

Wallace crinkled his forehead. "The dark one, I think."

"Where'd they go?"

"The dark one ran north."

"Toward the train station?" I asked.

"Yeah."

"And the light one?" Ernie asked.

"He came here."

"Here?" I said. "To the Seaman's Club?"

"Well, not inside. There was a cab parked outside. He jumped in the back, said something to the driver."

"Did you hear what he said?"

"No. I was too far away."

"Which way did the car go?"

"South."

"Toward the Port of Inchon?"

"Yeah. Toward the port."

We questioned Wallace a little longer, but that was all he knew. Still, we'd come up with a witness. I jotted down the particulars from his military ID and prodded him for his address and told him that we might need to question him later. He asked us to buy him a drink.

"Things are a little tight right now," he explained.

Ernie complied, slapping a buck on the bar.

Outside in the jeep we talked it over.

"The dark guy must've taken the money and jumped on the train to Seoul," I said. "Before the KNPs had time to react."

During the day, commuter trains from Inchon to Seoul depart about every fifteen minutes.

"Smart move," Ernie said. "A dark man alone would blend in with the Koreans easier."

"And the other guy?"

"If he had taken that cab to Seoul, he would've never made it past the road blocks."

"So he's still here?"

"Maybe."

"If you were a GI, hot, holed up in Inchon, where would you hide?"

"Some place where money talks," Ernie said, "and some place where there are plenty of foreigners and where people don't read the newspapers much."

There was only one place in Inchon that met that description. We both thought of it at the same time: The Yellow House.

4

The Yellow House was not a house. It was an area near the main entrance to the Port of Inchon set aside specifically for the entertainment of foreign sailors. Jammed with brothels, the entire fifteen- or twenty-acre area was as densely packed as the Casbah.

"Won't the KNPs check it out?" I asked.

"When they have time," Ernie said, "but not now, they're overextended. Besides, it would take a small army to search every little hovel in every little hooch in the Yellow House."

"We're a small army."

"That we are."

Ernie started up the jeep, backed away from the United Seaman's Service Club, and gunned the engine hard, swerving on dirty pavement, heading south toward what was perhaps the most notorious den of iniquity in the Far East: the Yellow House.

Last spring, on a bright sunny day, Ernie and I had cruised in his open-topped jeep through the narrow lanes of the Yellow

House. The two- and three-story brothels loomed on either side, and since it was late morning, the girls were out and about, not sitting in lingerie behind brightly lit display windows, as they were required to do at night. Instead they wore their regular clothes: house dresses, blue jeans, tight-fitting T-shirts. There were no foreign sailors about, so they were outside, their black hair tied up and held by silver clasps, munching on snacks or playing badminton or gossiping with their neighbors. Some of them held plastic pans propped against their hips, filled with soap and shampoo and washcloths, sauntering on their way to the public bathhouse. When Ernie and I approached, driving slowly through the narrow lanes in the jeep, they shouted, and more of them swarmed out of the brothels, and then they were all headed toward us like young girls on their way to a rock concert.

Quickly, our jeep was surrounded. Ernie shifted into low gear and barely crept forward. All the girls laughed and reached into the open-topped jeep and some pinched us and then squealed when we slapped their hands away. Others down the lane gazed out of their second- and third-story windows, waving and yelling at us.

You'd think they'd be sick of men, in their line of work. But to them young GIs are like saviors. Their usual clientele is surly merchant marines, most from Greece or the Philippines or Indonesia or other countries just as poor as Korea. They pinch every penny and pinch more than that. American GIs are the only men who have something in common with the girls who work the Yellow House: they're young, naive, caught in a world not of their own choosing, and quickly finding out, sometimes painfully, what life's struggle is about. GIs are for the most part clean and healthy, and they have more disposable income than the merchant marines. Most important of all, some GIs are young enough and foolish enough that they just might take one of the Yellow House girls away from all this. It's happened before, plenty of times, and that is why, on that fine spring day, the fresh round faces of the young whores of the Yellow House were so playful when they saw Ernie and me. And so full of hope.

This time, Ernie parked the jeep two blocks away from the Yellow House, and we approached on foot. Ernie checked the .45 under his coat. Without thinking, I checked mine and was momentarily shocked to find my shoulder holster empty. Then I remembered. He had it, the dark thief.

Did Ernie and I have a plan? Not exactly. We'd enter the Yellow House as we normally did, sniff around, pretend to be shopping for a girl. Try not to raise any alarms. Try not to scare away the thief. We wouldn't Bogart our way into the Yellow House like twenty or thirty KNPs would. And while we were shopping for girls, we'd look for anything unusual. Anything that might give us a lead.

Night had lain its purple blanket over the City of Inchon. As Ernie and I navigated the cobbled pedestrian lanes, yellow street lamps buzzed nervous greetings. Ahead, sandwiched between a row of brick buildings, loomed the dark opening to one of the many narrow alleys leading into the Yellow House. Ernie flashed me a thumbs-up, turned, and entered the gloom.

I followed.

A cold mist from the Yellow Sea began to roll into the city. Soon, we were wading through a blanket of fog. The walls seemed to lean forward, closing in around us.

I was still trying to figure if the crooks who robbed the Olympos Casino bought my badge and gun on the black market, or if they were somehow in on the theft of those items from the beginning.

As far as I knew, and as far as the Korean National Police knew, there was no black market in guns in Korea. The penalty was too harsh. Death, as a matter of fact. The only people daring enough to traffic in weaponry and explosives were the highly trained Communist agents who infiltrate into the south from North Korea. But that's a military operation, conceived and controlled by the People's Army in Pyongyang, and there's no way a couple of miscreant GIs could've bought my gun and my badge from North Korean agents.

More probably, they'd obtained the .45 and the badge from the smiling woman herself. But what's the chance that a poor, half-caste prostitute would just happen to know two guys who were in the market for a pistol and were daring enough to rob the Olympos Casino? It was unlikely that she'd lured me into an alley, convinced some guys to bop me over the head and help her steal my gun and badge, and then—within a couple of days—just happened to find two buyers for those items who just happened to be planning a robbery.

More likely, the two thieves who robbed the Olympos Casino and shot Miss Han Ok-hi had been in cahoots with the smiling woman from the beginning. From the moment one of them came up with the evil idea until she drugged my glass of beer and lured me into that cold Itaewon alley, she'd been part of a team. A team with a plan.

I'd been targeted.

Would they have bopped Ernie over the head if they'd been given the chance?

Probably. But, as usual, Ernie was surrounded that night by a bevy of women. The smiling woman hadn't bothered competing with that. Instead, she'd turned her star power on me. The lone and drunken and morose George Sueño. The perfect target for a beautiful blonde Asian woman with blue eyes and a smile that advertised madness.

And I'd walked right into her trap, like the fool that I am.

* * *

She said her name was Suk-ja.

She sat on a plump red cushion, wearing see-through pink silk panties and a frilly silk upper garment of the same material. Her face was overly made-up, but the goop couldn't hide her ready smile and curious expression. While listening to Ernie talk, she alternately wrinkled her brow and contorted the lines around her full-lipped grin, until she looked like a white-faced mime performing in front of a close-up camera. But she wasn't mugging for laughs; she was genuinely interested in what Ernie had to say and what he and I were doing here in House Number 59 in a narrow alley about as close to smack dab in the middle of the Yellow House area as it was possible to get. So far, House Number 59 was the sixth brothel we'd reconnoitered.

"You want girl?" Suk-ja asked.

"Maybe," Ernie replied. "First we checky checky every woman."

Ernie waved his hand to indicate the entire expanse of the neighborhood known as the Yellow House.

"You *dingy dingy*?" Suk-ja asked, circling her forefinger around her ear. "Too many woman. No have time checky checky all."

Ernie shrugged, grinned, and glanced at me. "Maybe me and my *chingu*, we try."

Suk-ja rolled her brown eyes. "Every GI think they *big* deal. Every GI think they number *hana*."

She pressed one elbow against her crotch, stuck her forearm straight out, and fisted her palm.

"Too *skoshi*," Ernie replied. Too small. "Me *taaksan*."

He spread his open palms apart, as if describing a huge fish.

Suk-ja laughed and covered her mouth with both hands.

"Every GI same same," she said. "All time bullshit."

"No bullshit," Ernie replied.

Suk-ja rolled her eyes toward the varnished rafter beams.

While they bantered, I'd been looking through the window at

the shadowy figures pacing the narrow alley. Men. Hands in their pockets, shoulders hunched against the cold, damp mist. Koreans? Greeks? Japanese? In the fog-filled gloom, I couldn't tell.

Suk-ja wasn't the only woman on display in this brightly lit room on this warm, vinyl-covered floor, wearing nothing but see-through undies. There were about a half-dozen girls seated near us, some of them listening absently to Ernie and Suk-ja's conversation, others watching—like me—anxiously out the window. They for a customer. Me for a thief.

The other girls didn't speak English as well as Suk-ja—she'd been here at the Yellow House for a few months already, she told us. When we'd first arrived at House Number 59, I'd asked the women in Korean, as casually as I could, if they'd seen an American, someone who looked like Ernie. They stared blankly, wishing they had, wishing they could earn some income to contribute to their ever-growing mountain of debt.

The mama-sans here charge them for everything: room and board, even the flimsy clothing on their backs. And once they amass a bill, which they inevitably do, the mama-sans charge interest on top of that.

Ernie didn't flash his badge. We wanted to pretend that we were just two GIs on the town. Observe. See what we could find out. Gossip spreads fast in the Yellow House, and if the word was put out that two strangers were looking for a fugitive, chances are that the fugitive would disappear into the ocean mist.

The mama-san of House Number 59 wasn't much help. She was suspicious of us from the start, what with our coats and white shirts and ties, and since we hadn't spent any money yet she was doing everything she could to show us her displeasure: turning on a water faucet in the alley out back, clanging pots and pans loudly just as Ernie and Suk-ja started to talk, clearing her throat of what must've been huge wads of phlegm whenever she tottered through the room.

Soon she'd tell us to either choose a girl and cough up some dough or get lost.

I pulled on my earlobe and Ernie understood the signal: time for us to move on. There were, after all, over forty houses of prostitution registered in the Yellow House area, all of them numbered and inspected regularly by the Inchon Municipal Health Department. We had a lot of ground to cover before the midnight curfew.

We said our goodbyes and were halfway down the cement stairway to the front door, when Suk-ja, wooden sandals clomping, came running down after us. From the harsh yellow light streaming in from outside, her slim figure was outlined in perfect symmetry beneath her flimsy pink negligee. She grabbed Ernie's elbow.

"You CID, right?"

So much for cover. Ernie was amused. "What makes you say that?"

"When you come in," Suk-ja said, "you look at shoes."

As in most Korean homes, one is obliged by custom to take off one's shoes before entering. So at the entranceway to House Number 59, there was a large assortment of footwear. Each pair either brightly colored or spangled with glitter and sequins. There was only one pair of men's shoes, not mass-produced like GI shoes, but handmade. About the right size for a Korean man. Maybe the mama-san's husband or live-in boyfriend. But no evidence of Greek sailors. Or GIs.

"Yes," Ernie said. "So what if we did?"

"You checky checky shoes," Suk-ja replied, "because you wanna know who's inside House Number 59. And then when you talk to me, this guy . . ." She pointed at me. "He don't look at girls. He stare out window." Suk-ja squinted, mimicking my gaze. "Checky checky every man who walk by. Either he like boy or he CID. Gotta be."

Ernie guffawed. "Maybe he likes boys."

Suk-ja eyed me more carefully. "No." She shook her head vehemently.

"Okay, Suk-ja," Ernie said, placing his hands on his hips. "What of it? What if we are CID?"

"I hear about girl get shot. Radio say. Good girl. Work at Olympos."

This woman who called herself Suk-ja was no idiot. She'd not only figured out who we were, but why we had ventured into the Yellow House. I stepped back from the doorway and glanced up at the brightly lit window of House Number 59. Inside, the girls sat in various states of undress, heads hanging down or cocked to the side, staring listlessly at the parade of furtive men outside.

Suk-ja, however, missed nothing.

"I help," she said.

"How can you help?" Ernie asked.

"I hear something today. All woman naked, they talk too much."

"What do you mean 'all women naked?'"

"At bathhouse, *pyongsin-ah*." Retard. In mock-reproach, Suk-ja slapped Ernie on the forearm. "Woman take shower, woman talk. One woman, she work at House Number Seventeen. She complain *taaksan* about man come this afternoon. He no look for woman, he look for room."

Ernie stared at her, waiting.

"He only want one room, this woman say. No like any other. Got to have window. Got to be high-up. Other things too, but she don't know all. Mama-san ask him why he care about room so much but he get angry."

"Is he an American?" I asked.

"Yeah. GI. But hair too long. Here and here."

She pinched the back of her neck and her sideburns. The guy needed a trim. If he was a GI, he hadn't stood inspection for a while.

"So why was this woman gossiping about him?" Ernie asked.

"Huh?"

"Talk. Why did she talk about him?"

"Oh. Because she get mad. He take her room, but then choose another girl to stay there with him. She no like. She want to get clean clothes take to bathhouse, but this man he busy all time with other girl. Too much boom boom. Mama-san say she no can go in, maybe he get *taaksan* angry."

"Was this guy wearing a suit like us?" I asked.

"I don't know. She no say."

"What's this woman's name?"

"I don't know. But she new. That's why she got room top floor." Suk-ja raised a hand above her head. "Away from customer."

"Where's House Number Seventeen?" Ernie asked.

"I show you."

"No. Just tell us."

Before Ernie could grab her, Suk-ja scurried away, back into House Number 59. She glanced over her shoulder and said, "*Chom kan man.*" Just a moment.

"Looks like she's going with us," Ernie said.

I nodded.

In a few minutes, Suk-ja emerged, wearing blue jeans and sneakers and a pullover wool sweater. Her hair was tied back in a tight ponytail. But what was most surprising was that she had slipped on a pair of black, horn-rimmed glasses that looked extremely attractive on the smooth oval of her unblemished face. Had she been carrying a book and a slide rule, I would've sworn she was a college girl.

"*Bali,*" she said. Hurry.

We trotted after her through a narrow, fog-filled alley. Ernie kept his hand on the hilt of his .45. I kept my eyes on shadows, suspicious, waiting for one to move.

* * *

Ernie held Suk-ja back.

We stood in the mouth of an alley gazing up at House Number 17. It was a ramshackle gray building made of rotted wood planks broken out in pustules of peeled paint. The fog hovered low to the damp, flagstone-covered lane. Behind the brightly lit plate glass window on the first floor a few women shuffled about. They seemed to be older, some slightly overweight. One wore pajamas.

"*Kuji*," Suk-ja said.

I'd learned the word on the streets, not in my Korean language class. Some would translate it as "dirty," but that wasn't quite right. "Squalid" came closer. In brothels, as in everything else in human life, there are hierarchies of quality.

Ernie caught my attention and motioned with his eyes. Most of House Number 17 was dark. But on the third floor, a dim light shone.

Ernie and I'd discussed it on the way over here. This guy Suk-ja had heard about in the bathhouse could be a GI, but maybe not. He could've had something to do with today's robbery, but maybe not. Either way we wanted to talk to him. Should we call in the KNPs? No. Too early for that. This could be nothing, a false alarm. Until we had solid information, we didn't want to bother Lieutenant Won with unnecessary requests for assistance.

We'd check out the guy ourselves.

"That's her," Suk-ja said, pointing at one of the women sitting behind the front window. "The one I talk to in bathhouse. *Paran seik.*" Wearing blue.

I translated for Ernie

"I go checky checky," Suk-ja said.

Once again, Ernie held her back. "We'll go," he said.

I studied the lit window on the third floor. No movement. A fire escape ladder attached to the outer wall ran up to the roof. As in most Korean apartment-type buildings, this one was flat, designed to allow extra space to store earthenware kimchee jars or to hang laundry. There was no movement up there, but it would be an easy jump to the roof of the next building. And from there to the next, and so on. Then down some interior stairs, and whoever had insisted on a room on the third floor of House Number 17 would be walking the streets alone, and safe.

Ernie saw it too. If the Korean National Police stormed House Number 17, the room at the top provided at least the hope of escape.

"Are you sure there was only *one* GI?" Ernie asked Suk-ja.

"That's what she say."

If this was the right guy, we had to be prepared for the fact that he would be armed. Probably with the pistol the thieves had stolen from the security guard at the Olympos Casino. Ernie pulled out his .45 and jacked back the charging handle. Suk-ja jumped away from the clang.

"Sorry," Ernie said.

Someone shouted. I peeked around the corner of the alley.

Sailors. Merchant marines. Speaking some sort of gibberish. Not English. Not Spanish. Not Korean. They crowded around the front steps of another house of prostitution. Some smoking, some swigging from brown bottles of OB Beer. All were talking, playing grab-ass. One pulled out a pocket knife and waved it around. The others hooted.

Suk-ja's hot breath warmed my elbow.

"*Shila,*" she said. Greek.

I looked down at her. "You understand?"

"Have to," she replied.

"They all stay at one house?"

"Yes. Sometimes whole ship take one house. Mama-san give, how you say?"

She slashed her hand as if cutting something.

"Discount?"

"Yes. Discount. Maybe all women old and ugly. Then mama-san must give big discount."

I studied the sailors again. They were just having fun. Still, it was a rough-looking bunch. Best to steer clear of them.

"I'll take the front," Ernie told me. "You enter there." He pointed to the house on the other side of House Number 17, away from the Greek sailors. "Go up to the roof. Cut him off if he tries to escape."

"No good. What if you run into trouble? It'll take me too long to run back down the steps."

Ernie sighed with exasperation. "Sueño, you aren't armed. What the hell good are you if the guy starts shooting?"

He didn't intend to be cutting, I knew that. Ernie was simply stating a fact.

"I go up on roof," Suk-ja said, pointing at her nose. "If he come, I hit him with kimchee jar."

Ernie and I looked at one another. It wasn't a bad idea. If she could just slow the thief down, give him something to think about, we'd be across the roof and on him in no time.

"Okay," Ernie said. "But stay low. If he has a gun, you just hide. You *arra*? You understand?" He swooshed his down-facing palm through the air, like a bird in flight. "You let him run away."

Suk-ja nodded, and then, before we could change our minds, she trotted off across the alley to the building next to 17. She disappeared through the front door.

"Okay," Ernie said. "Are those Greeks going to be any trouble?"

"I think they're preoccupied."

A woman's laughter pealed through the night. As if it were a signal, Ernie and I crouched low and trotted across the fog-shrouded alleyway.

5

Maybe it was the wood creaking beneath our feet. Maybe it was just nerves. Whatever it was, Ernie sensed something and halted, holding me back with his arm. Listening.

We were crouched in the third floor hallway of House 17, swatting at fleas, our feet squishing into damp carpet. The place reeked of urine and garlic and sex.

A grunt. A man's voice. And then a high female squeal of pain.

When we'd entered downstairs, through the front door of House Number 17, several overly made up women accosted us, clawing at our sleeves, cooing, promising us various sorts of sexual delights. Ernie tried to shush them as best he could, and while he was busy, I pulled the mama-san aside and spoke to her in Korean. We were here to see our *chingu*. An American man. I described him, then told her that we thought he was staying up on the third floor.

"*Isang han saram,*" she said. A strange guy.

"How so?" I asked.

"He stay in room all day long," she told me. "No come out. Order food from Chinese restaurant, make boy leave noodles outside door. My girl, he won't let her come out. I think she *taak-san* tired."

Robbing casinos must be good for the libido.

After a few more questions, I determined that the guy had checked in alone. He'd had no visitors, and he'd arrived on foot at about noon. Since carefully choosing room 33 on the third floor, and choosing a girl to accompany him, he hadn't emerged. There was no phone in the room—the Yellow House doesn't go in much for phones—and no one else had visited.

I handed the mama-san a red Military Payment Certificate note. That's what the U.S. Army uses as currency overseas rather than greenbacks. She stuck the crisp five dollar bill into her withered décolletage. Then she winked at me and waved Ernie and me up the stairs. What was she thinking? That we were here to bust her customer? If so, she didn't much give a damn.

In the hallway outside of room number 33, Ernie waited a few more seconds. Listening. Then we heard another squeal. Louder this time. More desperate. Whoever the girl was, and whoever this guy was, he was hurting her. I didn't like it. Neither did Ernie.

Without warning, Ernie took three steps forward and kicked in the flimsy wooden door.

I charged in past him, unarmed, but ready to dive head first into whoever was there. Ernie crouched in the doorway, pointing his .45 straight ahead and shouting, "Freeze!"

A blast sounded, and I dove toward the foot of the bed. The blankets were wrinkled and damp but there was nobody on the mattress.

Then I heard Ernie's .45 behind me. It barked once, twice.

When I raised my head, I saw that the window was open. A naked Korean woman cowered in front of it, her arms crossed over her chest, tears streaming from tightly clenched eyes. To her left, a shoe-clad foot stepped rapidly up the ladder attached to the outside wall.

Ernie fired above the girl, but his bullet hit cement, sending a cloud of dust billowing into the air. She screamed and collapsed to the floor, covering her head, kicking in panic with naked feet.

I pulled myself toward the window sill, stuck my head out, and looked up.

Again, the same shoe. A black oxford, Army-issue. It disappeared over the roof's edge. I stretched out toward the ladder, swung around, and started to climb. Up on the roof, shoe leather pounded cement.

Somehow, the guy had known we were coming. He had been dressed and ready, and he'd waited until the last moment, until we were too close to cut him off outside, to make good his escape. Had somebody warned him?

I climbed. And when I reached the edge of the roof, I peeked over, then pulled my head back down, remembering what I had just seen. An empty roof, dark, lined with earthenware kimchee jars.

He must've already jumped over to the neighboring roof. Would Suk-ja be able to slow him down, or would she just get herself hurt? Suddenly, I regretted having allowed her to help. This was our job, not hers.

Ernie was scrambling up the ladder behind me.

I clambered up onto the roof, helped pull Ernie up, and then we were running toward the far wall. Just as I was about to leap off the edge, onto the neighboring roof, Ernie grabbed me.

"Hold it." He pointed at a glimmer of light peeking around a brick chimney behind us. I shrugged him off and prepared to jump. I didn't want to leave Suk-ja over there alone, without help.

"No," Ernie said. "Look. He's not there."

I glanced across the next roof and then at the roof beyond that. No one. Not even Suk-ja.

"He's hiding," I said.

"He wouldn't," Ernie replied. "He'd keep running. Come on."

He dragged me back over to the brick chimney. On the other side was an open wooden hatchway. I looked down. Another metal ladder led down into the hallway of the third floor.

"He probably already reconnoitered," Ernie said. "Knew that we'd expect him to hop from roof to roof, but instead he doubled back. Come on."

He lowered himself through the hatchway and then let go and dropped down to the creaking floor below. I followed, and we ran down the hallway until we found the stairwell. We flew down to the first floor.

The women in front of the window were up now, terror showing in their eyes, all of them pointing through the light-smeared glass. A dark figure flashed down the street, heading toward the gang of Greek sailors blocking the walkway.

In seconds, Ernie was out on the street, running after him, me right behind.

Twenty yards ahead, I saw the dark figure smash into the unsuspecting Greeks. Men cursed and spun out of the way. A beer bottle crashed to the ground. Someone shouted and threw his hands up. I couldn't understand a word, but the guttural sounds of cursing were unmistakable. And then our quarry was through the Greeks and past them and already disappearing into the mist.

Ernie didn't slow down.

One of the Greeks shouted. They all spun, staring at Ernie, who was plowing toward them. The men stepped together and formed a phalanx, as if responding to an ancient instinct left over from Alexander's army. Before Ernie could dodge them, they walked forward and reached out for him. Momentum rammed his body into the men, who grunted and gave and then held. They began to push back.

I could've run around them. Even through the dark and the fog I could still see the figure about thirty yards ahead, gaining speed, turning around a mist-shrouded corner. But the Greek sailors were pummeling Ernie. A knife glimmered in the yellow light of the street lamp.

I veered and rammed into them.

Men screamed and cursed, and I punched and kicked, happy, at last, to be set free. For the past few days, I had been holding everything inside: pining over a lost weapon and a stolen badge; putting up with the sneers of cops who play it safe, who stay on the compound near headquarters, afraid to put themselves at risk in the dark shrouded alleys of Asia. But now I was able to fight, to feel the satisfying crunch of fist on skull. Moving as fast as I could. Acting on instinct alone. Punching, kicking, screaming.

And then there was more shouting and Ernie was pulling me away, even while I still jabbed and cursed, and then my eardrum shuddered with the blast of his .45.

As if encountering a thunderbolt, the Greeks retreated.

Ernie pointed the .45 at them and cursed and kept jerking on the back of my coat and we backed off, until finally we were enveloped by the glow of the street lamp in front of House Number 17. Suk-ja was there, reaching for us, pleading with us to follow. The next thing I knew, we were running once again through the endless dark. I was enjoying the trip, feeling light-headed, flushed with the giddy rush of having released so much tension, until suddenly the world became smaller. Pinpoints of light spangled a blanket of fog. The lights faded. The fog closed in on me. A lonely foghorn moaned far out at sea.

And then I was leaning on Ernie and my feet grew numb. Suk-ja was helping. I'm not sure exactly when, but I must've collapsed.

Damp cobbles pressed against my cheek. People jerked on my arms, but I couldn't get up.

I'd been stabbed.

The cut wasn't deep, and the blade hadn't hit any vital organs but it hurt like hell nevertheless. The doctor told me it was a slice more than a stab wound. She actually used those words.

"Slice your rib," she said, pointing at her own rib cage. "Not stab into you lung."

Her name was Dr. Lim. A bespectacled woman, middle-aged, about the size of your typical twelve-year-old American boy. But the girls at House Number 59, including Suk-ja, bowed whenever she looked at one and backed up in the hallway to make way for her as she passed. They treated her like a visiting potentate. Why? The doc was a savior to the girls in the Yellow House area. Suk-ja told me that she was in charge of the city VD clinic, a clinic that years ago set up business only a few blocks away.

Dr. Lim swabbed my wound with rubbing alcohol, then gave me a tetanus booster and a shot of antibiotic. When I asked her what kind of antibiotic it was, she grew impatient and said, "You be quiet."

I did. In the Third World doctors are gods. Not to be questioned.

Then she sewed me up. Three stitches. Without anesthetic.

All the while, I lay on the warm vinyl floor of Suk-ja's room in House Number 59, on a rolled out cotton sleeping mat. Suk-ja, the mama-san, Ernie, and about a half-dozen of the House Number 59 girls looked on, the girls still wearing their flimsy lingerie.

Life is a communal activity in Korea. Everyone believes they have a right to know what's going on.

Ernie paid Dr. Lim out of his own pocket. After she left, Suk-ja fetched a bottle of Kumbokju brand *soju*, and she and Ernie and

I sat in her room toasting one another, tossing back thimble-sized shots of the fierce rice liquor, talking about the fight, laughing, speculating on who the guy was who got away.

I passed out first.

"You smell like a sewer," Ernie said.

"You're not much better."

The time was oh-dark-thirty. The sun still hadn't come up, and Ernie and I were winding our way through the walkways of the Yellow House, heading back to House Number 17. Both of us were feeling pretty gamey, what with all the activity of the last twenty-four hours. Now, early in the Inchon morning, unable to perform our morning GI rituals—a shower, shave, and change into clean clothes—we were each becoming more uncomfortable by the minute.

Before we left House Number 59, Suk-ja had done her best to wash me up, bringing a pan of heated water for what Koreans call *seisu*, scrubbing of the hands and face. But it wasn't the same as being in the barracks and standing under a luxuriantly hot shower for twenty minutes.

The Koreans consider Americans to be unclean. Most Koreans don't have much more than one faucet or well outside to provide water for their home, therefore they don't shower every day. But when they do shower, it's with a vengeance. At a public bathhouse, they might spend two or three hours, rubbing and grinding and pelting their raw skins until every pore in their bodies is free of grease and grime.

We stood in the dark street in front of House Number 17.

The Greeks were gone. The narrow alley, where one of them had sliced me, was empty and silent. Ernie stepped up to House Number 17 and pounded on the locked door until the mama-san opened up. I explained that we wanted to talk to the girl who'd spent time yesterday with the criminal who'd escaped last night. She agreed but asked for ten more dollars. I turned her down flat. When she complained, I told her that if she preferred, I would call Lieutenant Won of the Korean National Police and she and the girl could both talk to him downtown. That was enough to make the frowning mama-san open the door and let us in. She told us to wait and went upstairs to fetch the girl.

Five minutes later, the frightened young woman knelt on the warm vinyl floor in the front room, dressed in lumpy blue jeans and three layers of upper garments, topped off with a thick wool sweater that she clutched across her chest. When we'd seen her last night, she'd been naked and screaming, while bullets whizzed past her head.

Her name was Mi-ja, she told me. Beautiful Child. I held out the sketch of the Caucasian man who'd robbed the Olympos Casino.

When she reached for it, her hand shook, as it had last night when she'd attempted to cover her nakedness. Before she grabbed hold of the flimsy construction paper, she closed her eyes and pushed it away.

"Come on, Mi-ja," Ernie said. "You have to look at it sometime."

Apparently, Mi-ja didn't understand. So far, she hadn't done anything other than kneel before us and bow her head. I spoke soothingly in Korean, asking her to just take a look at the sketch. She kept her face down, and then I realized that she was crying.

I explained that more people would be hurt if she didn't help us capture this guy.

Without looking up, Mi-ja raised the left sleeve of her sweater. There, in a straight row, red and angry, were half a dozen holes in her flesh. All about the size of the tip of a burning cigarette. She continued to hold out her arm. Nobody spoke. Nobody breathed.

Slowly, I reached out my hand, feeling the ache of the slice in my side, and, as gently as I could, I touched the fingertips of her hand with mine. We lingered like that for a few seconds, flesh on flesh, and then Mi-ja pulled her arm back and rolled down her sleeve.

I held out the sketch again. This time she took it, sat it in her lap. While she studied it, fat tears splashed against the deft pencil lines. Finally, she handed the sketch back to me. Then she nodded.

It was him.

When she finally started to talk, she told me everything.

Hundreds of commuters, maybe thousands, stood in orderly lines along the cement passenger platform next to the tracks of the Inchon Main Train Station. They were silent, barely shuffling their feet. Occasionally someone coughed.

The cut in my side didn't hurt much. Actually, my head hurt more, and my stomach still roiled from last night's *soju*.

Another blast of cold, salted mist rolled in from the Yellow Sea. Then a buzzer sounded, and the tracks rumbled, and a few seconds later a train rolled up, brightly lit inside. It stopped, two dozen doors slid open, and the people standing on the platform rushed in, spreading themselves quickly over the seats and benches.

"Seems like the whole damn city works in Seoul," Ernie said.

I braced myself against a metal railing, supporting about half my weight with my arm, trying to keep the pressure off the slice below my armpit.

"Any *Miguks*?" I asked.

"Not that I could see."

Ernie had just returned from a stroll down the loading ramp, reconnoitering the crowd. But in the dim morning light and with so many people, it was difficult. The Korean National Police were out in force. Lieutenant Won figured that the Caucasian fugitive who'd gotten away from us last night might use the morning rush hour of workers commuting to Seoul to escape from Inchon. The roadblocks had been called off. The KNPs had decided it was too disruptive to keep them on this morning. Our only chance was to get very lucky here at the train station. So far, luck didn't seem to be going our way.

In an hour, the rush hour had subsided. I bought a copy of the *Korea Herald*, an English language daily. Miss Han Ok-hi, the young casino worker who'd been shot, was still in critical condition, according to the report.

Before we reached the train station, Ernie and I flashed the sketches of the two thieves and the smiling woman to all the vendors who sold newspapers and dried cuttlefish and warm barley tea outside on the street in front of the station. None recognized anyone in the sketches, and all claimed to have been asked the same questions by the Korean National Police yesterday. But our persistence paid off.

One old woman pushing a wooden cart supporting a cast iron stove shouted her lungs out trying to interest passersby in warm chestnuts. When I showed her the sketches of the two men, she claimed to have been shown copies yesterday by a Korean policeman. She hadn't recognized the two men then; she still didn't recognize them today. But the new sketch, the sketch of the smiling woman, intrigued her.

"*Boasso*," she said, gravely nodding her head. I've seen her. "Before noon yesterday," she continued, "rushing toward a train. I noticed her because she was tall and had a wool scarf tied over her head which I thought was unusual for such a young woman. And she clutched a canvas bag."

"That's the only reason you noticed her?" I asked.

The woman blushed slightly.

"Also," she said, "she's different."

"How so?"

"Like you guys," the old woman said. "Maybe she's American."

"Was she alone?"

"No. Someone was with her. A man, I think, but I didn't pay attention."

They'd hurried right past her and hadn't stopped to buy chestnuts. Still, the half-American blonde Korean woman had been unusual enough for the old chestnut vendor to notice.

"Had you ever seen her before?" I asked the old woman.

"Never," she said. "And not since. But if I spot her again, I'll grab her and hold her for the police."

Her eyes gleamed as she told me that. Something about her enthusiasm made me feel uneasy. I shivered in the cold morning air.

I boarded the next train for Seoul.

Ernie would drive the jeep to Seoul *yok*, the Seoul Train Station and pick me up there.

Why was I taking the train back to Seoul? I wanted to experience what the smiling woman had experienced. I wanted to put myself in the place of two people—one of them clutching a bag full of stolen cash, the other knowing he'd just shot an innocent woman—and see what they'd seen on the train ride back to Seoul.

People glanced at me as I boarded, but most were polite and turned away. I strode up and down a few of the cars, just to get a feel for the train. Wooden benches lined either side of the compartments, and in the center two rows of leather straps hung from metal railings. The train wasn't too crowded now since it was past 8 a.m., so I found a spot on a bench and plopped down to watch the scenery roll by.

Ernie and I had pretty much nailed the sequence of events. At least to my satisfaction.

The smiling woman, along with two male accomplices, had decided to rob the Olympos Hotel and Casino. To make it easier to bluff their way into the casino's cashier cage, they needed law enforcement badges and a weapon of some sort. They cased Itaewon. For how long, I don't know, but eventually the smiling woman found her chance and managed to sit alone with an armed man: me. That's when she slipped something into my beer. In the alley, her accomplices knocked me over the head, stole my badge and my .45, and three days later, robbed the Olympos Casino.

After the robbery, the two men split up. One of them fleeing for the anonymity of the Yellow House, the other keeping the money and joining the smiling woman for the train ride back to Seoul. Why the train? It would be leaving right away, it wouldn't be subject to KNP roadblocks, and the police would be looking for two men traveling together—not a man and a woman.

Had the thief planned on shooting Han Ok-hi? I doubted it. More likely his target had been the owner of the Olympos Casino, probably because he expected there to be more money hidden in a safe in his office. But the owner had fled through the escape hatch in the back wall, the thief had fired in an attempt to stop him, and poor innocent Han Ok-hi had stepped in front of a bullet that hadn't been intended for her.

That's the way I saw the case so far.

The next question was, where would the dark thief and the smiling woman go?

Somewhere in Seoul, no doubt. Somewhere they felt safe. Home, probably. But where was that? In a city of eight million people, it wouldn't be easy to pinpoint them. But there were ways. There had to be.

Once we left the outskirts of Inchon, the train picked up speed. Small stations flashed by: Jeimul-po, Dong-am, Pupyong, Buchon. But we didn't stop at any of them. This was the express. Seoul Station was our destination. Nothing less. A half hour later, we slowed as we rolled through the densely populated district of Yongdung-po, and then we wound our way onto a bridge that crossed the blue expanse of the Han River. There, on the far river bank, rose the mighty city of Seoul. Green-topped Namsan Mountain loomed to the right, the skyscrapers of the downtown district were straight ahead and to the left. Behind them, craggy granite peaks had long protected the ancient capital from marauding nomads from the north. The train slowed as it reached the far bank and the tracks rose slightly and we rumbled through the southern district of Yongsan. Finally, two miles later, we came to a halt behind the stately old Seoul Station. It was a round-domed building, made of brick, and looked like something out of *Doctor Zhivago*. It had been built in the 1890s by Russian architects, supposedly a gift to the Korean people from the Czar.

I jumped off the train onto the cement platform and strolled along with the flow of the crowd, surveying directional signs, keeping my eyes open for anything that might give me a hint of where the smiling woman had gone.

At a long row of turnstiles, I stood in line and handed my ticket to a uniformed Korean conductor. The white-gloved man squinted at me curiously but made no comment. Inside the main hall of the station, people hustled back and forth: women balancing bundles on their heads, men pushing carts laden with wood-framed boxes, school children in black military uniforms with square backpacks slung over their shoulders.

Outside, rows of vendors. Six times as many as at the Inchon Station. Systematically, I worked through every stall, showing the sketches of the two men and the smiling woman. Just as systematically, I was told no one had ever seen them before. I showed the sketches to the two policemen working traffic in front of the bus and taxi stands. Again, the response was negative.

The entire left wing of Seoul Station was occupied by 8th Army's RTO, the Rail Transportation Office. Inside was a counter for traveling GIs to buy train tickets, a small PX, a snack stand, even a barber shop. A little piece of America. Ernie's highly polished jeep, with its distinctive leather tuck-and-roll interior, sat parked out front. He was waiting for me inside, but somehow I couldn't bring myself to enter 8th Army's RTO. It would be too much like leaving Korea. I wanted to stay with the people—Koreans—as the smiling woman and the dark thief had done. So, instead of searching for Ernie, I walked down a cement stairway and joined the crowd in a pedestrian tunnel crossing beneath the busy thoroughfare that ran in front of Seoul Station. There were more vendors on the far end of the underpass and more negative responses. I continued walking into the heart of Seoul. In the distance, I saw the green tile-roofed edifice of Namdae-mun, the Great South Gate, a meticulously preserved remnant of the stone wall that had once surrounded the entire ancient capital. Skyscrapers loomed over dark alleys lined with canvas lean-tos. People swarmed everywhere. Signs hung from brick walls covered with the neatly stenciled *hangul* lettering or the elegantly slashed characters of Chinese script. Squid tentacles boiled in oil, dumplings steamed in straw baskets. Only a few of the Koreans strolling past me gawked at the tall *Miguk* wandering lost through their bustling city.

I felt alone in this multitude. Where had she gone? Where was the smiling woman?

A horn sounded from behind. Ernie leaned out the driver's side of his jeep.

"What are you, Sueño, lost?"

I turned away from him and stared into the endless passageways, inhaling deeply the garlic and green onion and rice powder wafting in the air.

Ernie was right. I was lost. As lost as a little half-American girl who'd grown up in this indifferent city. A girl who didn't belong here. A girl who probably hadn't even been able to afford to go to school, who hadn't worn the same dark skirts and tunics and white blouses as the other school-age girls, who hadn't been welcomed at the playground or the sports field or patted on the head fondly by a bald Buddhist monk. A girl who'd grown up in this teeming city apart. Alone. A girl who'd grown up, despite all her travails, to become a beautiful woman. Beautiful, mad, and dangerous.

Ernie honked again. He parked the jeep, jumped out, and ran after me. Seconds later, he grabbed me by the elbow.

"What the hell's the matter with you, Sueño? Couldn't you hear me?"

"I could hear you," I said.

"Then come on! Eighth Army's had MPs out looking for us all morning."

A finger of cold fear poked into my stomach. "What's wrong?"

"Don't know yet. They won't tell me. But we have to get our butts back to the CID office right away."

"Why?"

"The CG," Ernie said. He meant the Commanding General of the 8th United States Army.

"What about him?"

"He wants to talk to us."

"Us?"

"That's what I said."

Ernie tugged me toward the jeep. This time I followed.

6

Tango.

That is the military code name and what everybody calls the place. Also known as 8th Army Headquarters (Rear). It's a huge cavern carved out of the side of Mount Baekun, fifteen miles south of Seoul. If and when war broke out with North Korea, this would be the place our heroic military commanders and their bureaucratic staffs would retreat to. It's a small city unto itself, with offices, communications facilities, sleeping quarters, a chow hall, and even a PX to make sure that no one runs out of chewing gum or cigarettes. They say that Tango's inner concrete walls are thick enough to withstand a direct nuclear blast of thirty megatons. Now, in the late afternoon haze, twenty-foot-high sliding steel doors stood open, like the welcoming jaws of a hungry dragon.

A squad of MPs approached our Army-issue sedan.

"What's this all about, Top?" Ernie asked.

Ernie and I were sitting in the back seat. Up front, behind the wheel, was the Provost Marshal's white-gloved driver, Mr. Huang. Next to him sat our immediate supervisor, the First Sergeant of the 8th Army CID Detachment.

As soon as Ernie and I had returned from Inchon and reported to the CID headquarters in Seoul, all hell broke loose.

"Where you been?" was the main question, interlaced with various four-letter Anglo-Saxon expletives. We heard it from Staff Sergeant Riley, from the CID First Sergeant, and a few minutes later, from Colonel Brace himself, the Provost Marshal of the 8th United States Army.

Neither Ernie nor I answered. They knew where we'd been. Investigating a crime. What they really meant to ask was "What took you so long?" and "Why weren't you here when I needed information from you in order to avoid bureaucratic embarrassment?"

They knew all about the robbery of the Olympos Casino. It was big news this morning at the 8th Army Command briefing. Mainly because an Army issue .45—probably mine—had been used to shoot a female Korean bystander. A GI had probably pulled the trigger. This was also the crux of the story splashed all over the Korean newspapers, television, and radio that day.

The *Pacific Stars & Stripes*, official newspaper of the U.S. Department of Defense, had yet to find the story interesting enough to run. They were, however, featuring a full-page spread on the new outhouse built by a combat engineer unit at an orphanage in Mapo.

Ernie and I had just started to type up our report when the First Sergeant emerged from his office, wearing a freshly pressed dress uniform. We were ordered out to the Provost Marshal's sedan, told to climb in the back seat, and then Mr. Huang drove us south across the Han River. Once we left Seoul, we continued south down the Seoul-Pusan Expressway. Ernie and I were both too stubborn to ask questions. If the First Sergeant wanted to push us around and not tell us what was going on, so be it. We were soldiers. We followed orders. To the letter if we had to. The First Sergeant sat in front with his shoulders back, staring straight ahead. For the entire thirty-minute drive we were quiet, all of us, admiring the brown rice paddies that stretched toward gently rolling hills.

Finally, when we pulled up in front of Tango, this huge bomb shelter that is 8th Army Headquarters (Rear), Ernie couldn't stand the silent treatment any more. He spoke up and asked what this was all about.

The First Sergeant cleared his throat. "Go with the MPs," he said. "Somebody wants to talk to you."

"Who? The CG?"

"Just answer the questions straight, Bascom. Don't offer any information that isn't requested. If you don't know the answer to something, say you don't know. Don't try to bullshit the man. And, most importantly, no mouthing off."

An MP swung open the rear door. When Ernie hesitated, the MP leaned in and grabbed him by the arm.

"Keep your hands off!" he shouted. "I'm coming."

With that, Ernie climbed out. So did I. The MPs fell in on either side of us, and without a verbal command, we all marched toward the huge looming doors of Tango, 8th Army Headquarters (Rear).

Mr. Huang shoved the sedan in gear, performed a wide, slow U-turn, and he and the First Sergeant drove off toward the expressway leading back to Seoul.

Neither one of them waved.

Our little detail walked down one of Tango's endless carpeted hallways. There was dim fluorescent lighting, portable walls, and a feeling of cold immensity above. And no doubt that we were in the hollowed-out center of a mountain. The MPs stopped at the end of the hallway, and one of them knocked on a double door made of paneled wood. In the center hung the red-and-white four-leaf-clover patch of the 8th United States Army.

Ernie and I and the small squad of MPs stood for what seemed a long time. Finally, from within, a hollow voice shouted, "Enter!" The MP saluted and he and his fellow MPs stepped back, forming a single file in the center of the hallway. As one, they performed an about face and marched back down the corridor.

Ernie and I glanced at one another. "I've had plenty of ass-chewings before," Ernie whispered, "but no one's ever gone to *this* much trouble." Then he stepped past me and pushed through the door into the room.

I followed, frightened at first by the darkness.

When my mother lay dying, when I was a child barely able to talk, her room had been dark like this. Women stood by, lace mantillas covering their heads, and a priest hovered near her bed. They brought me forward. My mother's face, which had once been smiling and vibrant, appeared wan in the flickering candle-light. She grabbed my hand. Her fingers were cold. So cold I pulled away. But she beckoned and I stepped forward and grabbed her hand in both of mine. Her fingers, and then her palm, became warm again and she smiled at me, a smile as radiant as the wings of a flight of angels.

Suddenly I was back in Tango, shoving such thoughts out of my mind, forcing my concentration back to my immediate sur-roundings. I'm an adult now. A soldier. A CID investigator. Time to do my job. And accept my ass-chewing if that is what I was here for.

There was a box with a handle on a desk. It was metal, larg-er than a construction worker's lunch box, and sticking out of the top was a six-inch-wide bulb. It lit up the desktop but nothing else. The rest of the room was dark. Still, there was enough light to see the man who sat behind the desk. He was thin to the point of emaciation, his receding gray hairline cut so close to the scalp you couldn't be sure where his forehead ended and the top of his skull began. He wore highly starched fatigues with a razor sharp crease running from the top of the shoulder down to the wrist. On his pressed collar were four black stars. His name tag said ARMBREWSTER.

Ernie and I both knew who he was, as did every American GI in country. General Frederick K. Armbrewster, Commanding General of the United Nations Command, U.S. Forces Korea, and the 8th United States Army.

Bony fingers shuffled through stacks of paperwork. Much of the paper had already been placed in a box labeled "Out." More was stacked on the other side of the desk, next to a box labeled "In."

"Bullshit," General Armbrewster said. His voice sounded dry. Crackling. As if he needed desperately to gulp down a glass of water. "That's what it is," he continued. "All paperwork is bullshit. Designed by the politicians and lawyers to keep themselves rich."

Then he looked up at us, his mouth set in a straight line.

Ernie and I saluted, both feeling awkward, what with our unshaven faces and grimy clothes. General Armbrewster didn't seem to notice. Listlessly, he returned our salute and told us to sit on two folding metal chairs in front of his desk.

He didn't bother to explain the lighting, or why he had to work with a battery-powered lamp on his desk. This was a man who didn't bother with trifles.

He continued to finish up the paperwork in front of him, hardly noticing us. But he hadn't made Ernie and me remain at attention while he worked. That seemed out of character. Usually, when we received ass-chewings—and Ernie and I were experts on them—the person doing the chewing took every opportunity to humiliate us; to keep us standing at attention while they leisurely finished their task. That was standard procedure. In the army, humiliating subordinates is what lifers live for.

General Armbrewster was different. He hadn't brought us here to chew us out. Such minute disciplinary detail would be beneath his dignity. He'd brought us here for another reason. Something that had to be done face to face.

Suddenly, I was nervous. Much more nervous than I had been before.

The General finished with the paperwork, slipped a metal clip on a short stack, and tossed it into the "Out" basket. Then he stared at us, each in turn, long and steady.

"First," he said, "forget all the bullshit."

I sat with my back ramrod straight in the chair.

He turned his attention fully to me. "They're going to bring a Report of Survey down on you, Sueño, for losing your forty-five. A Report of Survey that could lead to court-martial." He stared at me for a few moments. I stared back. He turned toward Ernie. "And an official reprimand against you, Bascom, for being the senior man and allowing it to happen."

He waited for a reaction, but Ernie and I were still too stunned at being in the presence of a four-star general to say anything. Ernie shows no reverence for anyone alive. And I've seen him mouth off in circumstances that were bound to get him slapped in the stockade or even killed, but he chose to mouth off anyway. Threats don't scare him. Yet even he knew that now was not the time to say anything. A private audience with the Commanding General of 8th Army was not something two lowly CID agents experienced every day. It was as if we'd suddenly been shoved in a cage with a Bengal tiger.

"I believe in redemption," General Armbrewster declared. "We all make mistakes. The test of a man is whether or not he corrects them."

He paused and seemed to want a response to this. Was he saying that neither Ernie nor I would be punished if we caught the people who stole my .45 and shot Han Ok-hi? I think he was. However, I was afraid to say so out loud. Negotiating with a four-star general was not something I was used to. The silence grew longer. Finally, I found the courage to speak. "Yes, sir," I said. Nothing more.

Armbrewster nodded his bony head, taking my statement as complete acquiescence. Which, of course, it was.

"On the other hand, if one doesn't correct one's mistakes . . ."

The General let the sentence trail off, spreading both his hands, as if allowing sand to sift through his fingers.

His meaning was clear. If Ernie and I don't catch the people who perpetrated these crimes, he'd allow all charges to be brought against us. The full force and power of the Uniform Code of Military Justice would hammer us senseless.

These weren't idle threats. In the military justice system, the commanding officer performs the same function that the district attorney and the grand jury do in civilian proceedings. He decides who is going to be prosecuted and who isn't. In addition, he appoints the officers who will preside as judges over the trial. And often there's an understanding as to what the CG expects the verdict to be. So the Commanding General functions as the district attorney and grand jury and also—if he chooses to—as the judge and the jury. Ernie and I were toast if the CG decided against us, and we both knew it.

When General Armbrewster was satisfied that we understood what he was saying, he crossed his arms and leaned back in his swivel chair.

"He's a killer."

Ernie and I both jerked forward. My first thought was for Han Ok-hi—she hadn't made it, after all—but the General said, "A traveling man."

"Where?" Ernie croaked.

"Up in Songtan."

We knew the place. The village outside Osan Air Force Base, the largest U.S. Air Base in Korea.

"I don't know much more about the victim yet," General Armbrewster said. "An old hag who works the streets, they tell me."

"Who told you, sir?" Ernie was already investigating.

"The Korean National Police Liaison Officer," Armbrewster answered. "He says the KNPs are worried because they don't have access to our compounds or much good intelligence amongst the GIs who work mischief off base. He's going to need American help."

"How do the KNPs know it's the same guy?" I asked.

"The way she was killed. Raped, strangled, stabbed, and then she was . . ."

"But that's not the way Han Ok-hi was hurt," Ernie interrupted. "Not at all."

"I'm not finished." Armbrewster stared at Ernie until he quieted. "Once this cretin was through with the old bag, he put a hole in her skull. With a forty-five."

My side was still throbbing from the knife wound last night. In fact, I was worried it had started bleeding again. But now it felt as if another hot blade had been shoved into my stomach, by the same guy who had pulled the trigger of my pistol.

"It could be anybody's forty-five," I said. "The KNPs couldn't run a ballistics test that quickly."

"No, they couldn't," Armbrewster agreed. "But they also have this."

He shoved a small piece of cardboard wrapped in plastic across his desk. Then, while Ernie and I leaned forward, he lifted the portable lamp and shone the beam directly onto the document.

It was made of rectangular white cardboard. Wallet-sized. Perforated edges. A standard 8th Army Form: USFK 108-b, Weapons Receipt. The card that was needed by every GI when he checked out his weapon from his unit's arms room. This one described the type of weapon authorized—.45 pistol, automatic, one-each—and next to that the serial number of the specific weapon.

I recognized the serial number. I had memorized it over a year ago, when I'd arrived in Korea and been assigned to the 8th Army CID Detachment.

I also recognized the name typed into the top square: Sueño, George (NMI).

There was a thumbprint on the card. Brown. Probably dried blood. Clear. As if it had been purposely placed there by a professional.

I looked back at General Armbrewster, still too stunned to speak. Ernie spoke for me.

"He wants us to catch him," Ernie said.

General Armbrewster nodded his skeleton-like skull.

"Yes. On that, if nothing else, I and this cretin agree. I want you to catch him. Now. Not tomorrow, not the next day, but now! I saw your MPRFs." Military Personnel Records Folders. General Armbrewster took a deep breath. "You're both a couple of fuck-offs. You never do anything right. Your black market arrest statistics are for shit, and you're always embarrassing some staff officer with a lot of scrambled eggs on the brim of his cap. Why? Because you don't care about a damn thing except catching crooks." He looked directly at us, eyes blazing. "Good work, goddamn it! Keep the bastards on their toes. You two are the only cops I've got who can find out anything in the ville. All the other investigators are like the assholes who work for me here in the headshed. Always trying to impress somebody, disdainful of going where the real soldiering is. This case fell on you two like a ton of latrine waste. God only knows why. But it's yours now. You solve it. You catch this creep. You do it now. Not later. Now! Before he kills again. And if anybody gives you any bullshit, any bullshit at all, you contact me. You understand?"

We both nodded.

He handed us each another wallet-sized card. This one clean, no blood on it, only his name and personal phone number and his radio call sign. English on one side, Korean on the other. The card was stamped "Secret."

"Don't stop until you find him."

We both stood and were about to salute again when General Armbrewster waved us off. "I told you. Forget about the bullshit. Get this guy. Get him now."

We turned and started to walk out, but he called me back, as if he'd forgotten something.

"Sueño," he said. General Armbrewster was standing. "One more thing. Sorry to have to break this to you, but that casino dealer in Inchon, the woman named Han Ok-hi. Bad news. She died less than an hour ago."

He twisted the portable lamp, aiming it at the paperwork on his desk until his face was again deep in shadow. Then he sat down and began reading, ignoring me completely. I thought of Han Ok-hi's parents. Their daughter was gone. I thought of my own responsibility. I wanted to speak, but what was there to say? So I stood there, silently, the only sound in the room the scratch, scratch, scratch, of a fountain pen on parchment.

7

A squad of Military Police vehicles, sirens blaring, escorted us south, away from Seoul, away from Tango, toward the town known as Songtan.

"VIP treatment," Ernie said. "About time."

We were in the back seat of yet another Army-issue sedan. This time with two MPs up front, one driving, the other holding an M-16 rifle across his lap.

Ernie leaned forward. "You guys ever seen two GIs being treated better than this?"

"Yeah," the driver drawled. "When we transport them in chains down to the stockade."

The other MP guffawed. Ernie sat back in his seat and turned to me and smirked. "Jealousy is a terrible thing."

But I wasn't so sure the MPs were wrong. We'd just been handed a hot potato by the Commanding General of the 8th United States Army and we'd just been given permission to ride roughshod over any military staff officer who dared to stand in our way. In the Machiavellian world of the 8th Army bureaucracy, such power had to be used with caution. Staff officers have long memories. And they know how to bite. Not to mention that failure meant court-martial. But I tried not to think about that.

We were off the expressway now, on a country road leading south toward Songtan-*up*. The town of Songtan. "*Si*" on the end of a place name means city, "*up*" means town, and "*li*" or "*ni*" means village. The farther down the hierarchy you go, the farther out in the country you are. Rice paddies stretched away on either side, and the MP convoy occasionally was forced to swerve around an ox-drawn cart laden with piles of moist alfalfa. The weather was cold and hazy, the way I like it. When I was growing up in L.A., we didn't experience many days like this: overcast, fresh air, a brisk chill invigorating a gentle breeze. What we got mostly was blazing hot sidewalks and smog thick enough to make breathing painful when we tried to play.

It was autumn now. According to ancient poets, the most beautiful time of the year on the Korean Peninsula. The time when the name Chosun, the Land of the Morning Calm, seems most appropriate. When leaves turn brown and red and yellow, and farmers harvest the last dry fields of grain, and rice paddies are flooded in preparation for the winter freeze. Autumn is the time of Chusok, the harvest moon festival, on the fifteenth day of the eighth lunar month. When families gather and perform the *seibei* ceremony and then trek out into the countryside, toward grave mounds dotting round hills, to commune with the dead. To eat a family lunch with long-departed relatives and provide them with updates on the progress of the living. It's a warm time, a family time, a time of bounty and good cheer. And a melancholy time for an American GI alone in a strange country. But I'm used to that. I grew up in foster homes in L.A., and I felt alone in a strange country there too.

Straw-thatched huts lined the two-lane road but they soon

gave way to tile-roofed buildings. Behind a line of hills was the vast acreage of Osan Air Force Base, the largest American air base in Korea.

At the edge of Songtan, we passed the open parking lot of the bustling Songtan Bus Station and hung a right across a double line of railroad tracks. The one-lane road narrowed, and we slowed to a crawl. The road became even narrower, and we spotted the first pool halls and beer joints, and finally the lead jeep pulled over. The MPs parked their vehicles, leaving one MP behind as a guard, and we stepped into the maze of passageways and alleys that branched out from the main road.

Shops filled every nook and cranny: brassware emporiums, leather goods stores, sporting equipment outlets, and then, at last, the bars. One nightclub after another, each with brightly colored neon just now blinking on in the late-afternoon dusk. Business girls, most freshly made-up for their night's work, loitered in bead-draped doorways. They waved at the MPs, inviting them in, laughing, cooing at us. A few of the MPs waved back.

The NCO in charge barked: "Knock off the bullshit!" The MPs turned away from the girls and resumed their grim-faced expressions.

There was no doubt where the crime scene was located. The entire walkway had been roped off, and two Korean National Policemen stood guard. Ernie showed them his CID badge, and I flashed my newly-minted military identification card. When they hesitated, Ernie said, "He's with me." He grabbed me by the arm, lifted the white police tape, and before the cops could react, the two of us ducked through.

Behind us, scantily-clad business girls flooded out of the front doorways of every bar lining the alleyway.

"Set up a perimeter," the MP sergeant shouted. His men scurried, preparing to protect this crowded little walkway from the threat of a pack of mini-skirted Korean bargirls.

Why had General Armbrewster sent such a large contingent of MPs with us? I suppose because he wanted to show that he meant business. The murder of an innocent young woman had struck a nerve here in Korea, and the honchos of 8th Army were always wary of bad publicity. Ernie and I were to be provided with the resources we needed to conduct this investigation as we saw fit. Actually, we hoped to ditch the MP escort as soon as possible. Grabbing a lot of attention was good for advancing a military career, but it wasn't much help in solving a murder.

Three men in khaki stood outside the mouth of a dark alley. As we approached, they watched us expectantly. Korean cops. One of the men I recognized. Captain Noh, commander of the Songtan contingent of the Korean National Police. We'd worked with him once or twice before. Results had been mixed but, fortunately, Ernie hadn't pissed him off. Not much anyway.

We shook hands and rapid introductions were made. Without further ado, Captain Noh led us down the alleyway.

He was a grim-faced man with a lugubrious expression and a no-nonsense, by-the-book way of doing his job. Last time we'd worked with him he'd told Ernie and me that he'd been prowling the streets of Songtan for more than twenty years, since the end of the Korean War. Crime had gotten worse, according to him. After the war, people were starving, and they stole, robbed, and maimed in order to feed their families. Now, he said, they were becoming westernized. They stole, robbed, and maimed simply for kicks.

Ten-foot-high brick and cement-block walls loomed on either side of the narrow pathway. Behind the walls, pots clanged and radios blared. Families at home, hidden behind their barricades, cut off from the raucous world of the GI bar district. Every half meter or so, a brick-lined channel in the center of the cobbled lane was punctuated by three-inch-wide air vents. Sewage bubbled through subterranean passageways, reeking of ammonia and soap suds and waste. The air in the walkway was pungent not only with the smell of sewage, but with clouds of charcoal gas billowing out from beneath the warm *ondol* floors that heated the homes behind the walls.

The alley curved and then curved again. Sinuous, like a dragon winding its way through a stone maze. Finally, in front of a red tile-roofed overhang in the center of a red-brick wall, Captain Noh stopped. The wall didn't look too welcoming. It was topped with rusted barbed wire and shards of glass embedded in mortar. Captain Noh rapped on the varnished wooden gate and shouted, "*Na ya!*" It's me!

Immediately, the door in the gate opened.

Inside, a uniformed KNP came to attention and saluted. Captain Noh returned the salute as he ducked through the door. The rest of our entourage followed him inside. Before entering, I paused to study the recessed gate. Embedded in the cement wall next to the door was a metal speaker for an intercom system, and below that a brass placard. I pushed the buzzer. It worked. I pulled out my notebook and jotted down the name etched in the placard: Jo Kyong-ah, written in phonetic script. Jo being the family name, Kyong-ah a given name for a female. After the name, etched into the brass, was a Chinese character. I copied that down also. A complicated character, twenty strokes, female radical on the left. As I scribbled, the pronunciation and meaning of the word came to me: *yang*. The Korean word for "Miss." Whoever owned this house was announcing to the world that she was a woman, and an unmarried woman at that.

Unusual in Korea. For an unmarried woman to be successful enough to own a home and then, more unusual, to be proud of her unmarried status. Whoever lived here—or *had* lived here—was a person who didn't give a damn what other people thought.

I ducked through the small doorway.

Opulence. That's the word that jumped to my mind.

Usually—at least in Itaewon—these hooches behind big walls

are not much to shout about. Wood or brick tile-roofed buildings, single story, with a dusty courtyard containing a chicken coop and an outside cement *byonso*, usually stenciled with the letters "W.C."

But this place was something else.

The garden was well tended with neatly raked gravel, spotted with those stunted trees you see in Japanese travelogues, and in the center, a gurgling, stone-lined fountain. Golden fins splashed through water running blue. Arrayed along the walls, a row of three-foot-high earthenware jars stood at attention, freshly dusted, probably containing a bounty of cabbage and turnip and cucumber kimchee.

The raised floor of the hooch itself was freshly varnished and immaculately clean. To the left, a door opened into a large storeroom. The overhead bulb was switched on, splashing artificial light onto piles of cardboard boxes emblazoned with English and Japanese lettering. Each box touted the contents within: color TV sets, stereo components, electric fans, radios, tape recorders. Whoever lived here was running her own electronics shop. I stepped closer and inspected the boxes. None bore a Republic of Korea customs stamp.

Captain Noh and the other cops slipped off their shoes and stepped up onto the raised floor. As Ernie and I followed, the first thing I noticed was the odor of something burnt. Neither Captain Noh nor Ernie nor the other cops paid any attention to the smell, but I paused and inhaled deeply. The aroma was faint but unmistakable. Something cooked. Overcooked. Something natural, some sort of wood, or maybe an herb. Was it pine? I compared the odor swirling about me to the cloying sweetness of scented air freshener. This was much harsher. Sizzled sap. Nothing artificial about it.

The sliding doors leading to the main living room had been pulled open. Handle-level, the oil-paper in the latticework design was ripped open. Captain Noh pointed at the tear with his ballpoint pen.

"Somebody climb wall, break in here."

Ernie knelt and examined the inner hasp. "Busted," he said.

"Yes," Captain Noh replied. "But look. No scratch."

The metal hasp was still in pristine condition, but the wood around the hasp had been splintered inward.

"He didn't use a tool," Ernie said.

"Right. He just push." Captain Noh mimicked the action of shoving the sliding door inward.

"That would've made a lot of noise," Ernie said.

"Yes. Lot of noise."

"So the people inside, they must've woken up."

"Yes." Captain Noh nodded. "Only one person inside. Woman. She wake up. She fight."

In Korea, the custom was that if a burglar broke into a home, and the home was empty, he had every right to take whatever he wanted. After all, if the owner valued those possessions, he would've left someone home to guard them. If, however, someone inside the home made their presence known—by coughing or banging on doors, or otherwise preparing to confront the burglar—the burglar was obliged, by tradition, to withdraw. If the burglar was in the process of withdrawing and the homeowner chased and beat him, the homeowner could be charged with assault. On the other hand, if the burglar refused to withdraw when he discovered that someone was in the home, he was compounding his crime, and the punishment he could expect would increase by an order of magnitude.

This burglar was one of those Westernized criminals Captain Noh found so repugnant. The homeowner had risen, confronted him, and he had refused to withdraw. To say the least.

We followed Captain Noh deeper into the hooch.

The next room was immaculate. Delicate celadon vases on shelves, low mother-of-pearl cabinets displaying books and hand-crafted artifacts that looked like antiques. Clocks, dolls in glass cases, brass incense burners, hand-painted porcelain dishware. Fragile works of art that wouldn't last five minutes in the barracks I lived in. But nothing had been disturbed.

We walked down a short hallway.

The odor of burnt pine faded slightly. The source was behind me now, on the far side of the house. Possibly in the kitchen.

When we reached the end of the hallway, Captain Noh paused at a closed sliding door. He reached into his coat pocket, and the other two Korean cops did the same. They pulled out gauze face masks and slipped them over their noses and mouths. Captain Noh pulled out two more masks and handed one each to Ernie and me. Without comment, Ernie slipped his on. So did I.

Then Captain Noh passed out sets of white cotton gloves. When all our hands and fingers were properly attired, he slid back the oil-papered door.

The stench hit me first. Blood. I knew what it was because I'd smelled it before. There must've been a lot of it to put out such a powerful odor.

Why hadn't I smelled it in the hallway? Because the wood-work in this home was handcrafted and everything, including the runners on the sliding doors, were shaped and planed and sealed with meticulous care.

Who was this woman who lived in such finery? Who owned so many precious things? And what did she have to do with the woman who stole my .45 and my badge and the men who robbed the Olympos Casino in Inchon? Was she just a random victim, or was there some method to this madness?

No sense thinking about those things now. Time to observe, gather facts. There'd be time to sort them out later.

Captain Noh switched on a tinted glass lamp, suffusing the room in a purple glow.

Opulence again. An armoire, of the same expensive mother-of-pearl design. A low dressing table. No bed, just another varnished wood slat floor: *ondol*, heated by steam running through stone ducts below. A thick down-filled mat had been bunched up and skewed away from the center of the floor. A silk-covered comforter, hand-embroidered with white cranes rising from green reeds, was wadded in a corner, smeared with blood.

Here, in this room, there was no neatness. Dozens of vases and bottles and vials of lotion and unguents and creams had been stepped on and smashed against walls and smeared on the floor, mingling with the jellylike coagulated blood.

"She fought," Captain Noh said. "Before they took her body away, I look." He held up his own hand and picked at the space beneath his fingernails. "How you say? Skin?"

"Flesh," Ernie corrected. "Beneath her fingernails. She scratched him?"

Ernie clawed the air like a tomcat.

"Yes. She scratch. She punch too. And bite. Knuckles bruised. Very dark. Two tooth broken." He opened his mouth and pointed at his incisors.

"She did a number on the guy," Ernie said.

Captain Noh stared blankly.

"She hurt him," Ernie said.

Captain Noh nodded. "Yes. She hurt him. And he hurt her."

Meanwhile, the other two cops were kneeling and studying the broken bric-a-brac around the room.

Everything was still dusted with fingerprint powder, and Captain Noh went on to explain that in the hours they had been waiting for us, not only had the body been taken away, but his technicians had already collected bits of flesh and broken fingernails and body hair. All evidence had been rushed to Seoul for evaluation in the main KNP lab. Results would start trickling in tomorrow.

A representative from the Songtan coroner's office had measured liver temperature and rigor mortis, and the other things that coroners measure, and estimated the time of death at sometime early this morning. Probably before dawn.

There was a bullet hole in the floor. The wood surrounding it had been singed upon entry. Already, the KNP technicians had pried out the bullet and it would be evaluated in the lab in Seoul along with the other evidence. The initial indication was that it had come from a .45 automatic pistol.

Like mine.

So far, the evidence seemed clear. The man had broken into the home, confronted the woman who lived here, wrestled with her, subdued her, raped her, and then killed her. Not necessarily in that order. The woman's purse lay next to the mother-of-pearl armoire, all contents dumped on the floor. Everything apparently there—Korean National Identification Card, keys, photographs, etc.—except no money. After robbing the woman, as a final farewell, he had shot her through the back of the head with a .45 automatic pistol.

A pistol that I believed to be mine.

Ernie and I looked at one another. The Caucasian criminal we had chased out of the Yellow House last night could never have made it here in time to commit this crime. Not with a midnight-to-four curfew enforced all over the Republic of Korea. All traffic stops—except for those vehicles with governmentally approved emergency dispatches. We had rousted the guy out of his hiding place less than an hour before midnight. He never could've arranged for transportation all the way to Songtan in that amount of time.

It had to be the other guy. The guy with the curly brown hair. The guy who looked like me. The guy who'd departed the Inchon Train Station in the company of the smiling woman.

Ernie read my mind. "Could be the brown-haired guy," he said. "Or maybe they sold your .45 and weapons card to someone else."

"Why the weapons card? What value does that have? And

even if they did give the card to someone, why would that person leave it at a murder site?"

Ernie thought about that for a moment, but didn't answer.

I believed that the guy who perpetrated this crime was the same brown-haired man who had robbed the Olympos Casino in Inchon and shot Miss Han Ok-hi in the back. He left my weapons card here because he wanted us to know that he had struck again.

Ernie felt the same as I did. He shook his head sadly.

"Whoever this guy is," Ernie said, "he's a bad boy. A very bad boy."

Captain Noh described how the body had been found.

"Here," he said, pointing to the center of the room. "Face down. Arms out." He raised his arms over his head as if preparing to take a leap off a high dive. "He shoot in back of head. But before he do, he try to strangle her. Here." He pointed toward the back of his neck, and then thrust his hands in front of him, leaning down, as if applying pressure toward the floor.

"He strangled her from the back?" Ernie asked.

"Yes. Rape her from back too. Push down very hard. Front of her neck touch floor, head, how you say, back."

He mimicked the motion again, twisting the top of his head back toward his shoulder blades.

"Her head was tilted back," Ernie said, "because he was pushing her neck down onto the floor."

"Yes," Captain Noh said.

In front of where the body had lain was a small foot-high table with folding legs. The type Koreans use for everything from eating dinner to putting on makeup. Set like sentries across the table were three jewelry boxes. One large—the one in the center—and two smaller, on either flank. It was some sort of display.

While the brown-haired GI had clenched her neck, the woman had been forced to her knees in front of this small table with the neat display of jewelry boxes. Then he had shoved her face down on the floor and had tried to strangle her from behind. It hadn't worked. Apparently, she was a determined woman. She'd struggled. And when he hadn't been able to kill her by strangulation, he'd pulled out the .45 and shot her in the back of the head. Her heart hadn't stopped right away. That's why all the blood.

But why try to strangle her from the back? From the front of the neck, a strong man can place his thumbs right over the windpipe and with enough force cut off all air, stifle sound from the vocal chords, and even in some cases snap the neck bone itself. This would be much more difficult to do from the back.

And why set up this little table with this jewelry-case display? It was almost as if it were some sort of shrine. But a shrine to what?

Another anomaly occurred to me.

"Where did he leave my weapons card?" I asked.

Captain Noh shook his head and held up one finger, to let me know that he'd answer in a minute.

We all backed out of the room, took off our gloves and our masks, and returned to the front room. I veered off toward the kitchen. It was a rectangular room, not much bigger than a large pantry in an American household, the cement floor lowered two feet below the wooden foundation of the rest of the house. On a low cement bench sat three propane burners. Atop one was a flat, round skillet. The fire below had been turned off and the knob dusted with fingerprint powder.

Captain Noh stood behind me. "He start fire," he said.

There was a box of stick matches next to the burners.

"Why?" Ernie asked.

Captain Noh turned to look at him. The three of us were jammed into the narrow kitchen doorway.

"He want cook something."

"What?"

Captain Noh pointed. I stepped down into the kitchen, sliding my toes into a pair of plastic sandals. In the round skillet was spread a single layer of charred black things that looked like needles. Using my thumb and forefinger, I picked up a few. They crumbled to dust in my hand.

Captain Noh said something in Korean. *"Solip."* I didn't understand the word at first, but then I figured it out. Pine needles. Roasted at a low temperature. That explained the burnt odor.

"Why?" I asked Captain Noh.

He shrugged. "Maybe because of smell." Then he turned quickly and walked away.

Ernie glanced at me and raised an eyebrow.

I felt the same way. Captain Noh wasn't telling us something. Why would he be so sensitive about burnt pine needles? I almost ran after him to question him further but stopped myself. No sense pressing. When Koreans decide to keep a secret from a foreigner, no power on earth can pry it out of them. Best to wait, figure it out for yourself. Usually, in due time, I can.

Out in the courtyard, Captain Noh and his cohorts waited for us in front of the *byonso*. It was in its own separate little cement-block building up against the northern wall. When Captain Noh opened the wooden door, the smell of ammonia jabbed into our nostrils like a sharpened fingernail.

"There," he said.

"Where?" I asked.

"Right there. Inside." He pointed down.

I stepped into the outhouse and gazed into the rectangular hole in the cement floor. Down into filth and blackness. Most Korean homes don't have commodes. They just come out here and squat and do their business. If you're a man urinating, you aim carefully.

"My weapons card?" I asked. "You found it here?"

"Yes," Captain Noh said, his face unreadable. "First he do something. Then he drop card on top of it."

Ernie crossed his arms, trying not to laugh.

"Thorough search," Ernie told Captain Noh.

Captain Noh nodded, taking Ernie's comment as a compliment. He turned and returned to his colleagues waiting in the courtyard.

I grimaced at Ernie.

"Apparently," Ernie said, grinning broadly now, "the brown-haired GI holds you in high esteem."

"Can it, Ernie."

Then, with Captain Noh and his two assistants, Ernie and I left the home of the woman known as Jo Kyong-ah. "Miss" Jo Kyong-ah.

Now deceased.

We spent the rest of the evening canvassing the bars and brothels of Songtan-up. The MPs were happy because they were able to loiter in the brightly lit alleys amidst blaring rock music and play grab ass with the Korean business girls. Ernie and I, however, were becoming less happy the more we learned.

By the time our little convoy left Songtan, we were downright morose.

The MPs drove us all the way back to Seoul. We stopped at various military checkpoints along the way because it was after the midnight curfew. We showed the stern-faced ROK soldiers our emergency dispatch and, holding their rifles at port arms, they waved us on. We approached the southern outskirts of Seoul, the Han River quiet and calm. Through glimmering moonlight, we crossed Chamsu Bridge, and the MPs drove us onto 8th Army's Yongsan Compound and dropped us off in front of our barracks. I thanked them for the lift and told them we would no longer need their services. There was some grumbling about that; every GI likes easy duty. The sergeant in charge took it well, however, and sped off, leading his little convoy back to their home in the cave at Tango, 8th Army Headquarters (Rear).

* * *

The next morning, Ernie and I were showered, shaved, changed into clean clothes, and back on the job at 8th Army CID headquarters. But there was a new attitude toward us now. Cool. Distant. Agents walked down the hallway, not looking at us, pretending we weren't there.

I knew, of course, why.

First, I'd committed the sin of losing my weapon and my badge. Something most cops swore would never happen to them unless they were dead. Second, Ernie and I together had committed the much worse sin of going "over the heads" of our immediate supervisors. Of course we hadn't intended to. The decision to lay the blessing of the 8th Army Commander on us had come, not from us, but from General Armbrewster, the 8th Army Commander himself. Still, in the army, it doesn't matter if you're not responsible for a bureaucratic breach. The sin has been committed. No amount of rational explanation can wash away the stain.

As always happens in military units, the attitude of the bosses flows downhill to the peons. Although they wouldn't state it directly, the orders from the Provost Marshal and the CID Detachment First Sergeant were clear. Sueño and Bascom are to be shunned. Anyone who associates with them will be guilty of disloyalty.

Even Staff Sergeant Riley, the Admin NCO of the CID Detachment, acted as if we were strangers. Ernie put up with this new attitude for about twenty seconds.

"You're the biggest drunk in Eighth Army," he told Riley, "and suddenly you're too good for us?"

Riley's skinny face looked shocked. "The biggest drunk?"

"What? Did I stutter?" Ernie asked. "If you hadn't started with lining up those shots along the bar at the NCO Club, none of this shit would've happened."

That was the night a group of us had gotten drunk, stumbled out to Itaewon, and I'd ended up losing my weapon and my badge.

"So it's my fault now?"

"It's always been your fault."

I interrupted.

"Let's get down to business, Riley. Show me the lists."

Sullenly, Sergeant Riley slid a stack of paperwork across his desk.

Ernie shot Riley a sour look and then turned and stalked across the room to the other side of the office. He sat down in front of the desk of Miss Kim, the attractive young Admin Office secretary. She ignored him, continuing to hammer away at the *hangul* lettering on her manual typewriter. Not that she didn't like Ernie. She liked him a lot. In fact, for the last few weeks they'd been dating regularly. But Miss Kim also had the Korean respect for harmony in the family—and in the work place—that's hammered into them from birth. She certainly didn't want to step into the middle of any dispute between Americans.

I plopped down on a vinyl-cushioned chair and started going through the lists.

At first I couldn't focus. I was still thinking about last night, the crime scene at the home of Jo Kyong-ah, and the gossip I'd heard about her from the bar girls and GIs who hang out in the back alleys of Songtan.

Miss Jo Kyong-ah was retired, people said. She'd been a big-time black-market mama-san in Seoul, in Itaewon to be exact, before something caused her to pack it all in and move down south to Songtan. Now, with a packet full of ill-gotten money, she'd bought a nice home and set herself up as a respectable citizen. Still, old habits run deep, and she'd continued to dabble in the black market, concentrating on high-value items, like the television sets and stereo equipment we'd seen in her storeroom. And her clientele, one of the owners of a local bar told me, were rich Koreans who could afford to buy the high-priced items. Her suppliers were field-grade Air Force officers who could write themselves up Letters of

THE DOOR TO BITTERNESS

Authorization to weasel their way around the strict 8th Army Ration Control regulations.

Why had everyone been so forthright with their information? Jealousy. Jo Kyong-ah was seen as a wealthy intruder who'd taken business away from the more longtime residents of Songtan. Still, she'd lived a quiet life, and no one could imagine a competitor going so far as to kill her.

As Ernie and I made our rounds, we flashed the sketches of the dark-haired shooter, the Caucasian thief, and the half-American smiling woman.

Nobody recognized any of them.

It seemed strange to me. Whoever had murdered Jo Kyong-ah—and I had no reason to think it hadn't been the brown-haired casino thief—had picked their target well. She was a wealthy woman. No telling how much cash and jewelry the killer might've gotten away with. But if the brown-haired man planned to pick out a wealthy target, he would've either had to have lived here—and known who had money—or he would've had to come to Songtan and gather information. Either way, someone would've noticed him.

Captain Noh and his legion of Korean National Policemen were having no better luck than we were. Instead of interviewing business girls and GIs, they worked the Korean side of the fence. Talking to citizens who lived nearby, who worked in the open-air Songtan Market. Even, he told me, wealthy local residents who were suspected of having bought black-market goods from Jo Kyong-ah. All dead ends.

Somehow, the brown-haired GI had slipped into Songtan unnoticed, gone directly to his intended target, beat her, raped her, robbed her, and murdered her. All without being noticed by anyone.

I put Songtan out of my mind and studied the lists Sergeant Riley provided.

AWOL GIs. Absent without leave. That was the first list and, I figured, the most likely to produce results. I decided to save that for last, and set it on the bottom of my pile of perforated onion-skin computer sheets.

Riley also ran a check at 8th Army Data Processing to see if anything had been purchased with my Ration Control Plate. I was worried that whoever had stolen my wallet would use my military identification card and my RCP to go on compound and buy duty-free goods out of the Commissary and PX. So far, nothing. But the computer punch cards were only collected once a week, so something might turn up on the next list.

I set that one aside and quickly studied the list of GIs on mid-tour leave back to the States and in-country leave here in Korea. Both lists were massive. What with over 50,000 GIs in country, five to ten percent were on leave at any given time. Neither list would be useful. They were both too long. I set them aside.

Finally, I was back to the list of AWOL GIs. There must've been close to five hundred names on it. Each entry showed the name of the GI, his rank, his unit, the date of unauthorized departure, and—in most cases—the date of return. American GIs in Korea don't usually stay AWOL long. Where were they going to go? The country only has one international airport: Kimpo, near Seoul. And the Korean authorities are always on alert and allow no one to enter or leave the country without being thoroughly checked. To leave Korea, an AWOL American GI would need a passport and a forged visa. Very few GIs have passports and even fewer of them are creative enough to forge the other documents. And what with the terrorism threat from Communist North Korea, there was no black market in forged passports and visas. The Korean National Police would never allow it. They come down hard on anyone who tries, and the jail sentences are unbelievably harsh. Like heroin smuggling and arms trafficking, passport forgery is a criminal enterprise that just doesn't exist in Korea.

So when their money runs out, most AWOL GIs return to their units.

A few stay out longer. Usually, they are well connected with the Korean underworld and manage to make a living buying from the PX and selling on the black market. There is a small trafficking operation for forged military ID cards and phony 8th Army Ration Control Plates. The KNPs don't crack down as harshly on these operations since everyone makes money and it's seen as being relatively harmless. Certainly no threat to national security.

It was those GIs I concentrated on. The ones who'd been away from their units for at least a week. After about a half hour of work, I'd jotted down a list in my notebook of two dozen names. Then I made a list of GIs who'd left more recently and hadn't yet returned. This provided another fourteen names. Now my list was manageable.

Then I started studying the units.

I was looking for the Field Artillery.

Why? Because of what Mi-ja had told me. She was the business girl who'd spent part of the night with the Caucasian GI at House Number 17 at the Yellow House in Inchon. I'd questioned her for almost an hour, trying to coax her into describing everything about him that she could remember.

She'd been nervous, still traumatized by being burned repeatedly with the tip of a lit cigarette. The fingers of her hand quivered as she talked. She pointed to various places on her body as she described the Caucasian GI who'd tortured her.

No, there were no red marks or calloused skin on his shoulders. That eliminated an infantry grunt, who had to hump a forty-pound rucksack on a twenty-mile road march. Yes, his hands were rough and bruised, so he worked physically, maybe lifting things. She hadn't noticed the soles of his feet, but she had noticed that he turned the radio up too loud—tuning in to AFKN, the Armed Forces Korea Network, to listen to the news broadcasts in

English. She stuck two fingers in her ears, to indicate how loud the radio had been. His hands and face were tan, much darker than his arms or chest or the rest of his body. That indicated that he worked outdoors, but wore clothing—probably a long-sleeved military fatigue uniform—while doing it.

Putting everything together spelled Field Artillery. He wasn't an infantryman; his hands were rough, and, most importantly, his hearing was shot. Standing next to the big guns, hearing the booms every day, being too lazy or insufficiently self-disciplined to keep his earplugs in at all times. All these things indicated that he was a gun bunny.

Still, all these things might be coincidence. He could be a supply clerk or a truck driver, or a concussed and deafened infantryman, for all I knew. But I had to narrow down the list somehow.

If we didn't catch him quickly, he and his brown-haired buddy might strike again.

To clear my mind, I stood up and walked over to the silver coffee urn, and pulled myself a mug of java. While I sipped on the hot brew, Ernie and Miss Kim made eyes at one another. She managed to keep typing as she did so, but at a slower rate.

What did she see in him? She was a good woman from a good family. A family that probably had high hopes of marrying her off to some well-educated young Korean man. A man who would treat her in the Confucian tradition as a respected wife and, eventually, a respected mother. What did she see in some wild GI who chased everything in skirts?

Excitement, I suppose. One thing about Ernie Bascom is that he was never boring. Ernie was a connoisseur of the insane. He loved people who didn't give a flying fart about what others thought, who were full of rage or passion or madness. They entertained him. And as soon as they stopped frothing at the mouth, he'd poke them—either verbally or physically—curious to see how they'd react. Like a demented kid torturing a beetle.

But Miss Kim couldn't get enough of Ernie Bascom. They'd already gone out together about a half-dozen times that I knew of. And maybe more, because when we weren't working Ernie had a way of disappearing and showing up the next day with a satisfied grin on his face. I tried not to give him the satisfaction of asking what he'd been up to. At least not too often. But occasionally my curiosity got the best of me. He told me once that he'd spent the night with Miss Kim, and then went on to describe her long-legged, statuesque body. Before he delved into too much detail, I changed the subject. Torment, I don't need.

I carried my hot mug of coffee back to my seat. Then I started going through my list of AWOL GIs.

Three out of the three dozen were in field artillery units. One at Camp Stanley in Uijongbu, another at Camp Howze near Pupyong-ni, and another at Camp Pelham near Munsan. I jotted down names. Of the three, two were typically Anglo-Saxon, and the third guy was named Jamal. I figured him to be black and crossed him off my list. That left two: Kevin S. Wintersmith at Camp Howze and Rodney Boltworks at Camp Pelham.

Which one to roust first? No way to decide. Geography was the tie breaker. Camp Howze was closer to Seoul, and if Wintersmith didn't pan out, Ernie and I could drive farther north on the Military Supply Route toward the Demilitarized Zone to Camp Pelham and check out Private First Class Rodney Boltworks.

I stuffed my notebook into my pocket, finished my coffee, and told Ernie it was time to go. He rose from his chair, unconcerned, but Miss Kim frowned, sorry to see him leave.

Staff Sergeant Riley remained hunched over his paperwork, and even as we stomped out of the office, he continued trying to pretend that we hadn't even been there.

8

The morning was wonderfully cool and overcast and in the open-topped jeep, as we sped north on the two-lane highway, a line of crystal blue hovered above brown rice paddies. Layered atop the line was a ceiling of churning gray clouds.

Camp Howze sat about a half mile off the MSR, on a hilltop overlooking a bar-spangled village. The Second Division MPs up here were more suspicious than their 8th Army counterparts back in Seoul and at the main gate they studied our identification and our vehicle dispatch carefully. Before waving us through, they radioed ahead to the Command Post to let them know we were coming.

As we pulled up to the sand-bagged bunker, a field-grade officer wearing a fur-lined cap stepped out to greet us. When we told him what we wanted, he marched us right into the Operations Center. In minutes, Private Kevin S. Wintersmith stood at attention in front of us. He had a short red crew cut, moist green eyes, and his fatigues, face, and hands were soiled and reeked of rancid lard from the grease traps he'd been cleaning. The major told us the story. Of his own volition, Wintersmith had returned to his unit two days ago and he'd been pulling KP—kitchen police duty—ever since.

Just to be thorough, I pulled out the sketch of the Caucasian GI and looked at it. So did Ernie. So did the major.

Not even close.

Wintersmith had never heard of the Olympos Casino in Inchon nor of Brothel Number 17 at the Yellow House. Nor of a teenage girl named Mi-ja whose arm had been lined with cigarette burns.

We thanked the major, returned to our jeep, and continued north toward the DMZ.

At the main gate of Camp Pelham, one MP and two uniformed Korean security guards studied our emergency vehicle dispatch. Behind them, a wooden bridge spanned a rock-strewn gully. Above the guard shack, a neatly painted arch said: *Welcome to the Home of the 2/17th Field Artillery.* Then in smaller letters: *Shoot, Move, and Communicate!* The MP tried to scratch his head, but his fingers were blocked by the rim of his black helmet liner.

"They're in the field," he told us, "the entire battalion. Left this morning on a move-out alert."

"How long ago?" Ernie asked.

"About zero six hundred."

They had a four hour start on us.

"Where were they headed?" I asked.

The MP shrugged. "Don't know. Classified."

I thought about it. No military unit leaves their headquarters compound completely deserted. Somebody would know where the Second of the 17th could be found.

"Where's your Operations Officer?" I asked.

This time the MP pointed. "The battalion head shed. Over there, on your right."

Ernie slammed the jeep in gear, and we rolled across the rickety wooden bridge, beneath the stenciled arch, onto the black-topped roads of Camp Pelham, home of the Second of the 17th Field Artillery. The MP was right. The place did look deserted: rows of Quonset huts, striped camouflage green, their big double doors padlocked shut. Occasionally, a lone firelight shone through the morning mist.

The battalion headquarters was larger than the other buildings. Three Quonset huts arranged in a T-formation, hooked together by covered walkways, the entire complex splashed with paint of the Army's favorite shade: olive drab.

We parked in the gravel parking lot. Only one door was open, on the side of the stem of the T. Inside, the long corridor was quiet. We stood still, listening. Finally, toward the cross of the T, we heard a toilet flush. We walked up the hallway toward the sound.

At the back of a large office filled with desks and tables and filing cabinets, a uniformed soldier was just walking out of the latrine. He glanced at us, still adjusting his fly.

"Can I help you?"

His eyes widened. Maybe it was the coats and ties. Maybe it was the fact that we were Americans and not wearing green fatigues like every other American up here near the DMZ.

Ernie and I approached him and showed him our identification. His name tag said Oliver, and the rank insignia on his collar indicated that he was a major. A stout man, he wore square-lensed glasses and an otherwise bushy hairline that was beginning to recede. We told him who we were looking for.

"Boltworks? He's the one who's been AWOL, isn't he?"

I nodded.

He walked over to a screen hanging on the far wall and pulled it back, revealing a green board with rows of names written in multi-colored chalk.

"Boltworks," Major Oliver mumbled to himself. He stopped at the right side of the board and pointed. "There he is. Charley Battery. Still being carried as AWOL."

"Did you know him?" Ernie asked.

Oliver shook his head. "No. There're a lot of troops in the battalion. I stay pretty busy here." He held out his arms to indicate the operations office surrounding us. Desks, chairs, and filing cabinets were surrounded by walls covered with charts, maps, and bulletin boards. In the corner, a squat olive-drab field radio blinked ominously with one red eye.

Ernie pulled out the sketch of the fugitive we'd been calling "the Caucasian GI." Oliver studied it, then shook his head.

"No. I don't know this person."

"But it could be Boltworks," Ernie said. "You don't know either way."

Major Oliver nodded.

Ernie pulled out the other two sketches and received the same reaction.

"Anybody else here," I said, "who might be able to identify Boltworks?"

"Not here," he said. "Division-wide move-out this morning. They're all in the field."

Ernie walked over to the chalkboard. "How long had Boltworks been assigned here?"

Oliver studied the list. "Almost ten months," he said. "Strange to go AWOL when you've only got a couple of months left on your tour."

"Maybe he didn't want to return Stateside," Ernie said.

Oliver looked at him blankly. Such a thought, apparently, had never entered his mind. I didn't want Ernie to go off on some odd tangent—comparing GI life in Korea to civilian life in the States—so I interrupted quickly.

"Boltworks will be known at the unit," I said. "Charley Battery, right?"

Oliver nodded.

"Then we need to talk to some folks in his unit. Where can we find them?"

Oliver shook his head again. "Long way from here."

"Show us."

He walked to the other side of the Ops Center, to another curtain. Before pulling back the curtain, he stared at Ernie and me.

"What's your clearance?" he asked.

"Top Secret," I said. "Crypto."

Cleared on a need-to-know basis for access to top secret information, including information generated through cryptography, highly classified codes. Actually, neither Ernie nor I were cleared that high. We had Secret clearances, that was it. But what Oliver didn't know wouldn't hurt him.

He slid back the curtain.

Arrayed before us was a massive, wall-sized map of the area known to the world as the Korean DMZ, the Demilitarized Zone. On the left flowed the blue Han River Estuary, leading into the Yellow Sea a few miles north of the Port of Inchon. On the right was the Korean coastline bordering the Sea of Japan—in between, the DMZ—its thick body wriggled through the Korean Peninsula like a burrowing python.

On the left side was a black dot for the city of Munsan, and close to that, less than three kilometers away, a bright red star that said "Camp Pelham."

Major Oliver pointed to the star. "We're here," he said. He traced his finger toward the East, along a road that divided a ridge of hills. After about twenty-five miles, his finger turned north, traveling another twenty miles until it reached a blue line that wound south of the DMZ. "They crossed the Imjin here," he said, "at Liberty Bridge, about zero seven thirty this morning." His finger continued north, toward an area adjacent to the DMZ, with no black dots representing cities or towns. "They're up here now. Exactly where, I can't say. The Second Division G-2 is simulating an all-out North Korean attack, so Charley Battery and the rest of the battalion are doing what they do best. They're north of the Imjin River, moving, shooting, and communicating."

"Can you pin-point their location for us?" Ernie asked.

"When I receive another radio call. But right now they're on the move. So far this morning, they've set up and fired live rounds three times. Each time, they break down all weapons and equipment, load them up on their trucks, and move out to the next firing position."

Sounded like a lot of work. Oliver grabbed a wooden pointer and used it to indicate an area higher up on the map, adjacent to the southern edge of the DMZ.

"It's clear where they're headed," he said. "Closer to North Korea. By tonight, they'll probably be operating in the largest military firing area in country." He slapped the pointer against the map. "Right here."

"So we can find them there?"

"It's a large area, but yes."

"Then that's where we'll go."

Ernie started to leave, but I stopped him and made Major Oliver give us the coordinates of the firing area he had just referred to. When I jotted them down, I said, "Do you have a map we could borrow?"

"You won't need one."

"Why not?"

"When you cross Liberty Bridge there will be checkpoints, plenty of them, all on the lookout for North Korean intruders. They'll guide you to the firing Operations Center. Don't bother with the coordinates. Just tell them you're looking for Charley Battery of the Second of the Seventeenth. And tell them they're at Nightmare Range."

"Nightmare Range?"

Oliver grinned. "Garden spot of the Orient."

Liberty Bridge was a low cement bridge with no railing to speak of, the roadway just a few feet above the churning waters of the Imjin River. MPs armed with M-16 rifles lined the bridge, on the look out for anything sinister floating downriver from the headwaters in North Korea. As we crossed, waves of cold water from the rapidly flowing Imjin splashed our tires. On the far side of the bridge, we followed the road upward, winding past granite cliffs and through tunnels hewn out of solid rock. Finally we emerged onto a long plateau. For a moment it almost seemed as if we'd left Korea. No rice paddies, no straw-thatched huts in the distance, no farmers leading ox-drawn carts to market. Only wilderness. The uncultivated wilderness of the militarily controlled areas south of the DMZ.

Occasionally, a big deuce-and-a-half or a box-like chow truck passed us, heading south toward Liberty Bridge, returning to civilization for re-supply.

Signs written in English and *hangul* guided us toward the Range Operations Center. Again, a sheet-metal Quonset hut, this one painted in darker shades of camouflage green. Inside were ROK Army officers. One of them, a Lieutenant Park, spoke English. When we asked him where we could find Charley Battery, 2/17th FA, he frowned.

"Moving," he said. "Far north. Where they stop, nobody know right now."

The war games were still on-going. They could last for many hours, until the generals back in their bunkers had enough data to keep themselves busy analyzing it for the next couple of weeks.

"Where are they now?" Ernie asked.

Lieutenant Park led us into a room filled with a topographical map spread out on a flat table. South of a red line, tiny tanks and artillery pieces were arrayed in a line facing north. Even more tanks and artillery pieces were arrayed north of the line, facing south. Lieutenant Park grabbed a wooden pointer and slapped the brass tip into the center of a broad valley surrounded by jagged hills.

"Charley Battery," he said.

Ernie and I studied the map. The valley was about fifteen kilometers from our current position. At the southern edge of the valley sat a village known as Uichon.

When I asked Lieutenant Park the name of the valley, he answered in Korean. I didn't understand, so he repeated the name in English.

"Nightmare Range," he said.

We thanked him and left.

Uichon was a dump.

One paved road, right down the center of town, wide enough for two big military re-supply trucks to rumble through without slowing down. Toddlers wearing wool sweaters, but no pants, stumbled through the muck on the side of the road, chasing chickens and an occasional small pig. Adults with wooden A-frames strapped to their backs hoisted hay, firewood, and gunny sacks full of cabbage toward the village's open-air market. On the outskirts of town, a few farmhouses were visible but not many. Some roofs were tile, like the whitewashed police station, but most of the hovels settled for the traditional straw-thatched roofs that had been used in Asia since the beginning of recorded time.

About a hundred yards on the far side of the village we came to a road that Lieutenant Park had told us we'd find. An arrow-shaped sign pointing north said USFK firing range No. 13, north 2km. The road was made of hard-packed mud and gravel and sat a few inches above the swampy grasslands surrounding it. Ernie shoved the jeep into low gear and made the turn.

"Hold onto your hat," he said.

He was enjoying this a lot more than I was.

Was all this effort really worth our time? What would the members of Charley Battery have to tell us? If the sketch we showed them wasn't Boltworks, all would be for naught. If it was him, we still wouldn't learn much. Since he'd been AWOL for over a month, it was unlikely that anybody in the unit would have any idea about where to find him. Still, we had to ask. That's what police work is all about.

Major Oliver back at Camp Pelham told us that Nightmare Range had been the site of a series of ferocious battles between the 8th United States Army and what was called, in those days, the CHICOMs, the Chinese Communist People's Army. Known to GIs as "Joe Chink." In the foreboding terrain we were traveling through now, I could imagine what it must've been like. Explosions everywhere, bayonet charges, hand-to-hand combat, men screaming, rolling through the cold mud and hot blood. And the mountains around us made things worse. They looked primeval: jagged, muddy, ringed with low-lying clouds that blocked the afternoon sun.

I shivered and hugged myself, wishing we were back in the cozy alleyways of Itaewon.

It took us ten minutes to drive the two kilometers the little sign had been talking about. When we arrived, we found a flat swampy area, but no field artillery unit.

"Charley Battery's moved out," Ernie said.

Fresh tire tracks were everywhere. I climbed out of the jeep and studied them.

"They're heading north, up this road," I said.

"Good work, Tonto."

You didn't exactly have to be an Apache tracker to see where they'd gone. The mud and gravel had been plowed up everywhere.

We continued after them. All that afternoon we followed Charley Battery of the Second of the 17th but each time we drew close, they had already loaded up and moved out. Finally, the sun went down. Ernie and I were just about to give up, when we had to swerve off the side of the road for a huge diesel refueling truck that was barreling down the muddy path. We pulled over and Ernie flashed his lights, and the trucker rolled to a stop.

I climbed out and talked to him.

"Charley Battery?" he said. "Yeah, up the road about three klicks."

The driver was a young Spec 4 from Dubuque, Iowa. He bragged that he knew the firing ranges up here like the back of his hand.

"You're in luck," he told me. "Charley Battery's been given clearance to stand down for the night. That's why I was able to refuel them. They've already put up the wire."

He meant set up a defensive perimeter and unraveled coiled concertina wire around the battery's position. When I asked him for directions, he started to explain, but the winding and turning grew too complicated. I pulled out my notebook and asked him to draw me a map. He did, using two sheets of paper. When he handed it back to me, I used the light inside his cab to read it and I asked questions to make sure I understood. Finally, we said our goodbyes, and he rumbled off down the road, red taillights fading.

"You know where they're at now?" Ernie asked.

"Yeah. Got the map right here."

Ernie started the jeep back up and, with his headlights on high beam, rolled north on the narrow lane. In the dim red glow of the dashboard, I studied the map again. At the end of the winding road, the fuel truck driver had drawn a large X.

Next to it, in childish script, he had written the words: Nightmare Range.

When we finally found Charley Battery, we didn't just drive right up to the concertina wire surrounding the perimeter. Instead, we decided to reconnoiter. Ernie switched off the high beams and approached with only his parking lights on. While we were still a hundred meters away, he parked beside a hill. We climbed to the top and gazed down on the encampment of Charley Battery, Second of the 17th Field Artillery.

Six 105mm howitzers. That's the first thing you noticed, long firing tubes glowing dimly in the moonlight. All six were covered with camouflage netting, and all six were pointing straight toward North Korea. Behind them, two rows of tents. Inside each, the faint glow of portable space heaters. Next came a row of two-and-a-half ton trucks. Eight of them. Six of the trucks were to pull the guns, one each, and also to haul each weapon's "basic load," its full complement of high explosive ammunition. One of the remaining trucks was for the maintenance crew and its associated equipment, and the last truck was for chow, a big box-like wooden cab teetering on its back.

Concertina wire was strung hapzardly around the entire bivouac.

Occasionally, some GI tromped from one tent to another. Spaced evenly around the perimeter, three armed guards, rifles carried at sling arms, paced within the wall of wire.

Why had we stopped to take a look? Call it cop instinct. Or more accurately, suspicion. We wanted a better idea of who we were dealing with before we barged in on this idyllic scene and started asking embarrassing questions. Like, why has one of your GIs seen fit to desert his unit? No commander likes to hear that one. And if Private Boltworks was our man, the Battery Commander would be even less pleased when he heard about a casino robbery and a shooting. A shooting that had resulted in death.

I was about to rise from my kneeling position and return to the jeep, when Ernie elbowed me in the shoulder. He pointed.

Something dark emerged from the reeds, about ten yards outside the concertina wire. One of the armed guards sauntered over.

"North Korean commando?" I asked.

"Not quite."

With his thick-lensed glasses, Ernie's eyesight was better than mine. I wished we'd brought some binoculars, but since we hadn't, I rolled my eyes and tried my peripheral vision and then refocused on the dark figure standing in front of the guard. A woman. The red moonlight behind her outlined long, straight hair. She seemed to be wearing thick clothing—a jacket or a sweater—and holding it shut. Instead of challenging her with his weapon, the guard stood in front of her casually, his rifle still slung over his shoulder, motioning for her to come forward.

They seemed to be chatting.

Ernie shook his head. "Even out here."

"What do you mean?"

"I've heard about it," he told me, "but I hardly believed it. In 'Nam it used to happen constantly. But here too?"

Ernie seemed surprised, not shocked, and maybe a little disappointed.

"That woman," I said, "who is she?"

"Girl, more likely. That's why they bring them out here. So they won't get busted by the KNPs for being under eighteen."

"What are you talking about?"

"Business girls. Out here to make a few bucks. Turn a few tricks."

"Out here?"

"Sure. They probably operate out of that village we passed, Uichon. Think about it. Units rotate in and out of these ranges constantly. Each one chock full of horny young GIs. And no competition. You take a few girls out here, and you have all that GI money to yourself."

I stared at him. Still trying to fathom who would voluntarily come out into this cold and mud.

"Look," he said, pointing. "Behind the girl, about twenty yards away from the wire."

I scanned the tall grass. The tips of the vegetation were illuminated by the three-quarters moon, swaying in a soft breeze. Judging from the position of the girl, and the guard she was talking to, the grass must've been four feet tall. But ten yards farther in, away from the wire, a square patch of grass was missing. I studied the patch, and then I saw something pop up, something round.

"See?" Ernie said. "More girls. Back there. Waiting to see what kind of business the other one can drum up. They'd send the prettiest one first."

I turned and studied Ernie. He was intent on the scene below us.

"How do you know all these things?"

"Years of research," he said. Then he shushed me and pointed again.

Another GI was now standing behind the guard. They were talking. The girl moved back into the high grass. Then the two GIs moved quickly. If I hadn't been watching, I might've missed it. The guard leaned down, grabbed a handful of concertina wire, and lifted. The other GI dropped to his belly and low-crawled forward. Within seconds he was through the wire, crouching and moving quickly into the grass.

"Come on," Ernie said.

He charged straight over the hill, veering to his right, away from Charley Battery's encampment. I followed. Within seconds we were on level ground, crouching and moving as quietly as we could through the same high grass that the GI and the girl were using for concealment.

Every minute or two, I poked my head up to see if the guards inside the Charley Battery perimeter had spotted us. I didn't particularly want to be mistaken for a North Korean commando. But the guard we had seen earlier had moved away from this side of the perimeter. There was no one in sight.

When we approached the rectangular opening in the grass, Ernie stopped and motioned for me to be quiet. I came to a halt, listening.

Giggles, whispering, the rustle of grass and clothing.

Ernie inched forward and motioned for me to follow.

It wasn't prurient interest that kept me moving forward. Not alone, anyway. But I knew that we had to talk to GIs in Charley Battery and preferably GIs who knew Private Rodney Boltworks. A guy like this GI, who'd leave his unit's perimeter and risk court-martial or Article-15 for deserting his post, is a guy who would most likely know a troublemaker like Boltworks. And if we caught this GI, whoever he was, in flagrante delicto, we'd have leverage over him. He'd have to tell us everything he knew, and tell it straight. At least that's what I was hoping for.

What Ernie was hoping for, I wasn't quite sure.

We crept ever closer to the mashed-down grass. Now we could hear heavy breathing. Ernie turned, looked at me, and in the moonlight I could see his grin. He raised three fingers and started counting down: One, two, three.

Ernie rose to his feet and burst into the clearing.

I expected the women to scream but they didn't. They were seasoned pros. But they did scoot back from their squatting positions, covering their mouths with their hands, and stared at us in wide-eyed astonishment. There were three of them, all bundled in thick jackets and mittens and wool scarves, as if expecting to be out in this cold weather for many hours. In front of them, on a blanket spread atop crumpled grass, lay a GI. All I could see of him was the back of his field jacket and his green fatigue trousers. Sticking out on either side of him were two small hands and two small feet. I noticed that the feet were incongruously shod with knitted wool socks.

Ernie grabbed the GI by the scruff of his neck and brutally jerked him backwards.

"What the . . . ?"

From nowhere, Ernie's .45 glistened in the moonlight, the tip of the oil-slick barrel pointing straight up into the GI's nostril. He was a black man, or at least partly black. Very light-skinned and slightly chubby around the jowls.

"Move and I'll blow your dick off," Ernie said.

The GI started cussing. The girl beneath him squealed and kicked her way back into the grass. Of the three women sitting across from us, two of them were young and one was old. Very old. I spoke to her in Korean, not bothering to use honorifics for the elderly.

"*Weikurei yogi-ei?*" What the hell are you doing here?

She answered in Korean, her withered hand pressed against her chest, and told me that Ernie and I had given her quite a start. I told her to shut up, while Ernie let the GI pull up his fatigue pants. I saw by the tag on his field jacket that his name was Taggard. He wasn't wearing any rank insignia. That meant that he was a private E-nothing. Busted down to the lowest possible military rank.

"Court-martial time," Ernie told Taggard. "Article Fifteen at least. You know you're not supposed to be out here. What if there's a fire mission? And the women out here are off limits. They probably don't even have VD cards."

Taggard cussed a little more, trying to regain some of the dignity he'd lost.

Ernie had referred to these prostitutes as women but they were, in fact, only girls. Fifteen or sixteen years old, I estimated. One still sported the Buster Brown haircut that middle-school girls in Korea are required to wear. Probably from poor families, sold to this old witch sitting here who was pretending to act so shocked at the intrusion.

Did the Korean National Police in Uichon know about this operation? Certainly, they did. A group of teenage girls living with an old crone, with no visible means of support? The KNPs knew. Worse, they were probably receiving a cut of the action.

"All right, Taggard," Ernie said. "That's your name, isn't it? Unless you borrowed somebody else's field jacket. No. Couldn't be. Nobody else in the unit could be that fat."

Taggard's cheeks bulged with anger. Ernie held the .45 aimed at his face, although I knew the charging handle hadn't been pulled back. Ernie couldn't have shot Taggard if he'd wanted to. Fortunately, Taggard didn't know that.

"I'm going to ask you some questions, Private Taggard," Ernie said. "After each one you're going to give me an answer. Understand? You're not going to give me any bullshit or any excuses about why you don't know. You're just going to give me an answer. Got that?"

When Taggard didn't reply, Ernie clanged back the charging handle of the .45, pressed it hard up against Taggard's nose, and repeated the question, pronouncing each word slowly.

"Do you understand that?"

Reluctantly, Taggard nodded. Beads of perspiration broke out on his forehead.

I considered jumping on Ernie, wrestling the .45 away from him. But that might cause the gun to go off. Would he really shoot Taggard? From the look on Ernie's face, I couldn't be sure. He was enraged. In Inchon, when we gazed at the wounded Han Ok-hi in her oxygen tent, and at the Yellow House, when we examined the cigarette burns along Mi-ja's arm, and then, in Songtan, when we saw the blood exsanguinated from the body of Jo Kyong-ah, Ernie had acted as if he were just a cop doing a job. No emotion showed on his face. But now his face was a mask of rage. He'd caught someone in the act of committing a crime: having sex for pay with an underage girl. What worried me most was that he was going to take all his rage and frustration out on a miscreant GI named Taggard. Maybe Taggard deserved to have his ass kicked. He probably even deserved time in the stockade, but he didn't deserve to be shot dead.

"Boltworks," Ernie said. "Rodney, K., Private First Class. Talk!"

"Asshole," Taggard said.

"Explain!"

"He was an asshole, that's all. Always messing with people. When he lost his ration control privileges, he started pestering everybody else—Let me use your ration card for this; let me use it for that. He beat up a few of the wimpy dudes in the battery and made them buy some shit out of the PX for him, but he knew better than to mess with me."

"I'll bet," Ernie said. "How long has he been gone?"

"Ask mama-san. She knows."

The old woman and her girls slid back even further into the grass. I told her in Korean to stay right where she was.

"What do you mean?" Ernie asked Taggard.

"Bolt was the first one out here."

"Bolt?"

"Yeah. That's what we called Boltworks. Every time we were in the field, he'd find mama-san and her girls. Had a nose for pussy until he smelled the wrong kind."

Ernie shoved the tip of the .45 back toward his nose. "Go on," he said.

On the other side of the wall of grass, I noticed some movement of lights. Probably just the perimeter guards.

"Why you want me to tell you?" Taggard said. "Ask mama-san."

"I'm asking you," Ernie replied.

Taggard sighed. A gentleman, hugely inconvenienced.

"Boltworks came out here for one particular girl."

"Pretty?"

"Better than these pug-nosed bitches. Boltworks was greedy. Kept her all to himself, alone, way over there in the grass all night."

Taggard pointed vaguely into the distance.

"Didn't Boltworks have guard duty?"

"He didn't mess with that shit. Told somebody else to pull it for him."

"Paid them?"

"Hell no. Boltworks was crazy. Guys'd pull his guard duty just so he wouldn't mess with them. Not me though. I wasn't afraid of him."

"Tell me about the girl."

"He used to take her every time we came out to Nightmare Range. Give mama-san here some *tambay* or something." Cigarettes. "And then one night we heard a lot of noise. Not screaming or crying or anything like that, but fighting. A couple of the other guys went over, and they found the girl bloodied up. She was too pretty, almost blonde, you know. She crazy though. Still smiling. That big smile of hers she always had no matter what."

I felt dizzy for a moment. The smiling woman, the one who'd sat at a table with me in the King Club in Itaewon, the woman who'd drugged me, the woman who'd escorted the dark GI onto the train at Inchon Station—that's who he was talking about.

"So what happened to Boltworks?" Ernie asked.

"Mama-san here wanted more money, for the blonde girl's hospital bills and shit like that, but Boltworks told her to go screw herself. Then she took her girls and left and the next time we came out to Nightmare Range, she and her little bitches weren't out here. Everybody was pissed, but nobody said nothing to Boltworks."

"Too scared?"

"*They* were. Not me."

"And that's it?" Ernie said.

"I told you, ask the mama-san."

"I'm asking you."

Taggard shrugged. "You going to turn me in, or what?"

"Depending," Ernie said. "Talk."

"So we come back to Nightmare Range and suddenly mama-san's back, with new girls and everything, and the blonde girl, she back, smiling as usual and she takes Boltworks by the hand and leads him out into the high grass and . . . "

As if a bolt of lightning had struck, the world was suddenly full of light. I covered my eyes, cursing myself for not staying alert.

"Freeze!" a voice shouted.

Shading my eyes from the glare of a half-dozen beams of light, I could still make out dark shadows standing in front of us. A few of them held long, dark objects. Rifles.

Ernie lifted his .45 straight up in the air.

"Set it down, mister," a voice said. "Slow and easy."

He did.

9

Something poked me in the arm.

With an effort, I opened my eyes. Something was pressing against my hip, my elbow and shoulder, and my neck was twisted at an awkward angle.

I looked up to find a stern-faced Korean man glaring at me. Wearing khaki. I sat upright.

Where was I?

Then I remembered. We were in the police station in the village of Uichon. Was I locked up? No. This was the police station lobby, in front of the desk sergeant's counter. Both Ernie and I had passed out on the wooden benches against the front wall. There were no hotels in Uichon; not even a *yoguan*, a Korean inn. So the local KNPs had allowed us to sleep here rather than in our open-topped jeep.

Ernie sat up and rubbed his eyes. The Korean cop stared, making sure we were awake. He was a slightly cross-eyed young man and the dull curiosity in his eyes made me understand how a gorilla in a cage at the zoo must feel when being stared at by tourists. The young cop turned and walked back behind the partition, where his desk overlooked the public entrance. Cold air poured in through open doors. Outside, the barest glimmer of gray appeared at the edges of a dark sky.

"I feel like shit," Ernie said.

"Don't ask me how you look."

Last night, while we were busy interviewing Private Taggard in the tall grass, the perimeter guards around the Charley Battery encampment had noticed something amiss. They'd alerted their commander, one Captain Floyd Lewis, and he'd organized a detail of men and surrounded us before we knew what was happening. After taking Ernie's .45, Lewis marched us back inside the Charley Battery area and sat us down on folding stools inside the ten-man tent that served as temporary Command Post.

I tried to tell him that the business girls outside the wire were getting away, but all he said was, "What business girls?"

Typically, he pretended he hadn't seen the women, and he also pretended that he didn't know what was going on outside his concertina wire. The brass monkey act: hear no evil, see no evil, speak no evil. The road to advancement in the United States Army. Captain Lewis was much more concerned with the fact that Ernie had pulled a gun on one of his soldiers.

We showed him our identification and told him why we were here. When Ernie mentioned General Armbrewster's name, Captain Lewis fired up his communications equipment. After a few minutes, he received confirmation via radio that he was to provide us with full cooperation. Butt first, Lewis handed Ernie his gun back.

After slipping the .45 into his shoulder holster, Ernie pulled out the three sketches and laid them on the wooden field table.

Taggard flinched. "What the hell did he do?"

Instead of answering, Ernie said, "You know him?"

"That's Bolt."

Taggard pointed at the sketch of the man we'd been calling "the Caucasian GI." We now had a name to go with the face: Private First Class Rodney K. Boltworks, absent without leave from Charley Battery, 2nd of the 17th Field Artillery.

"How about her?" Ernie asked

Taggard studied the sketch of the smiling woman.

"She looks a little more cleaned up now," he said. "But that's her. The blond bitch who used to work outside the wire."

"She'd been one of *them*?" Ernie asked.

"Yeah," Taggard answered. "Same crew. Same mama-san. Everything."

"What happened to her?"

Taggard shook his head slowly. "Bolt liked her. Used to hog her, matter of fact, like I was telling you. Not give the rest of us a shot. Got so bad he started beating on her when she complained about not making enough money. Then one night a couple months ago, he took her out in the bushes, and while he was out there, somebody started beating on *him*."

Taggard grinned at the memory. One of his front teeth was missing.

"Who?" I asked.

"Don't know. But Bolt was bruised up pretty bad. Must've been a good fight. Wouldn't tell us who did it to him."

"And the girl?"

"She disappeared. Later that night, so did Bolt."

Captain Lewis stood with his arms crossed, rocking on his heels, not liking this testimony at all. He was a tall, lean man with a short crew cut.

"How about it, Captain?" Ernie asked. "Is that when Rodney Boltworks disappeared?"

"Almost two months ago. July seventeenth," he said. "While we were camped in this area. Haven't seen him since."

I spoke to Taggard. "So Boltworks goes out in the bush with this business girl. He gets in a fight with somebody who wastes him pretty bad. He limps back to the encampment and, later that night, he disappears?"

"Exactly what happened."

"Why?" I said.

Taggard grinned again.

"Why?" Taggard repeated. "I don't know for sure, but I think he liked it."

"Liked what?"

Taggard's grin grew wider. "I think he liked the ass-kicking he got."

Ernie and I glanced at one another, not sure how to proceed on that line of questioning. Ernie pointed at the sketch of the dark man with the curly brown hair.

"Do you know who this guy is?"

Taggard shook his head. So did Captain Lewis.

I wasn't surprised. The sketch was pretty vague. A dark man with an oval-shaped face and opaque sunglasses covering his eyes. He could've been a Korean, an American. He could've been a lot of things.

We prevailed on the good captain to bring every soldier in Charley Battery into the Command tent, one at a time. We paraded them past the three sketches. To a man, everyone knew Boltworks. A handful recognized the smiling woman, but not one recognized the dark man with the curly brown hair.

Afterwards, Ernie and I drove back to Uichon and asked the night duty officer at the Korean National Police Station to help us find the mama-san and the girls who worked the encampments in this area. The guy was adamant. He would give us no information, not without clearing it with his superiors. And since it was already past the midnight curfew, we would have to wait until morning to talk to the commander of the Uichon police station.

There was no place else to go, so Ernie and I sat down on the wooden benches and waited. And slept, until just before dawn.

Twenty minutes after we'd been woken up, the police station commander walked in. He was a young lieutenant named Cheon, rail thin, his khaki uniform pressed to a sharp crease. Most likely college educated. Probably a graduate of one of Korea's military academies. As he listened to Ernie and me explain what we wanted, he was even less happy than Captain Lewis had been. No Korean cop likes to admit that, right under his nose, underage Korean girls were being herded out into the bushes to have sexual relations with American GIs. We asked him about the mamasan and where we could find her. She was the only lead we had to the smiling woman and the AWOL GI known as Bolt.

Cheon pondered our request, probably trying to decide if he should just kick us out of his office. But if he did that, we would go to our superiors, they would contact his superiors, and then the shit would roll downhill, soiling both him and his little fiefdom. Less embarrassing to deal with the situation here, at our level, cop to cop. I had already worked through this line of reasoning but I waited for Lieutenant Cheon to figure it out.

He did.

Cheon grabbed his cap and told the desk sergeant he'd be back in a few minutes. Ernie and I followed him out the front door of the Uichon police station.

The sky was brighter now, though still gray. The air was clean and sharp and cold, laced with the tang of growing things, sliced, and piled and festering in green sap.

Somehow, amidst all this open countryside, the people of Uichon had constructed a slum. Arable land in Korea has always been precious. Although the peninsula is fertile and blessed with many lush river valleys, it is also ridged with mountain ranges and spotted with hills. Land that can be used for farming is scarce and conserved fiercely, even here in Uichon. Living space for humans is packed into constricted areas. The main drag of Uichon, with the two-lane MSR running down the middle, only stretched a block and a half. Behind that front line of buildings, the alleys dropped off into muddy pedestrian lanes. We tromped through one that headed downhill.

Lieutenant Cheon led the way, stepping across mud puddles, hopping deftly from a flat stone to a leftover slat of lumber, keeping his highly polished boots as clean as possible. Ernie and I tried to follow in his footsteps, but we were less successful. Soon, my trousers were spattered with mud.

A man pushing a cart filled with hay trundled past us, smiling a gap-toothed smile and bowing to Lieutenant Cheon. It was still too early for children to be up and about and on their way to school, and many of the homes behind the rickety wooden outer walls were dark. Occasionally we heard the scratch of wooden matches or the clang of a metal pot or the growl of an old man rising, clearing his throat.

Lieutenant Cheon stopped at a wooden gate that had been stained black with grease. He pounded his fist and shouted, "*Irrona-ya!*" Wake up!

He pounded repeatedly, until the splintered gate opened a crack.

A woman wrapped in a heavy wool sweater, so frail she looked made of sticks, peered up at us. I recognized the eyes. The same phlegm-filled orbs we'd seen last night while crouching in the reeds outside the concertina wire that surrounded Charley Battery. Those eyes looked worried when she saw Ernie and me. More worried when she recognized Lieutenant Cheon.

She pulled the wooden gate open. We entered.

This hooch was more like what we were used to in Itaewon. Muddy courtyard with nothing but a rusty pump handle. A chicken coop with no chickens, and three hooches on a raised platform, the wood rough and rotting. One of the oil-papered sliding doors was open and inside lay a jumbled pile of blankets. One naked foot stuck out from beneath the coverings.

"Better tell them to wake up," I told the old woman in Korean. "We're going to talk to everybody."

Ernie and I found two wooden stools. We sat on the flagstone edge of the courtyard beneath a tile-roofed overhang. The business girls came out, looking younger than ever. In the gray morning light, their naked faces showed pocks and blemishes invisible in moonlight. One of the girls had a milky eye, another a lame left foot. Gradually, this home for wayward girls was beginning to seem more like a hospice for the handicapped rather than a brothel for our brave American soldiers.

I took a deep breath and held it, trying to control myself. Pity doesn't help in a murder investigation.

One by one the business girls studied the sketches, and one by one they stared at the mama-san in worried concern, unsure of what to do or say. By now, the old woman had slipped on pajama-like black trousers and a tunic and squatted in the courtyard beside us puffing on a stale-smelling Turtle Boat brand cigarette.

I kept asking questions. The business girls stared, as if they didn't understand.

Lieutenant Cheon growled at them. " *Iyagi hei. Bali iyagi hei!*" Speak. Speak quickly!

He didn't like loitering in a whorehouse for foreigners any longer than he had to. But his instructions made the girls grow more reticent. They were frightened now, like a pack of chipmunks cornered by a wolf.

I caught Ernie's attention and, out of Lieutenant Cheon's line of sight, rolled my eyes.

Ernie understood. Soon he was talking to Lieutenant Cheon, his arm around the man's shoulder. Then he was walking him toward the courtyard gate. Together, they ducked outside.

The girls breathed a sigh of relief.

The mama-san stared after the two men, her eyes squinting into tight wrinkles. Her only reaction was to puff even more smoke up from the foul-smelling *tambay*.

"*Ajjima*," I said. Aunt. "Who is this person?"

I pointed at the sketch of the smiling woman.

The old woman stared at the drawing. She continued to puff on her cigarette. Finally, she spoke.

"I knew her mother," she said. "Long time ago . . . so many men that time, chase me and chase her mother. No woman that time look better than us."

"You were *jinhan chingu*," I said. Best friends.

She nodded. "*Nei. Jinhan chingu.* We all time together. All time take man, best man. Man with most money." She pointed at the top of her shoulder. "How you say?"

"The man with the highest rank," I answered.

"Yes." She waved her cigarette in the air. "Always top honcho. That's who we take. We catch him and we make pay."

She clenched her hand into a bony fist.

When this woman was young, the Korean War had been in full swing, and the country was swarming with foreign military officers, all of them away from their wives, all with extra combat pay and few opportunities to spend it.

"*Sajin issoyo?*" I asked. Do you have photos?

She smiled at that. Then she barked rapid commands in Korean to one of the girls. This girl was well-trained. She hopped up and scurried to a storage room next to the hooches. While she was inside, the mama-san barked more directions, and after a few minutes, the girl brought out a brown cardboard box wrapped with pink string. She set it in front of the mama-san and backed away.

The mama-san stared at the box for a while, still puffing on her cigarette. Then, with trembling hands, she reached forward and untied the pink knot. When she opened the box, a small cloud of dust and dried moth's wings puffed out. It smelled of ancient secrets. All buried now. Forgotten. Except for a few ugly things, of which this wicked old woman proceeded to speak.

The Uichon mama-san told me that about three months ago, the smiling woman had come to her looking for a job.

"Her mama die long time ago," she said. "Nowhere to go."

"How old was she when her mother died?"

"Fourteen, fifteen."

"How old is she now?"

The mama-san shrugged. "Nineteen. Maybe twenty."

What had she done all those years? How had she survived? I shoved the questions out of my mind, because worrying wouldn't help me put a stop to further killing.

"What about her mother's family?" I asked. "After her mother died, didn't they help?"

"Family no see her mother many years. Mother *yang kalbo.*" *Yang kalbo,* a prostitute for foreigners. "They no wanna talk."

"And her father's family?"

The mama-san laughed. The laughter gave way to coughing, and then wheezing, as she tried to regain her breath through the cloud of cigarette smoke.

"Her daddy GI," she said. "Maybe meet her mama during Korean War. He long time go."

Long time go. That was the story for tens of thousands of foreign soldiers during and after the Korean War, most of them American. They fathered children, sometimes they even took care of them for a while, and then they left. Never to return. Never to do so much as send a Christmas card to their abandoned children. Of course, many Amerasian children were adopted, through the good offices of charitable organizations such as the Pearl S. Buck Foundation. But not all. A percentage of these

Korean mothers, for one reason or another, did not put their children up for adoption.

Now, twenty years after the end of the Korean War, more and more Amerasians were seen around Seoul. Usually working menial jobs: hauling bricks, digging ditches, delivering truckloads of charcoal briquettes to homes and businesses. They stood out in a crowd of Koreans because of their unusual body shapes or their long noses or their odd hair: either stringy light brown, or black and heavily curled.

In school, few Amerasian children made it beyond the sixth grade. By definition, they came from poor families who couldn't afford the tuition to go higher. More importantly, Amerasian children were taunted brutally in school, for their racial difference and for the circumstances of their birth.

There were increasing numbers of Amerasians these days in the brothels. Wealthy Korean men and Japanese tourists liked them. So did American GIs. The girls, at least the better looking ones, were making money.

When the Uichon mama-san took the smiling woman under her wing, there'd been only one job opportunity available to her.

"She already know how to do," the mama-san told me. She exhaled and a puff of smoke passed through the gaps in her black-edged teeth. "Before, her mama's boyfriend teach her."

"Her mother's boyfriend?" I was incredulous.

"Yeah. Some GI."

"Didn't her mother try to stop it?"

"How? They need money. If boyfriend run away, no money."

My stomach churned but I picked up the sketch of the smiling woman anyway. I thought about her that night, sitting across from me at the cocktail table in the King Club in Itaewon. I remembered how she'd never stopped smiling. No matter what she said, or what I said, her smile remained constant. Eager to please. Offering no offense. Offering no resistance.

How could men do such things?

Roughly, I shoved the question out of my mind. Not for me to figure. I'm a cop. My job is to catch bad guys. Quickly, before my imagination conjured more pictures of grief, I willed myself to recall the murder scene in Songtan, the blood smeared on the floor, the broken antiques. And I thought of the now-deceased Han Ok-hi, back when she'd been in a coma under an oxygen tent in that hospital near the Yellow Sea.

Better to think about the victims.

The smiling woman I'd think about later.

The Uichon mama-san barked roughly at her girls, telling one of them to break a pile of dried sticks, another to start a fire in the kitchen. They would eat this morning, not well, but something to fill the belly: rice gruel and dried turnip. More than some people.

Ernie and Lieutenant Cheon were still outside somewhere, Ernie keeping the Commander of the Uichon Police Station busy to give me a chance to coax this old woman to talk candidly.

She called one of her girls over and told her to sit on my lap. The girl's face was pockmarked, but she was buxom and she giggled and kissed my neck. Her age? Eighteen if she was lucky. I knew what the mama-san wanted to do. She wanted to compromise me. Make me just another of her customers. Gently, I pushed the girl off my lap. With a full-lipped pout, she stared sullenly, then marched off.

The Uichon mama-san scratched a wooden match on a dirty brick and lit up another Turtle Boat cigarette.

The smiling woman's name was Yun Ai-ja, she said. Love Child Yun.

It was the name she'd used at the King Club. So it hadn't been phony, but it wasn't officially registered either. I didn't interrupt; I let the old woman tell it her way.

The family name was Yun. After her mother gave birth to

Ai-ja, her firstborn, she asked her older brother to include the child on the Yun family register. Koreans don't have individual birth certificates as we do in the States. Every live birth is instead recorded on a family register, along with all other members of the clan. And, without the permission of the senior male of the clan, no new name can be recorded. If the smiling woman's mother had married a Korean man, both she and her new baby would've been recorded on her new husband's family register. As it was, she had to beg her brother to grant her the honor of having her baby's birth recorded with the family Yun.

"He say no."

The Uichon mama-san shook her head sadly.

"Miss Yun, everybody call her." The Uichon mama-san was referring, once again, to the mother of the smiling woman. "She very famous in Itaewon. Everybody know her. *Best* looking woman." She dragged out the word "best," as the Koreans do when emphasizing a point. "Me," the Uichon mama-san said, pointing to her nose, "I was her *jinhan chingu*." Best friend. "Everybody call me Nam. Miss Yun and Miss Nam. All big shots call us anytime big party."

The Yun and Nam Show. They must've been something. The mama-san waved and shouted at one of her girls. "*Sajin boja.*" Show us the photos.

The girl crouched in front of the small cardboard box that had been tied in pink ribbon, pulled out a handful of photos, and handed them to the Uichon mama-san. The old woman studied each photo judiciously, tossing some aside, handing those approved to me.

The first was a black-and-white snapshot of two young Korean women wearing matching evening gowns. Even my untrained eye could tell that the gowns were cheap, but the women were knockouts. They stood in front of a wooden stage in what must've been some bar or small nightclub. Both women were too thin, gaunt around the cheeks, but good-looking nevertheless. I studied the shorter one, then looked at the Uichon mama-san squatting next to me. Smoke filtered through her flared nostrils, and the wrinkles around her eyes tightened. She seemed amused, watching me work it out. It dawned on me slowly. One of these good looking women, the shorter one, was her.

"*Onjie?*" I said. When?

"War almost finish. Some GI buy what you call . . . cloth . . . out of PX."

"Material," I said.

"Yes. Material. We makey."

So the evening gowns were homemade, as I had guessed. I held the photo out and pointed at the taller woman.

"Ai-ja *ohma*," she said. Ai-ja's mother. The mother of the smiling woman.

Where the Uichon mama-san had been cute in her youth, in a hard sort of way, this woman was truly beautiful. Her face was smooth and unblemished, oval-shaped, and her black hair hung like silk to her shoulders, framing doe-like eyes that stared at the camera lens with a mournful challenge.

"That time," the mama-san told me, "she already pregnant."

"With her daughter?"

"Yes."

"Why didn't she give the baby up for adoption?"

"No can do."

"Why not?"

"Some woman," the Uichon mama-san said, "no can do."

I thought of the smiling woman's mad expression. "It would've been better for her daughter, don't you think, if Miss Yun would've turned Ai-ja over for adoption? She could've grown up in the States or in Europe. She wouldn't have ended up here, working for GIs."

Still squatting, the Uichon mama-san puffed on her cigarette for a long time. Finally, she said, "Better, yes." Then she pounded her fist on her chest. "But inside, never better."

"What happened to your friend, Ai-ja's mother?" I asked.

Without looking at me, the Uichon mama-san slid a skinny finger across her throat.

"Killed?"

"Die."

"What happened?"

She told me, and I took notes, but not many. I kept thinking about Ernie stalling Lieutenant Cheon, and about Private Rodney K. Boltworks out there somewhere still on the loose. The story was upsetting, but it was all a long time ago. It didn't seem to have anything to do with our current investigation, so finally I interrupted.

"The daughter of Miss Yun, this young woman named Yun Ai-ja, where is she now?"

The Uichon mama-san shrugged. "She go. GI beat her up, then her brother come."

I stopped her right there. "Her brother?"

"Yes. *Dong seing*." Younger brother.

"What does he look like?"

She described him. I took notes, trying not to let my excitement show. I pulled out the sketch of the man in sunglasses that Ernie and I had been calling "the dark GI."

"Is that him?" I asked.

"Yes."

So that was it. All three of the people involved in the robbery of the Olympos Casino and the murder of the blackjack dealer Han Ok-hi were identified. At last. Now we just had to catch them.

"What happened after her brother arrived?" I asked.

"He *taaksan kullasso*." She raised two forefingers on either side of her head, indicating that he was angry.

"Why?"

"Ai-ja, she all hurt. Here, here, here."

She pointed at her face and shoulders and back.

"Bruised," I said.

"Yes. GI punch many times."

"Why?"

"I don't know. Ai-ja no do nothing. Never make GI angry. She out in grass with crazy GI. He move far away from us. Nighttime, so my other girls plenty busy. First, I don't hear nothing, then I hear fighting."

"She fought back?"

"You better believe-uh."

"But she didn't scream?"

"Ai-ja never scream. Never ask for help. I run over there, try to stop him. He no stop. Finally, GI tired of punching Ai-ja. He stand up, very happy on face. He give extra money, maybe ten MPC." Ten dollars in Military Payment Certificates. "Then he go back to Charley Battery. Say he no want any other man touch Ai-ja that night. But he don't have to say because she *manhi apo*." Hurt very much.

"Did you take her to the hospital?"

The mama-san shrugged. I took that as a no.

"And then her brother showed up?" I asked.

"Yes. Maybe two days later. He tough man. Very tough. Half-GI baby gotta be tough. He so angry, he come back next time Charley Battery come to Nightmare Range."

"How long ago was that?"

"Maybe one month."

"What did he do?"

"He tell Ai-ja wait for mean GI. She do. Together with mean GI, she go in bushes. Maybe mean GI he want to beat up Ai-ja again. But when he start, her brother jump on him." Her eyes gleamed at the memory. "Like tiger from mountain."

"They fought?"

"They fight. GI bigger, stronger, but Ai-ja brother, he tough. Very tough. He *taaksan* beat the shit outta GI. GI bloody, all beat up, but then something funny happen."

"What?"

"He laugh."

"The GI laughed?"

"Yes. He happy. He get beat up, he like. So Ai-ja brother, he do again."

"He kept beating on him?"

She nodded her head. "Until GI go back to Charley Battery. He have guard duty that night."

So much for military security.

"Later that night," she said, "Charley Battery have alert. Move to other side of Nightmare Range. We follow. Again they fight, all three. Ai-ja and her brother knuckle sandwich with GI."

"Ai-ja was fighting him too?"

The mama-san nodded.

"Next day, morning time, Ai-ja go."

"Where did she go?"

"Itaewon," she said. "That's where she grow up. That's where her brother grow up. They want to live there."

"They grew up in Itaewon?"

"Yes." She proceeded to tell me more stories about that, but I was impatient and interrupted.

"That morning, when Ai-ja left with her brother, the mean GI went with them?"

"Yes. He say he no wanna go back Charley Battery. Too much bullshit."

"So he followed Ai-ja and her brother?"

"Yes. Like, how you say, *kangaji*?"

"Puppy dog," I said.

"Yes. GI follow like puppy dog."

* * *

Ernie jammed the jeep into fourth gear and gunned the engine down the four-lane highway known as Tongil-lo, Reunification Road. We were heading south, back toward Seoul.

"So what'd she tell you?" he asked.

"I know who the dark GI is now. He's the smiling woman's brother."

Ernie shot me a glance. "How'd you get that?"

"She recognized him from the sketch. Boltworks beat up the blonde, and little brother came to the rescue. The mama-san was friends with their mother. She's got a million stories."

"Any other leads?"

"Maybe a couple," I said. "She was pretty vague."

"Aren't they all?"

He meant everybody a cop interviews. Nobody ever remembers much, and if you press them for facts, one of two things happens: They become defensive and clam up or, hoping to seem intelligent, they make up what they think you want to hear. Either way, a cop has to push past the first line of bull and search for the truth. That's what I'd tried with the old mama-san, but I'm not sure if I did it to her or she did it to me.

But I'd heard whisperings. Things not meant for my ears, said by the girls who worked for the Uichon mama-san as they struggled to get up and wash their faces and clean up the hooch while the mama-san and I talked.

Songsan-dong had been mentioned a couple of times. Star Mountain District. And *Ban Ban Suljip*. The Half Half Club. I rummaged through the canvas emergency bag beneath the front seat of the jeep and found what I was looking for. A U.S. Geological Survey map of the northern half of Kyongi Province. After five minutes of study, I found it. Songsan-dong was a suburb of Uijongbu, a city twenty miles north of Seoul, located in the middle of an ancient invasion route that military planners call the Eastern Corridor. And south of Songsan sat Camp Stanley. For security purposes, it was not on the map. DivArty, the GIs called it. Division Artillery. The headquarters of the field artillery brigade of the 2nd United States Infantry Division.

Songsan was out of our way, but when I told Ernie about the whisperings I'd heard and why I thought it might be worth checking out, he changed lanes and at the next intersection turned left toward the Eastern Corridor. I hadn't questioned the girls further, not in front of the mama-san. I knew they'd wanted to keep something secret, but I didn't know why.

We passed fallow rice paddies, white cranes winging toward a gray sky. In the distance the Bukhan Mountains loomed. We sped at fifty miles per hour toward a place known on military maps as the District of Star Mountain.

10

Camp Stanley sits on a ridge overlooking a broad valley full of rice paddies and straw-thatched farmhouses and narrow chimneys with smoke rising slowly toward the abode of ancestors. It was noon when Ernie and I arrived at the Camp Stanley main gate, and the day was still overcast, the air brisk. After being checked out thoroughly by the MPs, we cruised past truck parks reeking of diesel fumes. Huge tin-domed maintenance sheds lined the road to Camp Stanley's back gate. It was open only to pedestrians—a gate designed to let GIs on pass out into the village of Songsan-dong. We parked the jeep and strode toward the MP shed. When we flashed our military identification, the MPs guarding the gate stared at our civilian coats and ties suspiciously but waved us on. We had only taken a few steps before they cranked the canvas-covered field phone, reporting our movements to the MP Desk Sergeant.

Ernie didn't bother looking back. "Hayseeds," he said.

The truth was that an isolated base like Camp Stanley received virtually no visitors. Two CID agents from Seoul operating in the DivArty area would probably be enough to make the local Provost Marshal go into cardiac arrest. Like all military bureaucrats, his main job is to make sure the local commander looks good—under all circumstances and at all times. Having two outside investigators prowling around his back yard would almost certainly raise his blood pressure.

Not that Ernie or I gave a damn.

Hot grease popped out of deep fat fryers. American rock music vibrated out of warped speakers. GIs in uniform, wearing the Indianhead patch of the 2nd Infantry Division, paraded from one shop to another, some of them hunched over fried-chicken baskets at open-fronted eateries. Middle-aged Korean men and women slaved behind hot stoves. Young girls with long black ponytails carried trays back and forth, serving the hungry Americans.

Hundreds of GIs were lined up in front of the main mess hall back on Camp Stanley, waiting with their army-issued meal cards for free chow. But dozens came out here to eat, even though it would cost them. Mainly because out here in Songsan, it's just more fun.

Ernie and I strolled past the eateries until we came upon the inevitable tailor shops and brassware emporiums and sporting goods stores, and then we found what we were looking for. The bars. All shuttered now and locked up in the middle of the day. We checked out the signs: Gun Bunny Inn, The Royal Club, The Dragon Lady Bar.

I stopped a freckle-faced GI heading back toward the gate and asked him about the Half Half Club.

His round nose crinkled in confusion. "You want to go there?"

"Why not?" Ernie asked.

"You're white," he said.

"So?"

"The Half Half Club is for soul brothers."

He told us to continue down the lane another fifteen yards and there'd be an alley branching off to the right. We were to follow it for a quarter mile and watch for the signs.

"You can't miss it," he said.

Then he turned and continued his march toward the back gate of Camp Stanley.

Ernie and I followed his directions. We found the signs and were soon walking single file through a brick-walled walkway so narrow I had to angle in to squeeze through. The alley let out into an open flagstoned courtyard, then up a short flight of steps. At the top a sign above a door read: Half Half Club.

The door was locked but instead of pounding and demanding entrance, Ernie and I slipped around the side of the building to the alley behind the Half Half Club. The back door stood open. Laughter drifted out. High and shrill. Women's laughter.

Ernie and I stepped into the dark passageway. We strode forward, our GI-issue oxfords clattering on dirty cement.

A row of bulbs behind the bar cast a yellow glow onto a room equipped with a jukebox, a dance floor, and fifteen cocktail tables.

Some of the Half Half Club women wore shorts and T-shirts, apparently on their way to the bathhouse. Others sat on metal-legged stools around a table laden with steamed rice, cabbage *kimchee*, and *miyok kuk*—seaweed soup. They all looked up when Ernie and I entered; some with chopsticks halfway to their mouths, others in the midst of packing soap and shampoo and washcloths into small metal pans.

Once again, as had happened at the Olympos Casino, the

reaction was fear. Abject fear. As if the two tall strangers who'd walked into their midst were the most dangerous people in the world.

"*Anyong hashi*-motor pool," Ernie said as he strode forward, grinning like a hero returning home from a war. The girls gazed at him, mesmerized, wondering who in the hell he was.

The women of the Half Half Club were unlike any group of Korean women I'd ever seen. Why? Because they were not fully Korean; they were half-American, every one of them. All had dark hair and dark eyes, but some looked like their daddy could've been a coal miner from rural Kentucky, with a pointed nose and sunken cheeks and a sullen look that seemed to expect trouble. Others had faces that were full and noses more bulbous, and at least two of the girls had the tightly curled hair and dark complexion that indicated that they were partially of African descent. But none of the women were blonde. Light-colored hair had been subsumed by their Asian ancestry. And none of the girls dyed their hair blonde, trying to pretend they were more American than they were. Something told me that these women were proud to be Korean and maybe wished they could claim to be one hundred percent Korean. Then they wouldn't be working in this back alley in a low-rent bar called the Half Half Club, hidden away, as if there was something undesirable about them.

"*Meikju kajjiwa!*" Ernie shouted. Bring me a beer!

A space was opened for him, and he sat down with the girls at the table. One hustled over to the bar and returned with an ice-cold OB. Ernie pulled cash out of his pocket and ordered another beer for me, and then asked the girls what they were drinking. Cola and Orange Fanta were the main orders, and soon everyone had something to drink and Ernie sent one of the girls over to play a few tunes on the jukebox. Soul music: Jackie Wilson wailing an unrequited plea. Within five minutes, Ernie had the girls of the Half Half Club laughing and relaxed as if we were all old friends.

I appreciated his work. Relaxing them so I could start asking questions, but I knew I had to hurry. There were no GIs in the club right now, but once they started showing up later this afternoon, the girls would be distracted, and my chance at finding out what the Half Half Club had to do with the smiling woman would be diminished.

The first girl I talked to was tall and dark-complected and told me before I asked that her daddy had been a Creole from Louisiana.

"I never see," she said, "but my *ohma*, she show me picture many times."

I pulled out the sketch of the smiling woman.

The reaction of the girls was as if I had reached into a velvet bag and pulled out the Hope Diamond. They gathered around, oohing and aahing, jostling for a look.

"You know her?" I asked.

"We know," one of the girls said. "Yun Ai-ja. Best looking half-half *jo-san* in Korea."

Jo-san. GI slang, from Japanese, for a business girl.

"Do you know where she is now?"

They all shook their heads.

"But she used to work here," I said.

They nodded. She'd left, according to them, about three months ago. Approximately the same time she arrived up north at the doorstep of the Uichon mama-san.

"Why'd she leave?"

Eyes dropped, avoiding my stare. I waited, and when I received no response, I folded up the sketch and unrolled the sketches of PFC Rodney K. Boltworks and the other man, who was Yun Ai-ja's younger brother.

"Do you know either one of these two men?" I asked.

Everyone shook their heads no.

"Answer the man's questions," Ernie said gruffly. "Why did Yun Ai-ja leave the Half Half Club?"

The women who were standing backed up a half step. The women sitting bowed their heads.

There is much talk about Asian women being submissive. Maybe whoever said that wasn't talking about Koreans. I've seen Korean women stand in the middle of the street and exchange punches, toe to toe, with a grown man. And I'd never met a Korean woman who wasn't feisty when the need presented itself. But these women of the Half Half Club seemed particularly fearful, as if life had beaten them down and their only defense was abject submission to anyone who held the slightest hint of power.

Ernie repeated his question. Finally, the Creole girl sang out.

"Ask Fanny," she said. "She tell you."

"Fanny?"

"Yes."

Ernie stood up but I waved for him to stay put. He nodded, knowing that I meant for him to protect our rear. Two of the Half Half girls took me by the hand and led me to a dark corner beyond the bar. A flicker of candlelight revealed a steep stairway. They pointed up. I left them and climbed the creaking stairs.

As I climbed, an aroma sharpened, biting deeply into my sinuses. At first I thought it was incense. Then I realized the smell was too fierce and disagreeable to be incense. I took a deep breath and held it. *Hanyak.* Chinese medicine. Herbs and exotic ingredients boiled to within an inch of their fundamental essence.

Whoever this Fanny was, she figured to be sick.

The stairs of the Half Half Club squeaked. The sharp, almost toxic odor of *hanyak* grew unbearable. Holding my breath, I gazed down a varnished wooden-slat hallway. There, in a small room at the end, a brown earthen jar sat atop a flickering purple flame. I stepped closer. The spout of the earthen jar was covered with a thick wad of cheesecloth. Pungent steam moistened the cloth and bubbled upward, carrying the medicinal scent of ancient herbal remedies into the air.

"*Nugu ya?*" someone shouted. Who is it?

A woman's voice, in the room next to the small kitchen.

"*Na ya,*" I assured her. It's me.

I slipped back a flimsy wooden door.

She lay on a down-filled mat, rolled out on a floor covered with vinyl. Her back was propped against the wall. A small window was partially open, letting in fresh air and the midafternoon sun.

The young Asian woman stared at me with large hazel-green eyes.

She was thin, with long legs. But her cheeks were full, as if she might've been a rotund woman at one time. Her hands pushed down on the floor, straining. She was trying to rise, preparing for flight. But her legs couldn't join in the movement. They were atrophied, useless. And then I realized what she was and why she was sitting here alone. She was a cripple.

"Fanny?" I asked.

She nodded warily.

Her hair and skin were lighter than any of the women downstairs, though not as light as the smiling woman's. Her complexion was smooth and unblemished, but she was not a particularly attractive woman. She wouldn't have looked out of place in a Stateside supermarket or laboring in a barley field on the Russian steppes. Her age I estimated at about twenty.

I squatted slowly, and crossed my arms over my knees.

"My name is Sueño," I told her. "I'm looking for your friend, Yun Ai-ja."

Fanny stared at me without emotion. I wondered if she'd understood me. I decided to speak again, this time using Korean, when I realized her eyes had filled with tears.

It took a while to calm Fanny down. She didn't get many

visitors—that's what had upset her, or so she said, and when I'd asked about Yun Ai-ja. I'd brought back a lot of memories. The sound of laughter, from Ernie and the Half Half girls, drifted up the stairway. Before pestering her with more questions, I offered to take her downstairs. She hesitated, but after a little coaxing, relented. I called for the Creole girl and she and her friend came upstairs. While I waited in the hall, they helped Fanny dress. When she was ready, I carried her down. According to the Creole girl, Fanny hadn't been downstairs since the "accident" three months ago.

I sat her in a chair at a table in the ballroom. Ernie ordered Chinese food for everyone, and when the delivery boy arrived, Ernie and I moved three cocktail tables together. The boy laid out *yakimandu*, fried meat-filled dumplings; *chapchae*, noodles made of sweet potato flour; and *pibin pap*, rice and vegetables mixed with hot pepper paste. Then we sat down and me and Fanny and Ernie and all the girls at the Half Half Club enjoyed a small banquet.

A couple of hours later, the GIs started to arrive. They dropped coins into the jukebox and ordered drinks. Ernie and I moved to a table out of the way. But I kept Fanny in a chair next to me, and she told me of the night she'd been hurt and of the man who attacked her and knocked her down the stairs. And how in the melee the woman the man was after, Yun Ai-ja, managed to escape.

"She left everything," Fanny told me. "Her clothes, her money, everything. Except her mom."

"Her mom?"

"Yes. Her mom. You know, box hold her mom."

Not a casket, surely. And then I understood. "Her ashes?"

"Yes. Mom's ashes."

"She took a box filled with her mom's ashes and never came back?"

"Never."

"Who was the man who attacked her?"

"I don't know. She no tell. She very ashamed."

"Ashamed? Why should she be ashamed?"

Fanny shook her head. She didn't know.

"But this man," I asked, "this man who attacked her, it was someone who knew her?"

Fanny nodded emphatically. "Yes. Someone who knew her."

I showed Fanny the sketches of PFC Rodney K. Boltworks and the smiling woman's younger brother. "Was the man who attacked her one of these men?"

Fanny couldn't be sure since the attacker wore a ski mask and gloves. But her impression was that he was Korean. She also told me that he was not tall, but average height, and he'd attacked just after the midnight curfew, after all GIs had left the Half Half Club. He didn't have a weapon, but was brutal. He shoved Fanny toward the top of the stairwell, and she lost her balance and reeled backward.

"How can you be so sure," I asked, "that this man was after Yun Ai-ja?"

"I don't know. She know. She so frightened she crawl out window, almost naked, how you say . . . *nei yi?*"

"Underwear."

"Yes. In underwear. When man see Yun Ai-ja not here, he leave."

"And you?" I asked.

"Take go hospital. Stay two days. When no can pay more, Half Half women, they bring me back here."

There is no disability or workman's compensation in Korea. No welfare or food chits or universal health insurance. Fanny told me that her mother was dead, her father a GI whom she'd never known. Since she didn't have a family, this half-American woman was on her own.

At midnight, I carried Fanny back upstairs to her room and

lay her down on the cotton-covered sleeping mat. I was about to leave when she grabbed my hand and asked me to stay.

The next day, I rose early. Before she woke, I left all my travel pay—about seventy dollars worth of MPC—stacked in a pile on the dresser next to her bed.

11

━━━━
━━

Ernie and I didn't pull into the parking lot of the CID head-quarters in Seoul until noon. Two-story red brick buildings, built by the Japanese Imperial Army before World War II, rose above us. Ernie and I ran up cement stairs. When we entered the CID Admin Office, we discovered that the First Sergeant and the Provost Marshal were out to lunch. Lucky for us. Who needed them anyway? All they'd do is pester us for a preliminary report that, if our assumptions didn't pan out, they'd hammer us with later. Better to keep pushing on the investigation and report to them when we were sure of what we had.

Miss Kim sat behind her typewriter, a new pink carnation sticking out of a narrow vase on her desk. When she saw Ernie, she lit up, but then remembered how he'd been ignoring her lately and pretended to pout. Ernie strode across the room, plopped down in the chair in front of her desk, grabbed a copy of today's *Stars & Stripes*, and pretended to read. Furiously, Miss

Kim rolled paper into her typewriter and banged away on the keys, turning sideways from Ernie, pretending to be absorbed in her work.

Both a couple of frauds. But I had to hand it to Ernie, he was playing her like a violin. Or at least he thought he was.

I sat down next to the Admin NCO, Staff Sergeant Riley.

Miss Kim skipped lunch to watch her figure. Riley skipped lunch because the wasted lining of his stomach no longer tolerated food. He'd been boozing heavily since he was a teenager, and now, in his mid-thirties, he looked like a skinny old man two steps away from the intensive-care ward. Sometimes I worried about him, keeping a bottle of Old Overwart in his locker back at the barracks, hitting it hard every night. But he was an adult and the decision was his. And the honchos at 8th Army CID didn't care, because during the day, Riley worked like a Siberian tiger. Gathering information, nurturing contacts throughout 8th Army headquarters, handling all our pay and personnel needs with only the help of the diligent Miss Kim.

Riley stared at me balefully, withered lips pursed around a crooked front tooth.

"Where you been?"

"Up north," I said.

"The Provost Marshal's about to shit a brick."

"Why?"

"Because the Koreans are shitting a brick over the death of Han Ok-hi."

He handed me this morning's edition of the *Hankuk Ilbo*, the Korea Daily. Some of the big block Chinese characters in the headline, I recognized. The name, Han Ok-hi; the name of the city, Inchon; and finally *sa*, the character for death.

"The head shed wants answers," he said. "What can I tell them?"

"We're working on it," I said.

"That's not good enough, Sueño. Don't mess with their

minds. The Provost Marshal is already pissed off enough about you and Ernie being granted special access to General Armbrewster." Riley shook his head. "Going over their heads."

"We didn't go over their heads," Ernie said. "Armbrewster called us."

Riley shrugged. "Same difference. When this shit is over, you're going to be just a couple of no-rank CID maggots again. Nobody to protect you. Better tell the Provost Marshal something. Make him at least feel like he's in charge."

"Screw him," Ernie said. "And the First Sergeant."

I finished my coffee in silence. Riley had given up on Ernie, but he was still waiting for me to say something. I told Riley that Ernie and I were going to find some chow, and then we were going out to follow some leads.

"Give me more than that, Sueño," Riley replied. "I have to feed them some sort of line. Even if it's bullshit."

I paused at the door. "Tell them we're going out to Itaewon," I said, "to search for a woman who might be able to crack this case wide open."

Riley almost smiled. "You're that close?"

"We're close," I replied. "The only problem is, for the last four or five years, the woman's been dead."

Maybe it was his stomach. Maybe it was my answer. For whatever reason, Staff Sergeant Riley's mug turned sour again.

Ernie and I were wearing our "running the ville" outfits: blue jeans, T-shirts, sneakers, and jackets with an embroidered dragon on the back. My dragon embraced a map of Korea and said: "Frozen Chosun, Land of the Morning Calm." Ernie's dragon coiled itself around a beautiful Asian woman and said: "Served my Time in Hell, Korea, 1971-1973."

Without coats and ties, Ernie and I felt free again. That,

along with being fed and rested and, most importantly, back on our home turf: Itaewon, the greatest GI village that ever was.

It was late afternoon, the sun setting red and angry behind the western hills. We were checking *yak bangs*. The literal translation would be "medicine shops." The more accurate translation would be "pharmacies." Pharmacies in Korea, however, are different from pharmacies in the States. For one thing, customers don't need prescriptions. In fact, you don't necessarily need a doctor's advice at all. Many people, especially those who can't afford to see a Western-style doctor, simply stand in the *yak bang* and describe their symptoms. The man behind the counter probably isn't medically trained, and might not have even finished middle school.

That's what was happening now. A portly middle-aged Korean woman was grabbing her back in the lumbar region, ranting about the pain she suffered daily. She crouched, stood up, bent over, moved her arms as if swimming, all in an effort to make the Korean man behind the counter fully understand the pain she was experiencing.

The Korean behind the counter rubbed his chin and sucked in air and tilted his head, agonizing over his decision. He said something in Korean that I couldn't understand, and his wife, who had been standing patiently beside him, brought forth from the stacks in the rear of the shop a large brown bottle filled with pills. The three of them chatted loudly for a couple of minutes, and finally a dozen pills were poured onto a sheet of paper and the wife deftly folded the paper into the shape of a fat envelope. The middle-aged woman handed a short stack of wrinkled *won* notes across the counter. Then the pharmacist and his wife bowed to their customer, and the woman turned and slid open the door of the shop and walked out, the overhead bell tinkling after her.

The pharmacist and his wife turned their attention to me.

In the back, behind the rows of pills was a room with a warm floor and a television set, where two young children were watching cartoons.

I told them what I wanted. Their eyes widened. I explained again, using different Korean words this time, trying to insure that I was being understood. When I finished, the pharmacist breathed in deeply and shook his head.

Then he said something to his wife and she brought out a different brown bottle and poured out a few capsules for me to inspect. Ernie joined me now, sticking his nose in so close I was worried his hot breath might melt the gelatin.

The capsules were bright red, packed full of powder.

"Made in the U.S.A.," Ernie said. "Good stuff."

What we were looking at was what GIs called "reds." Barbiturates. Downers. A drug designed to relax you and put you to sleep. Taken responsibly, they're a perfectly legitimate medication. Taken irresponsibly, they can be lethal.

I asked the pharmacist again: how many reds would it take to knock out a GI as big as me who'd already been drinking? Knock him out so he could walk around for a short while, but in a few minutes be out cold.

The pharmacist told me it wasn't a good idea to drink and, at the same time, consume this drug. But if you did, probably two or three would be enough to incapacitate a man my size—if, that is, he'd already downed a lot of alcohol.

Then we showed him the sketches.

Ernie and I had played this routine in over a dozen pharmacies. This one was about three blocks from the nightclub and brothel area of Itaewon, but still close enough to attract an occasional GI customer. Theoretically, all Korean pharmacies are off limits to 8th Army GIs. Nobody pays much attention to the rule, however. Particularly since there are so many goodies in these *yak bangs* that GIs crave—and also because the rule was unenforceable. There aren't enough MPs to monitor every pharmacy in the Republic of Korea.

The man and his wife studied the sketches with interest. When the wife saw the smiling woman, her mouth opened in surprise.

"*Boassoyo*," she said. I've seen her. She glanced at her husband. "*Dok kattun kot sasso.*" She bought the same things, she said, pointing at the red capsules.

Then her husband remembered. "Yes," he told me. "She asked me the same question. How many would it take to knock out a big man who'd been drinking? I told her. Two. Maybe three."

"The same woman?" I asked again.

"Yes. I'm sure. She bought the same medicine as this."

"How long ago was she in here?"

He frowned and looked at his wife.

"Maybe one week," she said in Korean.

That sounded about right. This pharmacy must've provided the medicine she'd used on me.

"When you told her two or three capsules," I said, "how many did she buy?"

The pharmacist smiled. "That, I remember. She bought six. Twice as many as I recommended." Then his face turned grave. "I told her to be very careful."

I translated for Ernie.

The pharmacist interrupted. "She asked me to do an odd thing. She asked me to open all the capsules and pour the powder inside one wrapper."

"*I* did that," his wife said proudly. "My husband is very smart, but he's also very clumsy."

The pharmacist smiled as if he hadn't heard her.

I translated this exchange also.

Ernie slapped me on the back. "The Dragon Lady was careful, all right," he said. "She wanted to make sure you wouldn't wake up while she was robbing you. Good thing you're so big. Six reds on top of all that booze might've killed a lesser man."

It might've killed me too. But it didn't.

I asked the couple if they'd ever seen the woman again. They shook their heads emphatically. Never before and never since.

We thanked our friendly local pharmacists and left.

We stood on the streets of Itaewon. Gusts of cold wind threw whirlwinds of brown and yellow and red leaves into the heart of the nightclub district. I strained to see the stars, but could only make out a few. Mainly because of the glare from the main drag of Itaewon, which was likewise spangled with flashing neon: red dragons and golden butterflies, and even one sign with a blue and pink rotating yin and yang symbol.

Why had we returned to Itaewon when the two women had been killed in Inchon and Songtan? Because all the evidence so far pointed back to these hallowed grounds.

I'd been robbed here, my badge and my .45 stolen.

The casino robbery was only a thirty-minute train ride away on the most heavily traveled commuter run in Korea.

According to the KNP report from Songtan, the second victim, Miss Jo Kyong-ah, had been arrested numerous times over the last twenty years for black marketing. Where? Itaewon. A few months ago, she'd retired and moved to Songtan.

My final reason: Yun Ai-ja and her younger brother grew up here, in Itaewon. And their mother, while raising them, had worked for years as an Itaewon business girl.

Packs of GIs roamed the streets, their clean-shaven jaws chomping on chewing gum, their shiny eyes studying everything around them. Business girls stood in covered doorways, or in the beaded entranceways to the bars and nightclubs. They laughed and joked and called out to the GIs as they passed.

"Haggler Lee," Ernie said. "That's who we ought to talk to first."

Ernie was right. Haggler Lee was the biggest black market honcho in Itaewon. He'd been here for at least a decade. Since the murdered woman in Songtan, Jo Kyong-ah, had once worked the black market in Itaewon, Haggler Lee must know something about her.

"A surprise visit," I said. "Catch him off guard."

Ernie nodded, and we tromped up a dark alley, away from the nightclub district. We turned down one lane and up another. These roadways were only wide enough for one car at a time, but I knew from experience that a PX taxi could navigate up here easily. If somebody dropped off a load of duty-free military commissary and PX goods, cops like me and Ernie couldn't sneak up on them in our jeep. Which is why we did a lot of work in Itaewon on foot.

We turned down another cobbled street, and there before us stood the dark warehouse of Haggler Lee. *Kukchei Suchulip Gongsu.* International Import Export.

We walked around the side of the old brick building and squeezed through a passageway just wide enough to walk through single-file. At the end of the building, a candle flickered inside a dirty window.

Someone coughed. Ernie motioned for quiet. He edged closer to the back door of the warehouse.

Candlelight cast odd figures on the cement flooring. We heard urgent mumbling inside. Korean, but from this distance I could understand none of it.

Ernie knelt low. He peeked around the open door, then quickly pulled back. Motioning me forward, we entered the warehouse. After a few steps, we found cover behind a plastic-sheeted pallet of Pabst Blue Ribbon beer. Swirling dust clouds fogged my vision and made me want to cough. I fought the urge. Crouching, Ernie whispered in my ear.

"Move closer," he said. "So you can hear what they're talking about."

I nodded and, as quietly as I could, I duck-walked my way to the far wall of the warehouse. I found a gap in the piled merchandise and worked my way toward the voices.

When I was close enough, I peered around a pile of cardboard boxes full of Del Monte canned peaches. There, on a raised *ondol* floor, sat Haggler Lee—on his knees, as was his custom—wearing the traditional turquoise blue silk vest and white pantaloons of an ancient Korean patriarch. Lee, I guessed, was only in his early forties, but he acted as if he were a grandfather of venerable age. Maybe he thought it gave his black-market operation more class. Maybe he was just an old-fashioned guy. Who knows? What I did know was that the mumbling we'd heard wasn't conversation. It was chanting, coming from Haggler Lee. In front of him on a low table was a framed photograph, edged with black ribbon. On either side of the photograph, candles flickered. Lee mumbled some more, and then bowed, placing two palms flat in front of him and pressing his forehead to the floor.

I inched forward, hoping to catch a glimpse of the photograph. Squinting, I recognized the face. It was the same plain female I had seen in the crime folder in the Songtan Police Station: Jo Kyong-ah, the retired black marketeer who'd been murdered in her home by person or persons unknown.

All my concentration focused on Haggler Lee and the photograph and the ancient ritual that he performed.

Four dark shapes emerged from the rows of piled merchandise. Men. All holding something in their hands. Cudgels? Knives? From this distance, I couldn't be sure.

Shoe leather shuffled off to my right, probably Ernie.

The dark figures floated past and headed unerringly toward Ernie's last hiding place.

The blast of a .45 reverberated throughout the warehouse.

Haggler Lee sat on a silk cushion, shaking his head in dismay. "Why you shoot?" he asked Ernie. "Scare everybody?"

"Your men were coming after me," Ernie said, his neck a little too stiff.

"They only checky checky. See who's in warehouse."

The single shot fired from Ernie's .45 had, in fact, frightened the crap out of everybody, especially me. Ernie had held Haggler Lee's thugs at gunpoint until I determined that they were armed with nothing more than clubs and knives. When they put those away, we agreed to a truce and Ernie slipped his .45 back into his shoulder holster.

We sat on the raised wooden floor in the middle of Haggler Lee's inventory. Haggler Lee clapped his hands. A young Korean woman clad in traditional dress shuffled out of the darkness, slipped off her sandals and stepped up onto the platform. She set between us a small tray holding a round brass pot of hot water, a box of Lipton Tea bags, and a jar of Taster's Choice freeze-dried coffee. I took coffee, black. Ernie, too. He stirred sugar into his. The woman had a smooth, pleasant round face and was as cute as a porcelain doll and Ernie couldn't take his eyes off her. Both she and Haggler Lee ignored this rudeness. She bowed and backed away.

"Nice setup you got here, Lee," Ernie said.

Haggler Lee nodded and sipped from an earthenware cup. He was a frail man with long, tapered fingernails. In his traditional silk vest and pantaloons, he looked more like an ancient Confucian scholar than the head of a black-market operation. I waited until he set the cup down to ask my question.

"What are you so nervous about, Lee?"

He smiled at that.

"Besides your friend's pistol," he said, "only one thing. Someone murdered a very close friend of mine."

"Jo Kyong-ah," I said.

"Exactly. Before, long time ago, she black-market honcho.

When I come Itaewon, she helped me set up business."

Lee wasn't afraid to talk about illegal matters with a couple of GI cops. Although he was black-marketeering, almost exclusively, goods purchased from 8th Army PXs and commissaries, we had no jurisdiction over him. Of course, he had underlings handle all the day-to-day transactions but even if Ernie and I had caught Haggler Lee red-handed buying PX goods from a GI, we would have been unable to arrest him. We could arrest the GI, for violation of 8th Army prohibitions against selling duty-free goods to an unauthorized individual. And we'd busted many GIs for just such an offense and, in some cases, testified at their courts-martial. But Haggler Lee we couldn't touch.

The Korean National Police could arrest him but wouldn't. To keep the 8th Army honchos happy, they sometimes ran in some of the low-level Korean black marketeers, held them for an hour or two, and filed their equivalent of misdemeanor charges against them. Usually, the black marketeers paid a fine and were back in business the next day.

If the purpose of black-market restrictions was to protect the Korean economy, why didn't the KNPs take it more seriously? My theory was that a Korean just can't fault another Korean for trying to make a buck in a nonviolent way. Besides, everybody in the country—everybody who could afford it—bought American-made cigarettes and whiskey and imported foodstuffs; that included the rich, movie stars, and even politicians, those self-same politicians who signed treaties to limit the importation of such items.

The honchos at 8th Army, however, took black-marketing seriously. Why? They didn't want low-ranking enlisted GIs making money that way. Some GIs I'd arrested had made upwards of $40,000 per year black-marketeering. When a GI makes that kind of money, the brass loses control. It's hard to keep a young man enthusiastic about fighting war games in the snow and mud when he's making more than twice as much as the Captain barking orders at him. That's what 8th Army was fighting against, primarily. The loss of control over their own troops.

And if anything could tempt a GI to lose his dedication to duty, it was the easy money to be made on the black market in Itaewon.

Ernie and I never black-marketeered. It wasn't a moral thing. It was just that we both hated shopping. For Ernie, it was insulting to be in the PX and have a sweet-voiced announcer over an intercom refer to him as a "shopper." It enraged him. Even buying a bar of soap was a trial. I wasn't much better. Commercialism never appealed to me. And besides, we both had plenty of money. I cleared over $400 per month, more money than I'd ever seen when I was being shuffled between foster homes as a kid. Ernie had one more stripe than me and consequently he cleared $50 more per month. What we made, we spent on booze and women. Occasionally, when we got lucky, we received those things free. So who needed money?

I finished my coffee and asked Lee, "Why are you worried? Someone murdered Jo Kyong-ah thirty miles from here, in Songtan. What does that have to do with you?"

"Revenge," he said.

I waited for him to explain.

"In the black-market business some customers, when they run out of money, come to us for loans. Sometimes we give them loans. Have to. Otherwise people very angry. But I hate to give loans. Always causes trouble."

"People don't want to pay you back," Ernie said.

Haggler Lee nodded.

Ernie continued. "Because they think you're making so much profit off what they sell you out of the PX, that it's unfair for you to ask them to pay back the loan. So when you either collect or deny them another loan, they hate you. Over the years, you pick up a lot of enemies."

Lee nodded again.

"So," I said, "you think a disgruntled customer murdered Jo Kyong-ah, and you're worried that the same customer might come after you."

Haggler Lee said, "Sometimes people crazy about money."

I glanced at the piled goods in this dark warehouse and tried to calculate the cash they must represent. Tens of thousands of U.S. dollars, I imagined, and Haggler Lee was accusing other people of being "crazy about money."

"Who would've hated Jo Kyong-ah," I asked, "enough to kill her?"

"Lot of people."

"You, for instance?" Ernie said.

Lee shook his head vehemently. "No. She never cheat me. She can't."

"Why not?"

Lee straightened his back and thrust out his narrow chest. "I'm business man."

That explained that.

"So who else?" I asked.

"I don't know."

"Who would know?"

Lee thought about that, then shook his head. "I don't know."

I pulled out the three sketches and laid them on the floor in front of Lee. "Do you recognize any of these people?"

I watched his eyes as he scanned them. He skipped past Private Boltworks and the dark man, but his eyes lingered on the sketch of Yun Ai-ja, the smiling woman. Still staring at her, he shook his head.

"Her," I said, pointing at the smiling woman's sketch. "You know her."

"No," he said, but his voice sounded weak. Indecisive.

A thought hit me. Improbable, but worth a try.

"Think about this," I said. "What if her hair in this sketch was the same length but straighter, less wavy, and it was jet black."

He stared at the sketch again.

"Imagine her skinny," I said. "So skinny her cheeks were sunken in."

I sucked my cheeks in to demonstrate, but Haggler Lee wasn't watching. He stared intently at the sketch. As quietly as I could, I moved one of the candleholders closer. Suddenly, Haggler Lee gulped an involuntary intake of breath.

"Miss Yun," he said.

12

Haggler Lee took the unusual step of leaving his warehouse, along with his bodyguards, and escorted Ernie and me down to the nightclub district of Itaewon. While we stood on a dark corner, his bodyguards reconnoitered the area until they found the man they were looking for: Jimmy. A slender, middle-aged Korean who rode his motor scooter to Itaewon every night. With a big flash camera hung over his neck, he wandered from club to club offering his services to the GIs and business girls who snuggled together in dark booths, snapping a photo and popping the hot flash bulb into his white-gloved hand.

It was a living—the type of hustle that everyone had to make to get by in post-war Korea.

Jimmy stood before me and Ernie and Haggler Lee, eyes wide, crooked smile showing amusement at the attention. He nodded to Lee, but not deeply, Jimmy being older.

Lee spoke to Jimmy so rapidly I could barely keep up—

something to do with showing photographs to me and Ernie. Jimmy nodded, jumped on his motor bike, rolled up to one of the kimchee cabs that lined the streets of Itaewon, and gave the driver directions. Ernie and I hopped in the back of the cab. We followed Jimmy's scooter through the winding roads of Seoul.

Finally, in the riverside district known as Dongbinggo, Jimmy stopped on the flag-stoned sidewalk of a busy thoroughfare. He motioned for the cab to pull over, and we climbed out. Pushing his motor bike, Jimmy trudged up a pedestrian pathway that ascended a steep hill. The path was lined with wood and brick walls, behind which squatted teeming small hovels. When we were almost to the top, the road leveled off, and Jimmy turned and stopped at a rickety wooden gate. He banged on it with his fist.

"*Na ya!*" he shouted. It's me.

When the gate opened, two bright eyes shone out at us. A woman turned and shuffled off quickly, back to the hooch behind the wall. I helped Jimmy lift his scooter through the gate. We were in a small courtyard with the usual *byonso* on one side, earthen kimchee jars on the other. The kimchee jars flanked a cement-block building almost as large as the hooch. It seemed out of place in this Asian slum. Modern. Its red door and blue-tiled roof gleamed in the moonlight, and promised entry into another world.

Ernie inhaled the aroma of boiling red peppers wafting from the house the woman had disappeared into.

"Nice place you got here, Jimmy," he said, and I knew he meant it.

Below, headlights streamed down Han Kang Ro, the Han River Road. On the other side of downtown, a three-quarters-full harvest moon illuminated craggy peaks. I could just make out the symmetrical stone battlements that had once protected this ancient city from invasion.

Jimmy pulled out a ring of keys and opened the red door. He

flicked on a switch and the interior was bathed in red light. With his free arm, he motioned for us to enter.

When I was a kid in L.A., our grammar school once took a busload of us Chicano kids from the slums of Maravilla up to the scenic grandeur of Griffith Park Observatory. I was impressed with the granite monolith and the panoramic view of the Los Angeles Basin from its stone walkways. I was even more impressed by the show inside. We sat in comfortable chairs and the lights were turned lower and lower until, from horizon to horizon, the entire star-studded universe erupted from the darkness.

What I saw in Jimmy's photo lab that night was not nearly as magnificent. But in some ways it was more beautiful. For what Jimmy had done during his years since the Korean War—years spent wandering from bar to bar with a camera—was to chronicle a way of life. GIs pulled from their homes and thrust into the harsh and lonely environment of the United States Army, facing a four thousand year old Asian culture that was on the ropes, a country halved and reeling from thirty-five years of Japanese occupation and three years of vicious civil war, followed by a wary peace. Overly made-up Korean girls filled shot after shot. Girls who only weeks or days before had been squatting in muddy rice paddies, trying to harvest enough grain and pick enough cabbage to survive through the long months of the Korean winter. If the survival of their families meant they had to sell their bodies to American GIs, they would.

Jimmy stored the photos in long narrow boxes, each marked with a letter written in *hangul*. Without asking questions, he located three boxes buried under a table, lifted them up, blew dust off, and plopped them on the tabletop. He deftly thumbed through the photos, each sheathed in a brown pulp envelope. When he found what he was looking for, he slapped it up on a plastic-backed wall board and switched on the fluorescent light. He slapped another photo up, and then another, and Ernie and I stared at the universe before us.

The uniforms are what I noticed first. Archaic. Stiff old-fashioned khaki. The GIs wore black ties and their trousers were bloused into brown combat boots. Styles have changed. The haircuts are shorter now. The Rock Revolution, begun a decade earlier, prompted the army to tighten its haircut restrictions, so anything longer than a crew cut is frowned upon. The GIs in these photos from the fifties sported hair that looked shaggy in comparison.

Still, they were young and fresh-faced. There were many different GIs in the pictures, but the woman was the same. The same Korean face. She looked very much like the smiling woman, except her hair was black instead of blond, and her cheekbones were higher. She was skinnier than the smiling woman. On the edge of each envelope was written a single Chinese character: Yun.

And still there were more. The parade of GIs sitting next to Miss Yun changed as rapidly as an old film in a nickelodeon. Each one younger and more wholesome than the one before. And all the while, the woman known as Miss Yun kept her smile cranked up to full velocity.

Some of the photos that Jimmy slapped up for us weren't taken in nightclubs. Some showed Miss Yun outside the clubs, or on the shores of a lake, or standing with a Korean friend outside a bathhouse. I recognized one of her companions, the woman who was now the old hag known as the Uichon mama-san. And then a child: a toddler with straight blonde hair and a Korean face. As the child grew older and taller, a second child appeared. This one a boy. Dark. His hair curly, face scowling. Jimmy slapped another photo up and stopped.

"This her long time *yobo*," he said. Her long time American boyfriend.

He was beefy, with large hands and a scorched-earth crew

cut framing his bulging cheeks. He was homely, even in uniform, battle ribbons across his chest. Suspicious eyes glared out from behind thick Army-issue glasses. Miss Yun, although she was aging, was still much too beautiful for him.

Another photo. The booth was full. The beefy soldier took up most of the space. Sitting on either side of the couple were the children. The girl's hair was a little darker—light brown—and looked more Asian. His hair was wavy, no longer in curls. They boy had a strong square jaw. He sat with a non-committal expression, the big GI's paw resting on his shoulder. The GI's other arm was looped all the way around behind Miss Yun. His hand rested on the girl's head. His fingers were long, languid, fleshy. Possessive.

Miss Yun looked resigned.

The rank insignia on his khaki sleeve was SFC, Sergeant First Class. The name: Garner.

After that, the photos stopped. Except for one more that Jimmy found on the other side of his lab. It was from a much later date, because now both kids were teenagers, the boy maybe thirteen, the girl a couple of years older. Miss Yun stood between them, being held up. She seemed ancient now, skinnier than she had ever been, her face wrinkled, her eyes drooping as if exhausted from the effort of living. All stood in front of an ancient wooden gate. Above, three Chinese characters were slashed in red. Dirty snow lay in clumps at their feet.

"Where was this taken?" I asked Jimmy.

"At Buddhist temple in country. Called Hei-un Sa. The Temple of Cloud and Sea. Sometimes I go there pray. That time I see Miss Yun and her children."

"Why'd you take her picture?" I asked.

"Miss Yun made me much money for many years. Always ask GI take picture. Some say no. Most say yes. When she young, many GI like her very much. So when she ask me to take picture of her and her children, how can I say no? I take photo, give each one copy. Keep this one myself. Here." He handed me a copy of the photo. "I have negative."

Ernie was already restless. He didn't like nostalgia. He didn't like reminiscing about old times, and it was clear that both Jimmy and I were doing exactly that, even if it was someone else's old times.

"This big man," I said. "Sergeant Garner. Tell me about him."

"Lifer," Jimmy said. A career enlisted man. "He come back and forth Korea many times. Always *yobo* Miss Yun."

"*Yobo,*" meant lover. In GI slang, it meant to shack up.

"Are the two kids his?"

"No. Not his. They too good-looking. He know they not his. That why he all the time . . . *kullasso.*"

"Angry?"

"Yes. He don't want pay photo. This one Miss Yun order. When he no pay, she tell me she sorry. She no have money."

"But Garner was a senior NCO. He had money."

"He stingy. Still, Miss Yun tell me he feed her children."

"So she stayed with him."

Jimmy nodded.

"When did you last see her?"

"When I took photo." He pointed to the one of the withered Miss Yun standing with her almost-grown children in front of the Buddhist temple. "TB," Jimmy said.

"That's what killed her?" I said. "Tuberculosis?"

"I hear that. For sure I don't know."

Ernie crossed his arms, turning in a circle in the rouge-lit room, staring at the photos. Finally, he waved his arms.

"Why do you do this, Jimmy? Keep all these old photos of GIs and business girls?"

Jimmy shrugged. "Got to."

I thanked Jimmy for his help, and we all left his lab. He said goodbye to his wife, and I helped him carry his motor scooter out to the street. He putted off down the hill, leaving us behind.

Ernie and I walked to the main road. We waved down a cab and headed back to 8th Army's Yongsan Compound.

In the cab, Ernie was quiet. I kept staring at the photograph Jimmy had given me, of Miss Yun and her two children standing in front of the temple. It bothered me. The teenaged, half-American girl Yun Ai-ja was smiling, the beginnings of that unnerving leer.

13

The rising sun sent a dull glow over the mountain tops. Fog clung to fallow rice paddies. The engine of Ernie's jeep churned as we swerved around the occasional ox cart trundling down the road. I cupped my hands to capture the warmth radiating from under the dashboard.

"ASCOM City," Ernie said. "It figures. After the asshole ran away from us at the Yellow House, he probably caught a cab and headed straight to Pupyong."

ASCOM City. The village outside the main gate of the 8th Army logistics compound known as the Army Support Command (ASCOM). Both were located on the outskirts of the town of Pupyong, twelve miles southeast of downtown Inchon.

The asshole Ernie was referring to was Private First Class Rodney K. Boltworks, formerly assigned to Charley Battery, 2nd of the 17th Field Artillery, now absent without leave. Also, the young man we suspected of participating in the robbery of the

Olympos Casino, and the man who'd run from us when we almost collared him in Mi-ja's room in Brothel Number 17 at the Yellow House.

"He would've had to hide somewhere in Inchon until the curfew was over at four a.m.," I said. "Catch a cab to Pupyong. He's probably been holed up in ASCOM City ever since."

"With a pocketful of stolen money and no place to go." Ernie grinned. "I couldn't think of a better hideout myself."

ASCOM City was a notorious GI Village. High crime rate, high VD rate, rampant black-marketeering, and no one figured to bring the place under control any time soon. There were a couple of thousand GIs assigned to the ASCOM support complex, and plenty of soldiers on TDY who were there temporarily for various reasons. The village started at the front gate. Every bar and brothel and chop house and hooch was jammed into ten acres, cobwebbed with winding footpaths, with little or no space for motorized vehicles. The military police patrols were conducted on foot. On a payday night, the nightclubs were crowded with half-crazed GIs, and the MPs and the Korean National Police were outnumbered forty to one.

How had we figured Boltworks was there? Ration control records.

Staff Sergeant Riley, the Admin sergeant at the CID Detachment had been monitoring them for us. Boltwork's Ration Control Plate, or RCP, was still valid: we purposely hadn't closed it out. For whatever reason, he'd decided to go onto the ASCOM compound and make some purchases. Two quarts of Johnny Walker Black Scotch Whiskey, one case of Pabst Blue Ribbon beer, one jar of non-dairy soluble creamer, a 16-ounce jar of freeze-dried coffee, one pound of sugar, two cartons of Kent cigarettes, a large container of powdered instant orange juice, hand lotion, moisturizing cream, and two packets of nylon pantyhose. All prime black market purchases. Riley had cadged the list from a contact at the 8th Army Data Processing Unit.

When he saw the items, Ernie said, "He's shacked-up with a business girl." I agreed.

Ernie pulled the jeep off the MSR and rolled toward the main train station in downtown Pupyong. Even at this early morning hour, long lines of commuters were waiting to catch the next train into Seoul. We turned right, and three quarters of a mile ahead, we saw the main gate of the Army Support Command.

Ernie slowed to a crawl. Across the street from the high brick fences of the military compound, stood a sea of ramshackle buildings, none of them taller than two stories, with myriad alleyways leading down into the dark. Unlit neon lined the road: the Black Cat Club, the Yobo Bar, the Red Dragon Eatery, Mama Lee's Chop House.

"Lovely," Ernie said.

He meant it. He'd rather spend a week in ASCOM City than bask on the sands of China Beach, at Vung Tau.

According to 8th Army regulations, we should've checked in with the commander of the MP detachment of the ASCOM compound, to let him know we'd be operating in his area. However, Ernie and I had complied with that rule in the past, and all we'd received for our efforts was a bunch of long-winded speeches from pompous MP officers warning us not to mess with their troops. Bullshit we could live without.

Ernie cruised out past the sleepy village until we were seeing rice paddies again. Then he hung a U and turned right down the first cramped road leading into ASCOM City. This was the only route wide enough for kimchee cabs, and already a couple were parked in front of a small granary, their engines idling, waiting for the next GI miscreant who'd spent his night immersed in sin. Ernie parked behind the two cabs.

It would've been interesting to sit here and see who emerged, bleary-eyed and hung over, but we didn't have the time. The smiling woman's brother had killed twice already: the blackjack dealer at the Olympos, and Jo Kyong-ah, the retired black marketeer. My biggest worry was that he would kill again. Ernie and I talked it over.

"The first killing was a mistake," Ernie said. "The casino owner made a dash for the fire-escape hatch, our man pulled the trigger. Maybe Han Ok-hi stepped into the line of fire and took the bullet for her boss. So he knows he's toast. The KNPs are going to catch him eventually. Maybe not today, but soon. Once they do, his only choices will be hanging, or a life-sentence in a Korean prison."

For a young Amerasian man in a Korean prison, life would be unendurable hell.

"He'd choose hanging," I said.

"Right. So now, before we catch him, he decides to have a little fun. And, who knows, maybe he'll decide to have a little more."

"But why kill Jo Kyong-ah?"

"That part," Ernie said, "I haven't figured out yet."

I thought about the way Jo Kyong-ah's body had been left. Face down, the back of her neck bruised, spread out in front of a short-legged table. Despite the information I'd received from the Uichon mama-san and from Haggler Lee—and from the man Haggler Lee had introduced us to last night—I still had no lead that might help us find the younger brother. There were only possibilities. Find the smiling woman. Or find PFC Rodney K. Boltworks, his partner in crime.

Thanks to Sergeant Riley, we at last had a lead on Boltworks. So we sat in the jeep in the heart of ASCOM City, contemplating our moves.

"The KNPs?" Ernie asked.

"Maybe," I said. "See if there's been any incidents."

You'd think someone who'd just committed a serious crime like armed robbery, narrowly escaping the law, would need to hide. Keep a low profile, stay out of trouble. But every cop knows that when a criminal is hot, on the run and being pursued, he often does something to draw attention to himself. Maybe from stress, maybe from stupidity. No matter—it happens.

Ernie and I climbed out of the jeep and walked twenty yards to the modest, white-washed building flying the flag of Korea out front. The sign said: PUPYONG CITY POLICE STATION, WESTERN BRANCH.

The KNPs weren't happy to see us. They had enough trouble in this little corner of the world. When we asked about incidents, the desk sergeant rolled his eyes. Then he shoved a cloth-bound ledger across the counter and opened it to the most recent entries. I started studying it, and he went back to his paperwork.

There were no civilians in the station, just three cops and the desk sergeant. They were all bleary-eyed and half asleep and didn't seem too impressed to see a couple of 8th Army CID agents.

Ernie stuck his nose over the ledger. "It's all written in Korean."

I pulled out my notebook.

Ernie elbowed my left arm. "What you got?"

"A fight between a business girl and a GI. At a joint called the Asian Eyes Bar. Not last night, but the night before."

"Names?"

"Only one. The woman's name is Pak Mi-rae. The GI disappeared before the KNPs arrived."

"Descriptions?"

"A Korean business girl and an American GI. The KNP didn't bother."

ASCOM City was swarming with people of roughly the same description: American soldier, average height, average weight, light brown or dark brown hair, no identifying marks. Korean prostitute, dark brown or black hair, dark brown or black eyes, approximately five-foot-three inches tall, one hundred and fifteen pounds. Name: Miss Pak, Miss Kim, or Miss Lee. And—as the GIs would say—cute foreign accent.

So there was nothing to tie this incident to PFC Boltworks except for one thing. Ernie said it.

"Same night our man Bolt bought all that shit out of the PX."

We thanked the desk sergeant and found our own way out.

Two eyes were painted on a sign over the bar. Female eyes. Asian. Below the eyes, the sign said—predictably enough—Asian Eyes Bar.

The joint was located in the middle of the nightclub and brothel district known as ASCOM City. The walkways were paved with rough cobblestones. The buildings were packed tight. There was no room for a delivery truck to back in. All the supplies, like crates of beer and huge blocks of ice, must've been hauled in the old fashioned way: strapped to someone's back.

The bar district of ASCOM City sat in a depression half a mile long and a quarter mile wide, probably on top of what had once been ancient rice paddies. To reach either the road to the west, where the police station stood, or the MSR to the north, where the long walls of the Army Support Command Compound were located, you had to climb a gradual incline of a good twenty feet. Since we were in the well of a depression, the morning fog sat thick and sluggish. The overcast sky launched a splat of rain that hit the cobbled roads, an explosion of rust-flavored dirt. More splats followed. And more puffs of dirt.

"I expect a wolf to howl," Ernie said.

But none did. No one else howled either. The GIs were either snug in their hooches with their Korean *yobo*s or already back on the compound.

I tried the front door of the Asian Eyes Bar.

It was barred tightly from the inside. I was careful not to rattle the door too loudly. We didn't want to wake anyone. Not yet. Ernie and I reconnoitered.

One side of the building was flush up against the next bar, a joint called the Playboy Club—the establishments in ASCOM City don't worry much about trademark infringement. I squeezed through a brick-lined passage. In the rear of the building, the sign also read ASIAN EYES BAR. Up and down the alley were the backdoors of other saloons. GIs could enter one place in the front, and if they didn't find sufficient titillation, they could exit out the back, cross the alley, and immediately enter through the back door of another, equally raunchy dive. I imagined this alleyway at night, neon-lit, teeming with business girls and drunk Americans. Cigarette smoke, laughter, blaring rock music erupting out of the back doors. Not an area that an MP patrol would want to spend a lot of time in. At the moment, however, it was deserted, except for a rat who scurried into a subterranean drainage ditch.

The back door of the Asian Eyes Bar looked flimsy, easier to bust through, but no sense getting rough. After all, we had no reason to think Boltworks might be here. This was just a place to start our investigation, because we had to start somewhere. We wanted to talk to these people about the disturbance between a Korean woman and an American GI that had occurred the night before last. We had no reason to believe that the GI was Boltworks. Nevertheless, Ernie backed up, preparing to kick the door in.

"Why don't we just knock?" I said.

His eyes widened: the thought had never occurred to him.

I pushed past him and pounded my fist on the back door. One thing about Korean businesses is that they're virtually never deserted. Either the family that owns the enterprise lives on the premises, or they leave someone behind to protect it against burglars. I pounded for almost five minutes, until chains rattled inside and the door popped open. Ernie pushed it aside, and we strode into darkness.

"*Kyongchal. Bul kyo, bali!*" I said, announcing ourselves as police and ordering the lights turned on immediately.

Somebody did.

One of the benefits of operating in a police state is that civilians do what you tell them to do. Usually.

To the left of the hallway were *byonso*s, toilets, both men's and women's. Toward the front, a bar ran along the wall. A passageway opened into a larger area, red vinyl booths surrounding round cocktail tables covered by upturned chairs. In the middle of this main ballroom was a tiny dance floor. There was no stage, but refrigerator-sized stereo speakers were mounted along the wall every few feet. Near the dance floor stood an aquarium. Orange and white and purple fish swam serenely through green water. A blue glow filled the room. Behind us, harsh white bulbs lined the top of the bar.

"Kids," Ernie said.

There must've been a half dozen of them, both boys and girls. Not children exactly. Probably middle-school age, or just old enough to start high school. But these kids weren't students. They were staff here at the Asian Eyes Bar, responsible for the cleaning and bartending and serving and whatever else had to be done around the place. Possibly distant relatives of the owner, maybe just extra mouths to feed, from large rural families forced to sell them into indentured servitude. I wasn't going to bother to ask, because one thing's for sure: on personal matters—matters that cause shame—a foreigner never received a straight answer.

The oldest was a skinny boy. Straight black hair hung over his sleep-crusted eyes. He glared at us with a full-lipped sullen stare.

"*Wei kurei?*" he asked. Why are you doing this?

The other kids had been sleeping in the vinyl booths. Some

were up now, searching through a jumble of clothing on the red-carpeted floor. One girl lay still in her booth, a thin comforter pulled up over her nose, her black eyes sparkling with fear.

In Korean, I asked the oldest boy if the owner was here. He shook his head.

"What time does he come in?"

Again, a negative shake of the head.

Ernie took two quick steps and shoved the kid's back up against the wooden bar.

I walked over to Ernie. He knew I didn't like him getting rough with youngsters. He held his grip on the kid's collar and glared fiercely. I knew it was an act, the kid didn't. This gangly boy and the other children in the bar were frightened half to death. Who knew how many drunken GIs had come in here, terrorizing anyone they thought wouldn't fight back?

Still, if we were going to find Boltworks we needed information and quickly. ASCOM City is a small village and word of our arrival would spread fast. Once Bolt heard, he'd be gone. So we had to find out what this kid knew, and now. Every interrogator knows that there's only one effective tool to extract answers from people who don't want to talk: fear.

The kid tried to shove Ernie's fist away, but he wasn't strong enough.

I spoke in rapid Korean: "There was a fight here the night before last, between a Korean woman named Pak Mi-rae and an American GI. Tell me about it. Now!"

The kid started with the same disclaimer every witness uses. "I don't know. I didn't see anything."

Ernie tightened his grip and leaned into the kid's face. And the boy proceeded to tell us what he'd seen. I asked a few follow-up questions and was answered immediately. Ernie let him go.

The incident at the Asian Eyes Bar had been routine. A Korean woman claimed a GI had cheated her out of money she'd fronted him in a black-market deal. He claimed he didn't owe her anything, and she attacked. The GI, smart enough to know that he'd be in big trouble if he hit back, held her off. After about ten minutes of wrestling, he managed to escape the enraged woman's grip. Then he ran. Another smart move. No, they didn't know the soldier's name, but he'd been coming in for months. Therefore, the guy couldn't be our quarry.

Private Boltworks, before he went AWOL, was assigned to a field artillery base thirty miles north of here.

The other youngsters were up now, in various stages of undress. They lined up in front of the glowing aquarium. I pulled the three sketches out and held them to the light. One by one, I asked the children if they'd ever seen these three people. The eyes of two of the girls lingered on the sketch of the smiling woman. But in the end they shook their heads.

I believed them. They were too frightened and in too much awe of our supposed authority to lie. The oldest boy didn't recognize the sketched faces either.

Ernie sighed, frustrated at this waste of time and effort. He reached into his pocket and slapped a ten-dollar MPC note on the bar, not looking at any of the kids. He was ashamed of what he'd done, but he had to be certain that information would be surrendered quickly and accurately. With a killer on the loose, we had no time for niceties.

He was about to leave when I stopped him.

"Maybe these kids can help us another way," I said.

"How's that?"

"The woman involved in the altercation, she's a black marketeer . . . just a minute."

In Korean, I asked the kids if they knew where the woman who had been in the fight lived. All stood dumb except for one chubby girl. Almost imperceptibly, she nodded her head.

I asked again. "You know where she lives?"

"We all do," she answered.

The oldest boy frowned. I crossed the carpeted floor and slipped my arm around his narrow shoulders.

"*Bali kaja,*" I said. "Let's go."

Sullenly, he nodded. He slipped on a wool sweater to ward off the cold, and then Ernie and I and the boy left out the back door of the bar.

The sky had taken on a slightly lighter hue. As we wound through fog-shrouded alleys, Ernie leaned into me. "Why do you want to talk to this black-market woman? What's she got to do with all this?"

"Boltworks is on tilt. He's making purchases out of the PX. He knows eventually we'll cancel his Ration Control Plate. The time to buy is now. And if he buys, he has to sell. And quickly. Probably at bargain rates. The black market mama-sans in ASCOM City will be on him like vultures. The woman who started the fight at the Asian Eyes Bar is a black marketeer and a feisty one. And she has enough pull in the village to be released by the KNPs with nothing more than a warning. She'll probably know about a new GI in the village making *beaucoup* black-market buys. I'm willing to bet on it."

Ernie thought it over. "Maybe," he said.

The boy turned down a crack between two buildings. We angled in, emerging onto another alley. The boy stopped. He pointed at a wooden gate in a granite wall.

"*Yogi,*" he said. Here.

Nimbly, he hopped back, and then he disappeared. Ernie almost went after him, but I grabbed his elbow.

"Don't," I said. "The kid's not lying. He knows we can find him."

Ernie shrugged and stared at the gate. There was a black button with a wire running back into the hooch. Ernie reached to press it. Again, I stopped him.

I said, "Let's not knock."

Ernie's eyes widened, then narrowed. He nodded.

I checked for a brass nameplate embedded in the wall; there was none. Only two numbers on the door in black paint: "201 *bonji*, 36 *ku*." The address, but no name.

We searched around until we found a wooden trash crate. We set it on its end against the wall. Ernie was armed, his .45 snug in his shoulder holster, so he climbed up first and went over the top. He leapt, and I heard him grunt when he hit the ground. Then I was on the crate and atop the fence. I leapt down into a cleanly swept courtyard. The hooch was silent, its oil-paper sliding doors shut.

At the lip of the raised wooden floor, Ernie and I slipped off our shoes and stepped up onto the immaculate surface. A gleaming hallway led through an opening between the first few hooches. It emptied onto a courtyard, a well-tended garden paved with flagstone. The surrounding hooches faced inwards. All were silent. Sliding doors closed.

From behind, footsteps. I swiveled.

She wore a flower-print robe. Her feet were bare, her black hair ratted up in a sweaty disarray.

"What's the matta you?" she snarled.

Ernie and I stared. She must've been fifty, at least, with a wrinkled face and a round button nose that would've been cute when she was young. "Pak Mi-rae?" I asked.

"How you know?"

"You were in a fight at the Asian Eyes Bar the other night."

"Yeah. So what? GI owe me money. I knuckle sandwich with him."

A few of the doors around the courtyard slid open. Women lying on down-filled mats peeked out with sleep-filled faces. All were young, as Pak Mi-rae had once been.

Ernie grinned, looking around. He placed his hands on his hips. We were in a brothel, and he felt right at home.

I turned back to Pak Mi-rae. "Can we talk? You have coffee?"

She snickered. "You come my hooch, climb fence, wake up me, wake up all girls. Now you want *kopi*?"

"Yes," Ernie said, grinning broadly. "That's what we want. Part of what we want anyway."

He approached Miss Pak and pulled out his CID badge.

She stared up at him. "CID. Don't mean shit."

"Good. Then you won't mind fixing us some coffee."

She snorted, stared at Ernie for a moment, then swiveled and walked back toward her hooch. We followed. Ernie smiled and waved at the sleepy young women gawking at us.

A few, timidly, waved back.

14

Pak Mi-rae knew all about the retired black marketeer, Jo Kyong-ah, who'd been murdered in the city of Songtan.

"She treat somebody bad," Miss Pak said. "Me, I never treat nobody bad."

To her, punching out a GI who owed her money didn't qualify.

We sat in a large hooch near the front gate. Pak Mi-rae boiled water in a brass pot and poured us cups of freeze-dried coffee. We were cops. It was best to humor us. We sat on her warm *ondol* floor and used a foot-high table with folding legs. The table and the four armoires surrounding us were made of polished black lacquer inlaid with expensive mother-of-pearl designs. Miss Pak's bed was Western-style, with a hand-embroidered silk comforter hiding the wrinkled sheets. The place reeked of perfume. No sign of any man living there.

Ernie told her about the GI and his partner who'd robbed the Olympos Casino in Inchon and murdered a blackjack dealer. She knew about that too. Then he told her that we believed the GI's partner had murdered Jo Kyong-ah.

She thought about that for a while, stirring too much non-dairy creamer into her coffee.

"The GI's name is Boltworks," Ernie said. "Rodney K. He made a few purchases on ASCOM compound two days ago. He's dangerous, and we believe he's armed, with the pistol stolen from the security guard at the Olympos Casino in Inchon."

Ernie wasn't holding back on his English. Pak Mi-rae understood it as well as we. Her pronunciation and grammar, and liberal use of slang, was far from perfect, but we didn't have to talk down to her. And I didn't have to speak Korean. She'd probably been speaking English since she was a teenager, when she'd first arrived in some GI village to start work as a business girl.

She stared at her coffee cup, then ladled more sugar into it.

She knows something, I thought. Ernie sensed it too.

"We only want *him*," Ernie said. "We're not here to bust anybody for black marketing or anything."

She continued to stir, and then I noticed her hand was shaking. Behind us, I heard whispering. Quickly, I stood. Ernie too, instinctively going for his .45. But the whispering wasn't coming toward us, it was receding from the hooch, along with footsteps. I slid open the door of the hooch and, as Ernie was about to step past me with the weapon, Pak Mi-rae leapt at him. Screaming.

"*Ka! Bali ka!*" Go! Go quickly!

I tried to pull her off Ernie but she had dug her claws into his coat and held on like a snow leopard. We heard the front gate open, and then slam shut. With a fierce tug, I ripped Pak Mi-rae off of Ernie, and we rushed into the courtyard. We both remembered our shoes and skidded to a halt, but when we looked for them under the porch they were gone.

"Shit!" Ernie shouted. He stared at Pak Mi-rae standing in the doorway to her hooch and, without thinking, pointed his .45 at her. She cowered.

"Where are the shoes?" he shouted.

She retreated from the doorway.

"No time," I said. "Come on!"

In our stocking feet we ran across the courtyard, fumbled with the lock of the front gate, and burst into the alley, running full tilt, not sure which way to go.

"Did you see him?" Ernie shouted.

"No."

"Then where?"

"We'll never find him in this maze," I said. We stopped, looking around at the gaping mouths of dark, empty lanes. The morning fog had started to lift, but the sky was still a dark gray. "The MSR," I said. "That's where he'll go."

"How do we get there?"

I didn't know. Not exactly. I knew only the general direction. North, toward the long brick walls of the ASCOM compound.

We ran through the maze, past shuttered bars and quiet nightclubs, always heading north toward larger and larger alleyways. Finally, a curving pathway led sharply up an incline, past Han's Tailor Shop and Miss Goo's Brassware Emporium. Ernie stepped on a rock and hopped up and down, cursing. I kept going. Then we were on a sidewalk, and the walls of the ASCOM compound were across the street, and the MSR spread east and west in front of us. Two kimchee cabs sat about ten yards over. Ernie and I each chose a cab and ripped open the doors.

"*Migun*," I shouted in Korean—GI.

"*Kumbang.*" Just a moment ago.

"*Odi kasso?*" Where did he go?

Both drivers pointed straight ahead. East, toward the Pupyong Train Station.

Ernie and I jumped into the lead taxi. *"Bali ka!"* I shouted. Go quickly.

The driver glanced down at my stocking feet, but didn't comment. He started the engine and slammed it in gear. We lurched forward, shouting to go faster. He did. In a few seconds we were past the village, speeding into the still quiet edge of Pupyong proper.

And then, up ahead, we saw a kimchee cab. Ernie spotted it first.

"There!" He pointed, and the driver saw it and stepped on the gas. As we closed in, I reached into my pocket and pulled out a rumpled five-dollar MPC note. Too much. Way too much. And cops in Korea—at least Korean ones—have the right to commandeer any vehicle they want any time, as long as it's used for police business. I shoved the fiver back in my pocket. The driver would have to derive his satisfaction from doing his civic duty.

Ernie was shouting and pounding the back seat. "Faster! Faster!"

The driver understood, but the cab in front of us had realized it was being followed. It lurched right, toward the front of the Pupyong Train Station. Before it had rolled to a complete stop, the back door popped open and someone was out and running. Blond hair, short crew cut, stocky build. Civilian clothes that were a blur. Dark pants. Darker jacket.

"Boltworks!" Ernie shouted.

Our driver screeched up behind the other kimchee cab, and for a terrifying second, I thought he was going to smash into the rear bumper, but somehow he stopped in time, and Ernie and I were out of the cab, dashing flatfooted across cement, startling men in suits carrying briefcases. Ernie bounded up, trying to see over the growing crowd of morning commuters. I spotted it first. Not the blond head of Boltworks, but the dark-haired heads of Koreans being jostled out of the way.

"Over there," I shouted. "Heading for the trains."

The sign overhead had a fist with a finger pointing east. Beneath that, in *hangul* and English, the sign said: Seoul. If he hopped on a train, I knew we'd never find him in that teeming city of eight million.

We had just rounded the corner, running flat out, heading for the tracks lined with passenger cars, when a shot rang out.

Ernie and I flung ourselves to the ground. Ernie's .45 was out now, pointing ahead. All around us people screamed. Some threw themselves to the ground. Others ran back toward the front of the station.

Ernie was waving and shouting, "Get down! Get down!"

The train to our right, crammed with passengers, started to roll forward. Two cars ahead, we saw him. Private First Class Rodney K. Boltworks, pistol out, right arm wrapped around the neck of a struggling woman.

All I could think was how nicely she was dressed. Polished black shoes, naked legs, expensive knit wool skirt and matching jacket, and a beige overcoat that fell to her ankles. Her leather briefcase lay partially open on the cement platform, and her polished nails were clutching Boltworks' forearm, as if she were trying to loosen his grip so she could breathe. Thick-rimmed glasses were tilted at an angle across her flat nose. Her silky black hair swung as she struggled.

The train was barely creeping forward, but gathering speed.

Boltworks glanced between us and the metal steps in front of the next car that was rolling slowly toward him.

"When the steps get close," Ernie said, "he's going to let her go. When he does, you charge."

There was no time to think this over, no time for me to agree or disagree. What Ernie had said would be our plan. I raised myself to a crouch and edged forward. Boltworks was maybe twenty yards ahead of me now. How long would it take for me to cover that distance? Pro football players cover it in three seconds. I thought I could make it in four.

Still lying flat on the cement, Ernie raised his .45.

Boltworks glanced again at the steps leading up to the train, and I broke and ran. He turned back to look at me. As he did so, Ernie fired. The bullet ricocheted off the edge of the train. The Korean woman bucked and struggled, and Boltworks tried to point his gun at me and then at Ernie but he knew his shot would be wild, and the steps of the moving train were only a few feet away from him now.

He let go of the woman and raced toward the platform.

I ran as fast as I could, low to the ground, legs churning, hoping I wouldn't step on a rock. Another shot rang out from Ernie's .45, and Boltworks stopped, just for a second, only six feet from the onrushing metal steps.

Praying Ernie wouldn't fire again, I plowed into Private Rodney K. Boltworks. We slammed into the metal steps, falling forward onto them. The train rolled on, shoving us to the side. I twisted, holding onto Boltwork's neck. He twisted with me and the metal railing struck my back. I grunted and we were twirling through the air and falling backwards. The front wall of the passenger cab slapped into me once again. Boltworks and I twirled with the force of the blow, spinning like a top and rebounding once, twice against the side of the moving train. Startled Korean faces inside flashed by. Men, women, a few children. Mouths open. Eyes wide. And then the windows were gone and something metal slammed into us once again—into Boltworks this time—and we spun madly across the cement platform and crashed onto the ground in a heap.

Boltworks flailed, trying to rise and push me away but I held tightly. And then Ernie leaned over us, telling me to let go, grabbing Boltworks by the wrists and, finally, sweet sound of relief, metal handcuffs clinked. Boltworks let out a sigh of exasperation, and all the strength seemed to rush out of his thick body. I relaxed my arms.

I looked up at Ernie. He grinned. I passed out.

"I don't know where she is," Boltworks said.

We were in the Pupyong Police Station. One of their officers had patched up the slice in my side and once again stopped the bleeding. He also slapped a few poultices here and there over the bruised portions of my body and, most importantly, fed me a handful of unnamed painkillers, which helped some. Also, the KNPs had been kind enough to send a patrolman over to the home of Pak Mi-rae to reclaim our footwear.

Ernie and I wanted to escort Boltworks back to the ASCOM Provost Marshal's Office, but the local KNPs would have none of it. Bolt, as we were calling him now, had terrorized a Korean woman and half the morning commuters on their way to Seoul, amongst them many important and influential people. The KNPs weren't about to give him up. Not yet anyway. Not without orders from headquarters.

Bolt looked a lot less intimidating now. Of course, the KNPs had confiscated his stolen pistol, and they'd taken his jacket and his shirt and trousers. Bolt sat on a chair, wearing only boxer shorts and a sleeveless white T-shirt, his arms handcuffed behind him. His face was dirty and sweating, and I'm sure he fully expected to be beat up—maybe even tortured—by the Korean National Police. I doubted that, but I wasn't about to disabuse him of the notion. As I patiently explained to the morose Mr. Boltworks, his only chance of being returned to U.S. custody was by cooperating fully with me and Ernie.

"It's up to you, Bolt," Ernie said. "Me, I wouldn't want to spend no time in a Korean jail. Un-huh. Not after killing an innocent young Korean girl. No way."

"I didn't kill her," Bolt said for what must've been the umpteenth time.

"So your partner did. Same difference. You think those Korean convicts are going to give a rat's ass?"

Bolt didn't answer. He let his sweaty head hang. A hot bulb filled the cement-box interrogation room with light. Ernie and I stood, as did the five Korean cops.

The woman Bolt had taken hostage had been rushed to Pupyong Municipal Hospital. She appeared uninjured, but was suffering from shock.

"You know who your hostage was, Bolt?" Ernie asked.

Sullenly, he shook his head.

"The wife of the third son of the brother of the Mayor of Pupyong. You know how to pick 'em. Smooth move. Smoother than Exlax."

Private Boltworks' head hung even lower.

"Me and my partner have to go now," Ernie said. "We have things to do. Don't have time to sit here all morning chatting with you, no matter how much we'd like to."

Boltworks raised his head. "Don't leave."

"How can we stay? You haven't told us a goddamn thing. We want to get back to the compound, have breakfast. A cup of coffee. Because of you, we missed our bacon and eggs."

"Don't leave me."

"Sorry, Bolt," Ernie said, shaking his head. "You don't talk, we go."

"Okay," Boltworks said. "What do you want to know?"

Ernie smirked. I pulled out my notebook. In less than a half hour, we had the whole story.

We typed up our report at the ASCOM MP Station. It was past noon. We'd missed chow again, and Ernie and I were famished.

"Too bad you couldn't keep your promise to Bolt," I said.

"Screw my promise," Ernie said. "A maggot like that deserves more than lies."

"He'll get what's coming to him. That's for sure."

We'd left Private Rodney Boltworks in the custody of the Korean National Police. Since he'd committed crimes on their soil, and since he'd been apprehended off a U.S. military compound, by treaty, they had jurisdiction. Probably, in a few days, the ROK government would see fit to turn him over to U.S. military authorities. But that decision would come from on high. It wasn't for two lowly CID agents like Ernie and me to decide. If Boltworks hadn't been such a bonehead, he'd have realized that we really had nothing to offer him. But he'd been terrified of the stone-faced Korean cops who glared at him with such hatred. So he'd spilled his guts.

When we left him at the Pupyong Police Station, he'd squealed like a pig being left for slaughter.

A little betrayal didn't bother me, not at all. As we walked out of the station, I thought about the cigarette burns on Mi-ja's soft flesh. And I thought about the looks on the faces of Han Ok-hi's parents. A young woman struck down in her prime. PFC Bolt could go straight to hell as far as I was concerned.

I asked the MP Desk Sergeant if the PX snack bar was open, and he said it was open all day and gave us directions. We were about to leave the ASCOM MP Station, when the phone rang. The Desk Sergeant answered.

"It's for you," he called to us, holding out the receiver. "Seoul."

It was Staff Sergeant Riley.

"Top wants you back here," he said. "Immediately, if not sooner."

"We're gonna eat chow first."

"Chow can wait. You got bigger problems."

"*I've* got problems?" I said.

"Yeah, you. You're the one who had his forty-five stolen, aren't you?"

I didn't answer. The humiliation of having my weapon taken from me still burned deep.

"You there, Sueño?" Riley asked.

"I'm here."

"Back to Seoul—now. Both of you. Don't bother to stop at the compound, just head straight for Itaewon."

I stood straighter, suddenly alert. "Why? What's happened?"

"Nothin' good. You heard of a Spec. Five Arthur Q. Fairbanks?"

"Fairbanks? No."

"Yes, you have. You just don't know his name. He's the VD Honcho."

I knew who he meant. The medic at the 121st Evacuation Hospital who was in charge of the daily venereal disease sick call. Forty or fifty GIs every morning. The clap, herpes, non-specific urethritis, chancroid, even an occasional case of syphilis. Fairbanks and his staff took the complaints, conducted the tests, and turned the results over to an overworked medical doctor who reviewed the paperwork, then allowed Fairbanks to administer drugs to the routine cases. Only the most severely afflicted GIs saw a doctor. Fairbanks took care of the rest.

Naturally, GIs called him the VD Honcho.

"What happened to him?" I asked.

"Dead," Riley said. "Shot sometime early this morning. With a forty-five. We haven't done the ballistics yet, but we're betting it's yours."

"Why?" I whispered. "Why mine?"

Riley didn't answer right away. When he did, his voice came out softer, less gruff. "The way your luck's been running, Sueño."

I hung up the phone.

Ernie started to say something, but one look at my face, and he bit off whatever comment he'd been about to make.

"Another one," I said. "Itaewon, this time."

He didn't ask me to elaborate. Silently, we walked outside to the jeep. Ernie fired up the engine.

We sped back to Seoul, breaking the speed limit all the way.

During the interrogation at the Pupyong Police Station, Private First Class Rodney K. Boltworks had told us what he liked about the brother of Yun Ai-ja, the smiling woman.

"He kicked my ass," Bolt said. "I thought I was good, but he knows all kinds of karate moves and shit. You know, like Bruce Lee, except this guy doesn't whistle or flex his muscles, he just comes at you. He doesn't stop. His face is covered with little scars, and you should see his body. Knife wounds, the works. And man, don't look at his sister. He goes off."

"How does that work?" Ernie asked. "His sister's a prostitute."

"When he's not around. When he's around, she bows and serves tea and does all that kind of shit."

"What kind of shit?" I asked.

"You know. Lights incense. Bows to those statues they got."

"She's religious?"

Bolt shrugged muscular shoulders. "I never saw her go to church."

To him, religion was church. Anything else, he wasn't sure of.

"What made you decide to go AWOL?" Ernie asked. "And rob a casino?"

"Kong, that's what he calls himself."

"'Kong?'" I asked. "That's it?"

"Yeah. His sister said Kong is part of his full name. She told me the whole thing, but I forget."

Given names are almost sacred in Korean society. Not shared lightly. The fact that the smiling woman's brother only allowed PFC Boltworks to use part of his name said something about how much he trusted him.

"I was tired of Charley Battery," Bolt continued. "Tired of taking crap from lifers, and tired of getting up early in the morning. Kong told me that with an American to help him, we could make a lot of money."

"Help him do what?"

"You know, fool people. Make GIs relax when they saw me, and then Kong would bop 'em over the head."

"Did you do that?"

"A few times. But sometimes the GI fought back, and there were always too many people around."

"So you decided to switch to robbing casinos."

"Yeah. More money."

"Did you know that Kong and his sister are half-American?"

"I figured."

"You ever talk about it?"

"Never. Kong hates Americans."

"Did he hate you?"

Boltworks grinned. "Yeah. He and I were always about to fight, you know. But after a while, I learned a lot of his tricks, so he started to lay off me."

"Why would you hook up with somebody who hates you?" Ernie asked.

"We were making money. Besides, his sister didn't hate me."

"You were still boffing her?"

"When Kong wasn't around."

"Wasn't that sort of dangerous?"

"Yeah." Boltworks smiled. "Real dangerous."

There were certain lines of questioning that I didn't want to follow. Instead, I stuck to the more pragmatic questions. Bolt told us that after the casino robbery, he had split from Kong and, as planned, Kong kept the money and met up with his sister. Kong took off his sunglasses, changed clothes and put on a hat, and that made him look more Korean. She tied a shawl over her blonde hair. Together, carrying the money, they walked to the Inchon Train Station, merged with other commuters, and caught a ride to Seoul. Bolt holed up at the Yellow House at Brothel Number 17, and the idea was that after a few days, they would rendezvous in Itaewon and divide the money.

"You didn't keep any money?" Ernie asked.

"I was supposed to meet with them."

"Did you?"

"You guys screwed me up. Ai-ja was going to contact me at the Yellow House, but you guys chased me away."

"Didn't you have an alternative plan?"

Boltworks looked confused, and then remorseful, and then he shook his head.

"Did it ever occur to you," Ernie said, "that they never intended to give you any money?"

"No way." He sat up and pulled his hands against the cuffs behind him. "Ai-ja liked me. She told me she did."

"So what were you going to do?" Ernie said. "Wait in ASCOM City forever?"

"No. When the heat died down, I was going to go to Itaewon. To the coffee shop at the Hamilton Hotel. They like it there."

The Hamilton Hotel sat right on the MSR, across the street from the main nightclub district of Itaewon. The hotel featured a hundred or more rooms, and they were usually full of Japanese tourists and American GIs. The coffee shop was comfortable and well-appointed and probably the most popular meeting place in Itaewon.

"They go there often, do they?" Ernie asked.

"All the time."

"So all you'd have to do is sit there a few days, sipping on overpriced coffee, and eventually they'd show up."

"Two hundred and fifty *won* per cup," Bolt said. "That's not so much."

"No," Ernie said. "I suppose not. Not when you're a big-time gangster."

Bolt grinned. And he kept grinning until we started to leave. Which is when he started to squeal.

At the main drag of Itaewon, the jeep's engine churned up the incline. We passed the U.N. Club and the Seven Club and the King Club, and then hung a left about a block past the clump of nightclubs. A bunch of U.S. military vehicles—sedans, vans, MP jeeps—blocked all vehicular traffic. Ernie parked the jeep, chained and padlocked the steering wheel, and we climbed out.

We entered an alley leading into the bowels of Itaewon. Ahead, a gateway was open in a stone and brick wall.

As we approached, the hum of murmuring American voices grew louder. I ducked through the gate, and all talking stopped.

Eyes were on me. Gawking. Technicians and MPs and astonished Korean National Policemen turned their heads and stared. As if they couldn't believe I'd have the temerity to show up at this crime scene.

15

Ernie tried to stuff a fried dumpling into my mouth. I slapped it away.

"Come on," he said. *"Yakimandu.* I paid two thousand *won* for this stuff."

He motioned at the plate on the bar between us. A dozen meat-filled dumplings, fried in peanut oil, fanned out in a circle with a bowl of soy sauce in the middle. We were sitting at the bar of the Seven Club on the main drag of Itaewon. Night had fallen, and I'd already polished off four beers and two shots of bourbon.

Ernie lifted another dumpling, dipped it in the soy sauce, and offered it to me. "You haven't eaten all day, for chrissake. You need something."

"I'm not hungry."

"It ain't your fault," he said. "How many times do I have to tell you? They could've stolen anybody's gun and done what they did. You can't blame yourself."

Ernie was right, of course, but the crowd of MPs and other 8th Army officials who'd been milling around in the courtyard where the VD Honcho had been killed left no doubt as to who they thought was responsible: Me.

It was a brothel. Not surprising. Spec 5 Five Arthur Q. Fairbanks, the VD overseer, had been out in Itaewon early in the morning, trying to track down a woman who had reportedly infected five American GIs with gonorrhea. All he wanted to do was take her into the local health clinic. The U.S. government would pay for the antibiotics and the medical bills, a worthy investment if it helped keep our servicemen in fighting trim.

Why early in the morning? Because at night, these girls were almost impossible to find, and Spec 5 Fairbanks, by all accounts, was dedicated to his job. The Korean women present told the KNPs that Specialist Fairbanks had been talking to the infected business girl, explaining to her that the U.S. government would pay for everything, when a man in a ski mask entered the hooch. He stood just under six feet and wore a raincoat, nondescript slacks, and rubber-soled shoes. Some girls said the skin of his hands was white, some said brown, but they all agreed that there were tufts of black hair on his wrists. The man motioned with his pistol for Fairbanks to step into the courtyard, while all the business girls, most still in their pajamas or nightgowns, crouched on the edges of the horseshoe-shaped raised floor, with the open doors of their hooches behind them.

Fairbanks was terrified, the girls said. He began to cry and plead for his life. The man motioned with his weapon for Fairbanks to kneel. He did. The girls were ordered into their hooches. Some peeked through rips in the oil-paper doors.

The masked man reached into his raincoat and pulled out a stiff sheet of paper. Maybe cardboard. He set it on the ground and leaned it against the iron pump. Then he stepped back and ordered Fairbanks to bow to the paper. They weren't sure what language he spoke, they couldn't hear, but Fairbanks understood and did what he was told. He prostrated himself in front of the paper three times. While this was going on, someone joined them. Whoever it was slipped in through the front gate and stood next to the masked man in the raincoat. No one could see because of the angle from the hooches to the front gate, but they heard footsteps and a whispered, urgent conversation. They were too far away to make out what was said.

When the *seibei* ceremony was over, the masked man ordered Fairbanks to remain kneeling. Then he walked around behind Fairbanks and aimed the .45 at the back of Fairbanks' head and pulled the trigger.

Some of the young girls who witnessed this were so traumatized they'd been hospitalized.

After the killing, the assassin calmly replaced the pistol in the pocket of his raincoat, retrieved the piece of cardboard, and walked back out through the front gate with the other person.

Ernie and I spent the entire morning with the KNP crime-scene technicians, gathering evidence and then we spent the afternoon and into the evening listening to Captain Kim at the Itaewon Police Station interrogate witnesses.

Why did everyone believe that the .45 used in the crime was my weapon? Because it was the same type used in the shooting of Han Ok-hi in Inchon and Jo Kyong-ah in Songtan. The masked gunman matched the general description of the second bank robber who'd shot Han Ok-hi.

Why Fairbanks? Why kill Fairbanks?

That was what I kept asking myself.

And if it was the same gunman—this man called Kong, the brother of the smiling woman—why didn't he leave something behind to identify himself as he had at the killing of Jo Kyong-ah?

I puzzled over this all through the tedious gathering and

recording of evidence, the tear-filled interviews at the Itaewon Police Station. Late in the afternoon, the answer occurred to me.

At both the shooting of Han Ok-hi at the Olympos Casino in Inchon and at the assassination of Spec 5 Fairbanks in Itaewon, there'd been witnesses. No witnesses had been available when Jo Kyong-ah was murdered. So my weapons card had been left behind in the *byonso*, to make sure we knew who was doing this.

Why did they want us to know? What was his motive for all this carnage? And still the question remained: Why Fairbanks?

There had to be a connection between the Olympos Casino, the black marketeer Jo Kyong-ah, and Spec 5 Arthur Q. Fairbanks. I just wasn't smart enough to see what it was.

I shouted at the bartender. "OB *tubyong. Bali!*" Two bottles of Oriental Beer. Quick!

Ernie stared at me. I felt uncomfortable under his gaze but I knew why he was staring. It wasn't like me to be impolite. Even to a young man behind a bar.

"Okay," I said. "I'll keep my mouth shut."

He nodded and sipped on his beer. When the bartender arrived with our drinks, I tipped him heavily, which was unlike me too. Ernie was about to comment when we both smelled a warm, perfumed body. We turned.

Her face was too heavily made up, and she was wearing a sequined bikini with tassels hanging from a g-string. At first I didn't recognize her. Then I did.

"Suk-ja," I said.

She smiled broadly. "You no forget."

"How could I forget?" Then I turned to Ernie. "She helped us at the Yellow House in Inchon. She works at Number 59."

"Oh, yeah."

It wasn't surprising that we hadn't remembered her right away. At the Yellow House, Suk-ja had first worn see-through pink lingerie. Later, she'd changed into blue jeans and a pullover sweater and sneakers. Her face had been washed and she'd worn black, horn-rimmed glasses, with her hair pulled back in a pony-tail. She'd looked more like a college co-ed than what she truly was. Now she'd transformed herself again. The glasses were gone, her face was heavily made-up. A curly hairdo fell to her shoulders. Most impressively, she was wearing the barely legal outfit of an Itaewon stripper. The make-up I could live without, but in that skimpy outfit, her figure looked fabulous.

"First I do show," she said. "Then you buy me beer. Okay?"

She pointed at me and I nodded vigorously. "Okay."

She smiled and scurried back to the stage.

Watching her, I felt guilty again. One mad rush of sexual desire and, just like that, I'd forgotten about the murdered body of Specialist Five Arthur Q. Fairbanks. For a few seconds anyway. When Suk-ja disappeared behind the stage, guilt rushed back to replace the excitement.

The rock band started up with an out-of-sync rendition of "Satin Doll." Mercifully, Duke Ellington wasn't around to hear it. Suk-ja appeared on stage to a round of guffaws and proceeded to strut her way through her act. GIs were hooting, as were the Korean business girls, and then Suk-ja was almost naked and dodging grasping hands. Finally, the song ended, and she was off the stage. Twenty minutes later, the Suk-ja I had known at the Yellow House, in blue jeans, ponytail, and horn-rimmed glasses, sat next to me on a barstool.

We had a few more drinks.

Drunkenly, Ernie kept telling me not to blame myself. But the more he said that, the worse I felt.

Suk-ja ordered another plate of *yakimandu*. Using her polished fingernails, she raised a dumpling, dipped it in soy sauce, and popped it in my mouth. This time I ate.

* * *

I sat up in bed.

I was on a soft mat, and I could feel the heated floor beneath. A window was slightly open. An almost full moon shone. A soft hand touched my shoulder.

"What's the matter, Geogi?"

It was Suk-ja. We'd left the Seven Club together right before the midnight curfew and rented this room in the Seven Star Yoguan, a Korean inn.

"Miss Yun," I said.

"*Nugu?*" Who?

"Miss Yun. The woman who is the mother of the man who executed Specialist Fairbanks. And the man who murdered Jo Kyong-ah, and the same man who shot Han Ok-hi. They kicked her out of her home."

Suk-ja sat up. Her soft body was naked.

"What?" she asked. "Who did?"

"A mama-san up in Uichon told me. Miss Yun had two children, both half-*Miguk*. One a boy, one a girl. She caught tuberculosis, so they made her leave her home."

"She was a business girl?"

"Yes."

I told her the story.

The order for Miss Yun to be separated from her children and placed in a sanitarium had been executed maybe five years ago. The children were to be placed in an orphanage, possibly put up for adoption. Miss Yun fled the sanitarium. Somehow, she'd found her children and gone into hiding. A business woman without a home nightclub, where she could be registered with the authorities and receive regular health checkups, was reduced to avoiding the KNPs and walking the streets. With two children in tow, both just reaching adolescence themselves, she wasn't making enough money. Predictably, she tried to borrow. But after a few loans without repayment, she was turned down everywhere.

Her tuberculosis became worse, yet she couldn't go to a hospital. If she did, the authorities would be called, and she would be once again held as a risk to public health. Tuberculosis, small pox, venereal disease—these scourges had taken a terrible toll on Korean society during and after the Korean War. The government had no choice but to take draconian measures in an effort to curb their spread.

Miss Yun had remained on the street with her children until one cold winter night, she lay down on the frozen concrete and went to sleep. She never woke up.

Before dawn, her children tried to rouse her, to no avail. Her body was taken away, for reasons of public health, and burned. When the authorities tried to shuffle the kids off to orphanages, they escaped. When the smiling woman, the daughter of the late Miss Yun, showed up in Uichon asking for a job, she would not talk about the period after her mother's death. She did, however, always keep a white box wrapped in black ribbon. The Uichon mama-san couldn't be sure but she suspected that the box contained the ashes of the girl's dead mother.

I explained all this to Suk-ja. She listened patiently. I also told her about the smiling woman's sojourn at the Half Half Club north of Seoul near Uijongbu. How she'd been stalked there, and how she'd run away and hidden farther north with the Uichon mama-san. I wasn't sure who was after her or how this tied in with everything else. When I finished, Suk-ja rolled off the sleeping mat and, crouching on her haunches, poured barley tea from a brass pot into an earthenware cup. She offered the cup to me. I drank.

Then she lit incense in a bronze burner. Three sticks. Tiny flames burning brightly. Suk-ja pressed her palms in front of her nose and bowed three times to each red pinpoint of light. Miss Yun, her daughter and son. When she was finished, Suk-ja, one by one, snuffed them out.

* * *

The Chief Medical Officer of the 121 Evacuation Hospital was not happy to see two CID agents rummaging through the records of his Communicable Disease Unit.

"You are to remove nothing," he told us.

He was a portly man with a receding hairline, a gray mustache, and a white lab coat that failed to hide his paunch. Physically, not very impressive. What was impressive, at least to soldiers, were the silver eagles pinned to his collar.

"Yes, sir," I answered. "Only notes. That's all we'll be taking."

"See that you do. Before you leave, check out with Sergeant Whitworth, and I want to be briefed on whatever you find."

"Of course, sir," I said.

Fat chance. Eighth Army criminal investigation files are confidential, revealed only on a need-to-know basis. This pompous colonel wouldn't have a need to know unless we said he had a need to know. But no sense yanking his chain, so I just waited until he left.

"Asshole," Ernie mumbled.

"Someday you're going to say that too loud."

He shrugged.

We continued to look through files. VD records. Huge canvas-covered logs with every infected GIs name, rank, serial number, and unit. What type of VD, where he was infected, how long ago the contact was, and who had infected him. Many of the entries were blank, because if a GI was promiscuous, and many of the repeat offenders were, he couldn't quite be sure where or when or by whom he'd been infected. Ernie covered the most recent cases. After all, we couldn't be a hundred percent sure that the son of Miss Yun had killed him. Possibly Spec 5 Fairbanks had been involved in some sort of nefarious activity that had resulted in his death. We had to check that. Still, I doubted Ernie would find anything.

So did he. After half an hour, Ernie grew antsy and decided to walk out in the front office and chat with Sergeant Whitworth. She was a leggy blond, and Ernie hadn't been quite as lucky as I had been last night. He'd left the Seven Club alone.

Leftover fumes of bourbon and beer churned in my stomach and rose like hot air into my throat and nose. I had already taken four aspirin along with bicarbonate of soda, and I doubted that a cup of black coffee from the silver urn in the front office would help. My side was okay. It was healing nicely. No infection. That Greek sailor kept a clean knife. In a day or two, I'd pull the stitches out.

Outside the open door of the records office, white-smocked medics, nurses, and doctors paraded back and forth on their soft-soled shoes, hurrying to do the beneficial work of healers. They murmured and laughed and chortled, untroubled by visions of two children starving on the streets of Seoul while they watched their mother cough bloody guts onto a crystalline pile of ice.

I shoved such thoughts out of my mind and concentrated on my work.

I started with the records that ended two years ago. Why there? No particular reason, other than I had to start somewhere. And the Uichon mama-san had told me that she believed Miss Yun had died three or four years ago. But her memory could be wrong. Starting at two years ago, and working back from there, seemed safe.

I moved my finger name by name down the row of infected GIs, searching the columns to see where they'd been infected and by whom. Occasionally I slapped my cheek to keep alert, to avoid being mesmerized by the endless row of handwritten entries.

Most were in the hand of the late Specialist 5 Arthur Q. Fairbanks. He'd extended his one year tour time after time until, on the day he was shot, he had been in country almost five years.

This entire effort might be a waste of time. Possibly, if Miss Yun was involved with any of these GIs, they might not remember her name, or who it was that had infected them, or where they had met her. This would be particularly true once she was no longer working as an unpaid "entertainer" in a specific nightclub. A few of the entries said "streetwalker." I paused at each and studied it, but the information told me nothing.

A few of the entries had a red asterisk by the name of the "contact," the accused prostitute. I wasn't sure what the asterisk meant, but I'd figure that out later if I needed to.

After two hours, I passed the four-year mark. That is, the entries were now older than four years before today's date. As a reward to myself, I stood up and stretched and walked out to the front office.

Ernie sat on the edge of Sergeant Whitworth's desk, playing with the sharpened pencils she had placed upright in a coffee mug. He said something and leaned toward her, making her laugh. They ignored me as I walked past. Out in the busy hallway, I followed the signs to the men's latrine.

When I returned, Ernie and Sergeant Whitworth had disappeared.

I sat back down at my little desk, took a deep breath, and studied the thick clothbound ledgers again. I had only been working about ten minutes when I spotted it. The GIs name was Bombeck, Rufus R. His unit was the 501st Signal Battalion, and the point of contact was "streetwalker." But penciled beneath the entry was the name Yoon. And next to that was another red asterisk.

Quickly I jotted down the information and folded the top corner of the ledger page. I continued to work, but after two hours, and going back in the records another year, I found no similar entry.

I walked back into the front office. Still no Sergeant Whitworth. And no Ernie. I poured myself some coffee and waited. When they finally returned, Whitworth's immaculately white uniform was askew, her cheeks flushed red. Ernie grinned at me.

"Find anything?" he asked.

Whitworth scurried behind her desk and sat, immediately picking up the phone and making what must've been an extremely urgent phone call. While she chatted, I filled Ernie in.

"What the hell does the red asterisk mean?" he said.

I nodded toward Whitworth. When she'd finished her phone call, I asked her.

"Tuberculosis," she answered.

I sat quietly while she explained that when a prostitute was known to have an active case of tuberculosis, and Fairbanks found out about it, he routinely notified the Korean health authorities. Then a pickup was arranged.

"What do you mean 'a pickup?'"

"Four or five Korean health officials meet us here at the 121, and we convoy out to Itaewon, usually with the infected GI. He shows us where the woman lives, or at least where he had contact with her, and we take it from there. Usually, we find her, and the Koreans take her into custody."

"So," I said, "if a streetwalker with tuberculosis was picked up in Itaewon, Fairbanks would've been there to see her arrest. To see her being taken away."

"Oh, yeah. He had some stories. People crying, children screaming. You know, the whole works."

"By the way," I asked, "do you miss him?"

Her nose wrinkled. "Honestly," she said, "he was sort of a jerk."

Ernie and me and Suk-ja sat at a low-backed booth in the first-floor coffee shop of the Hamilton Hotel in the heart of Itaewon. Ernie sipped ginseng tea. Suk-ja and I drank coffee. She ladled plenty of sugar and cream into hers. Mine was black. She grimaced every time I took a sip.

"*Nomu jjia,*" she said. Too sour.

I explained to them what I thought, so far, about the case.

"First, Boltworks, the smiling woman, and her brother are running around Itaewon bopping drunken GIs on the head and taking their money." I sipped on my coffee, picturing the three of them in action. Then I set the coffee cup down. "But this can't last long, because Captain Kim and his men have dealt with crooks like that countless times, and I think the smiling woman was smart enough to realize they had to try something new. So they decide to go for a big score. A casino. But how? How do you gain entry and the confidence of a casino manager—get close enough to the cashier cage so you can force your way to the money?"

"That's where you came in," Ernie said.

"Right. They drug me, bop me over the head in an alley, and take my identification, badge, and sidearm."

Suk-ja looked as if the thought of me being hurt was causing her pain.

"So they rob The Olympos Hotel and Casino in Inchon," I said. "But while the robbery is going down, the owner makes a break for the fire escape. Without thinking, Kong, the brother, pops off a round. A young female blackjack dealer steps in the way and takes a bullet that should've landed in the casino owner's back."

"Okay," Ernie said. "I buy that. But why do you say 'without thinking?' This son of a bitch, Kong, is a cold-blooded killer."

"All right. Scratch the 'without thinking' part. But as far as we know, at that moment he had never killed anyone before."

"So he's in deep kimchee," Ernie said. "He takes the money and he and his sister run and hide."

"Right. But how long is that going to last? The KNPs are all over the case. And when Han Ok-hi dies, he knows they'll never stop coming after him. Maybe they don't have any leads, maybe they won't be able to track him down, because he left very little evidence at the crime scene."

"Other than a bullet from your gun."

"Yeah. Other than a round from my gun. But he knows that once he and his sister start spending the money, they'll be caught."

"Marked bills?"

"No. Not marked, but people remember half-*Miguks*, especially when they spend money and have no visible means. Eventually, they'd come to the attention of the Korean police."

"He should've thought about that before."

"And he knew Bolt would be caught. A GI on the run in the Korea—how long is that going to last?"

"Not long," Ernie said.

"Since they stiffed him of the money, they knew Bolt would spill his guts."

"They were right about that," Ernie said. "So why didn't he kill Bolt when he had the chance?"

"Maybe he was planning to. Maybe that's what the rendezvous in Seoul was all about, or maybe he planned to slip back into Inchon and murder Bolt at Yellow House Number 17."

"But we screwed it up by chasing Bolt away."

"Exactly."

Suk-ja stopped sipping coffee. Her smooth brow wrinkled in concentration as she stretched her knowledge of English in an attempt to follow our conversation.

"What about woman?" she said.

"The smiling woman?" I replied. "What about her?"

"She no have plan? She no say nothing?"

"I don't know," I said.

"Maybe she smarter than man."

"How do you mean?"

"Maybe her brother fight you, fight Korean police. When you catch him, she run away. Take all money, go."

"Maybe," I said.

But I didn't think so. The smiling woman had grown up with her brother under conditions that most of us couldn't begin to imagine. That would've made their bond impossible to break. But she had been fooling around with Bolt when her brother wasn't watching. What was that all about? And then I remembered her face. The eternal smile, the eternal willingness to please. Maybe she hadn't made a decision to fool around with Bolt, maybe he had simply made a demand.

"Sueño," Ernie said. "You still with us?"

I nodded and sipped on coffee. "Yeah."

I continued to explain that once the woman and her brother knew they were so hot they were bound to be caught, they had decided that—before being caught—they would take revenge on the people who had wronged their mother.

"Everybody murdered so far—at least after Han Ok-hi's death—has been somebody who was an important player in Itaewon during the years their mother operated there as a prostitute. Jo Kyong-ah was the biggest black-market mama-san in Itaewon until she retired less than a year ago. Spec Five Fairbanks was the VD tracker for the 8th Army. He wielded the power of life and death over some of these poor hookers. If he turned them in to the Korean health authorities, they couldn't work any longer."

Ernie sipped his tea. Suk-ja stirred her coffee.

"Makes sense," Ernie said. "But the big question is, who's next?"

"I'm not sure," I said. "But Haggler Lee seems awfully nervous."

"Maybe for good reason. Maybe he hasn't told us everything."

"Maybe. You finished with your tea yet?"

"Almost. Why?"

"Let's go check out a few *bokdok-bang*s." Real estate offices. "See if we can scare up somebody who remembers Miss Yun and her two kids. They lived here in Itaewon for years."

"Probably hopping from hooch to hooch," Ernie said. "That's a needle in the haystack, Sueño."

"We've got to try something."

"Good. You do that. Me, I'm taking the jeep in for maintenance."

"You can do that anytime."

"What else do you want me to do? Stand around while you speak Korean to a bunch of realtors? *Xin loy*. You do what you got to do, I'll do what I got to do."

Suk-ja stared into her coffee, embarrassed by the disagreement.

Ernie was burning out on this case, that much was clear. We'd made progress. Plenty of it. We knew who had perpetrated the murders, and we even had a pretty good theory as to why. The problem was that we didn't know where the woman or her brother were hiding and, even more importantly, we had no idea who in the hell they might choose as their next victim. The thought that they'd stop killing now, when they'd gone this far, seemed unlikely. Ernie was frustrated, so was I, and going back to talk to realtors sounded too much like starting from scratch. He couldn't deal with it. I was having trouble myself, but I was determined to drive on. If he didn't want to help, that was his problem.

"Okay," I replied. "Take care of the maintenance. But be back here in two hours."

Ernie stood up, buttoned his coat, and stalked out of the Hamilton Hotel Coffee Shop.

With the tips of her soft fingers, Suk-ja caressed my knuckles. I pulled my hand away, told her I'd see her tonight, and found my way out of the warm coffee shop. Alone, I walked the cold streets of the Korean red light district.

A sharp wind picked up beneath an overcast sky.

The torn shreds of a dried noodle wrapper tumbled past my feet. A few of the front doors of the nightclubs were open, and an occasional drunken GI stumbled in. All in all though, Itaewon was mostly deserted.

A little brown-faced girl with a Prince Valiant haircut appeared at my elbow.

"You buy gum?"

She held out a cardboard box crammed with an assortment of American and Korean brands.

"No gum," I said, sticking my hands in my jacket pockets. If I remembered correctly, there were real estate offices up the hill, beyond the nightclub district. In Korea, the *bokdok-bang*s are not just for buying homes. In fact, they're more often used as brokers for people trying to rent. Even one-room hovels were rented through a *bokdok-bang*. Ernie was right though, they changed personnel a lot. What was the likelihood that I'd run into an agent who had been working the Itaewon area four years ago and remembered one business girl out of how many?

But when I thought of Han Ok-hi and Jo Kyong-ah and Arthur Q. Fairbanks, and the weapon that had killed them, I knew I had to keep trying.

The girl selling the gum pressed my elbow.

I turned and said, "I told you, no gum!"

"*Solip*," she said.

"What?"

"*Solip*."

Then I understood what she was saying. The Korean word I had learned not too long ago. *Solip*. Pine needles.

"What are you talking about?" I asked the girl.

She pointed with a grimy finger.

"She want talk to you."

"Who wants to talk to me?"

"I show you."

Without warning, she scampered off. Into the mouth of a dark alley leading uphill into the jumbled hooches. When I didn't immediately follow, she paused and waited.

Pines needles. Who would know about the pine needles

that had been left on the stove to burn in the home of Jo Kyong-ah? Only the people who had murdered her. Should I stop and call Ernie?

Not only would it be tough to get in touch with him, but the little girl could run away at the slightest provocation. Was I armed? I hadn't been since the smiling woman led me into that dark alley. And now I was being led into a dark alley again, perhaps by the same person.

What choice did I have?

I shoved my fists deeper into my pockets and trudged on, following the girl into the dark heart of Itaewon.

16

The alleys of Itaewon cannot be plotted on a grid. They wind around and back, uphill and down, like the tentacles of a squid. I realized the girl had disappeared. I stood alone, behind a row of ramshackle wooden hooches, alongside a stone-lined drainage ditch fenced off by rusty, netted wire topped by coiled concertina. The ditch was six feet wide and just as deep. Filth flowed sluggishly through its channel. There were no lights, and although the sun had not gone down, the thick shroud of overhead clouds kept the world under a blanket of gloom.

I stood with my back against a dirty brick wall, facing the ditch. Nothing moved on either side. Most of Itaewon teems with life, but back here the world was holding its breath.

On my own, I never would've found this spot. Why come back here? Most GIs never wander far from the bar district. And when they did, they were escorted by a business girl directly to her hooch.

A glimmer of light appeared in the corner of my eye. Like a cartoon character, I swiveled my head in an exaggerated double-take.

She stood alone, on the opposite side of the drainage ditch, the ten-foot-high chain-link fence between us. She wore a plain beige overcoat that looked fashionable, with the collar turned up and the belt cinched at the waist. Her light brown hair fell to her shoulders, cascading in gentle waves. She stood so still that I blinked, wondering if she was imaginary. Her smooth unblemished skin set off the startling blue sparkle in her otherwise Asian eyes, and then I saw the smile. Broad. Too broad. As if the muscles of her face were incapable of assuming any other configuration.

Could I grab her?

No way. By the time I climbed the fence and hopped the ditch, she'd be long gone. Instead, I slowly moved a few feet, until I stood exactly opposite her. She didn't move, and she didn't stop smiling.

I stared into her eyes, she stared into mine.

"Why have you and your brother murdered those people?" I asked.

"Fanny likes you," she said.

I was startled. She meant the crippled woman at the Half Half Club in Songsan-dong.

"I like Fanny too," I said.

"You gave her money."

I shrugged. "She needed it."

The smiling woman stared at me in silence.

Finally, she said, "I have job for you. You don't want to do anything for me. I know that. No GI wants do anything for me. But this time you must do."

"Do what?"

She seemed pleased that I'd responded.

"You don't know. But when time to do job, you will do."

"How do you know that?"

She studied me. Weighing possibilities.

"You will do," she said, and took a step backward.

"Wait," I said. "Don't kill any more people. We can work something out for you. I know about your mom. About how she was cheated by Jo Kyong-ah. About how the VD guy dragged her away from you and your brother. I will testify on your behalf. The judge will be lenient. You can't go on killing."

She stopped, still smiling, but her leer now conveyed rage. Her neck was glowing crimson and she was about to blow her top.

"My mom?" she said. "My mom? You know *nothing* about her!"

With that she took two quick steps into the dark and was gone.

I leapt at the wire, clinging to the rusted coils, staring across the drainage ditch into the alley beyond. But she was in the wind.

17

The Yoju City Hall of Records was an old wooden building, probably built during the period of Japanese colonization, that had somehow survived the Korean War. Mementoes and plaques lined the walls, commemorating kings of the Yi Dynasty and victories over invaders stretching back to battles that were fought against Hideyoshi's invading army during the Sixteenth Century. I was staring at a hand-crafted bronze helmet when Ernie elbowed me in the ribs.

"This guy going to take all day?" he asked.

"It takes a while," I said. "All this stuff is filed on paper, the old-fashioned way. The archives down in the basement must be enormous."

"You'd love to look at them, wouldn't you?"

"Damn right."

Ernie rolled his eyes. "Figures."

Since seeing the smiling woman in that back alley yesterday

afternoon, I'd been in what psychologists might call a dream state. I'd managed to make my way out of the catacombs and re-enter the land of the living, but as I did so, I started to doubt if I'd really seen her, or if I'd just imagined the whole thing. Of course, I knew it was real. It's just that what she and her brother were doing seemed so unreal. Unreal, until you saw the blood.

Naturally, when in a dream state, I did what I always do—I wandered into a bar. By the time Ernie found me, I was pretty well gone. He slapped my face a little and made me drink some barley tea and drove me back to the compound in his jeep. Somehow, that night, I managed eight hours of sleep for the first time in a long time. The next morning, after a cup of hot Joe at the snack bar, it came to me what we had to do.

"We gotta find out more about her family," I said to Ernie.

"Her family? Why?"

"In case you hadn't noticed, Agent Bascom, that's what this entire mess is about. Family. And yesterday, that's what seemed to enrage her. When I mentioned her mother."

In one of the files at the 121 Evacuation Hospital, Specialist Fairbanks had kept a copy of the Ministry of Health records ordering the pick up of Miss Yun Yong-min, the mother of the smiling woman. According to the background information provided, Yoju was the *kohyang*, the ancestral home, of Miss Yun.

"If we're going to head off the next killing," I said, "we're going to have to find out more about the smiling woman's family."

What I didn't tell Ernie about the encounter yesterday was what the woman had said about having a job for me to do. I'm not sure why I didn't.

When the bespectacled Korean man who was the Yoju Clerk of Records emerged from the creaking staircase, he plopped an enormous leather-bound ledger on the counter. Photocopying was conducted in another office and would take a half hour, he said, but I told him I didn't need it. I just wanted to study the documents and take some notes.

Why had I started thinking in terms of family? A few things. The piece of cardboard that Specialist Fairbanks had been forced to bow to. A photograph maybe. Of an ancestor? And then someone joined the killer while Fairbanks was being forced to perform the *seibei* ceremony. The smiling woman, I presumed. She'd been present when her brother murdered Fairbanks. Had she been present when Jo Kyong-ah was similarly killed? I was starting to think that she had. These two were turning murder into a family affair.

The Uichon mama-san had told me that when Miss Yun's older brother refused to register her first child—her smiling daughter—on the family register, Miss Yun registered by herself as the head of her own family. No father, no grandparents, nothing. This is unusual in Korea, because the mantle of "head of the family" passes from father to oldest son to younger sons, to first daughter, to younger daughters, and finally to mother—in that order.

When one family member is seen to be shaming the rest of the family, they are sometimes banished from their hallowed place on the register. They're forced to return to their *kohyang*, the ancestral home, and request a new family register under their name alone. Apparently, that's what Miss Yun had done.

The family register the records clerk placed in front of me was the register where Miss Yun, the mother, was recorded. At the top were the stern-faced black and white photos of her father—the smiling woman's grandfather. Below, Miss Yun's mother—the smiling woman's grandmother. Both of them were marked deceased. Listed next were three sons. The first two were also deceased. I checked the dates. They had both died during the Korean War, a number of years before their parents. The only surviving son was Yun Guang-min. The photo showed him as a child of twelve years, stern-faced and sullen.

Yun Guang-min was older than his sister, Miss Yun, and had to be in late middle-age by now. His face was square, with high cheekbones, and bore little resemblance to the smooth contoured lines of his younger sister's face.

Miss Yun was the only daughter listed. She was a late child. Of all the faces on the family register, hers was the only beautiful one in the bunch.

"Seen enough?" Ernie asked.

"One more thing." I spoke to the clerk, explaining in Korean what I wanted. He nodded, took the ledger back, and returned it to the archives down in the basement.

"What is it now?" Ernie said.

"You'll see."

When the clerk returned, he brought a newer book, already open to a page that had the photo of a now-adult Yun Guang-min. Below him was his wife, a cute heart-faced young woman, and below that, four children. After his older brothers and parents passed away, Yun Guang-min opened his own family register with himself as head of the family. By tradition, his unmarried sister should've been listed on his register but, of course, she wasn't. Even Ernie understood why.

"His sister's children were half-*Miguk*," he said. "He didn't want anything to do with her."

"Right. He turned his back on all of them. And did nothing to help when she was working the streets and slowly dying of tuberculosis."

Yun Guang-min's treatment of his younger sister was harsh, no question about it, but not all that unusual. Sure, most people continue to support their daughter or sister, even if they're pregnant with a GI's baby. But other Koreans, the more traditional ones, didn't always act with such equanimity. There'd been cases, recorded by the Koreans themselves, in which a woman with a GI baby had been hanged by her father or brothers. The police, when they investigated, often wrote the whole thing off as suicide.

"I suppose," Ernie said, "this uncle will be the next victim on the smiling woman's hit list."

"Maybe."

"We'd better warn him."

"No need," I said.

"What do you mean?"

"He's already been warned."

"Already warned? How?"

"Look at the face again."

I pointed to the photograph of Yun Guang-min. The same high cheekbones and square face, but in this second family register, instead of being a boy of about twelve, he was a man in his early thirties.

"Imagine the face as a middle-aged man," I said. "Imagine gray hair, more wrinkles, a grim expression."

Ernie worked on it for a while, and then his eyes widened. "Holy shit," he said.

I thanked the records clerk, slid the ledger across the counter, and Ernie and I trotted outside to the lot in front of the Yoju Hall of Records. Ernie fired up the jeep.

"Don't worry," he said, "I know the way."

We wound through back country roads, heading west. The afternoon was once again gray and overcast. At an intersection, one sign pointed north toward Seoul, another pointed west toward Inchon.

Ernie turned toward Inchon and shifted into high gear.

Blackjack dealers looked up from their tables as Ernie and I waded across the carpeted floor of the Olympos Casino. I wanted to talk to the smiling woman's uncle, question him about the whereabouts of his nephew and niece, and maybe—just maybe—head off the next killing. The door of the cashier's cage was locked, but I pounded on it and told the cashiers inside that I wanted to talk to Yun Guang-min, the owner of the casino.

Their eyes widened, and they conferred with one another, and while they mumbled, the manager, Mr. Bok, appeared out of nowhere. He smiled and bowed and told me that unfortunately Mr. Yun Guang-min was not available. I asked him why. He said that he was currently engaged in a banquet entertaining honored guests.

"Where?" I asked.

Bok just kept repeating that Yun Guang-min was unavailable.

Ernie was fed up. He reached for Bok, grabbed his shoulders, and while the casino manager's mouth opened in shock, Ernie reached inside the man's expensive suit jacket and pulled out a leather-bound notebook. He handed it to me.

Bok struggled to grab it back, but Ernie held him off.

I riffled through the pages. It was an appointment book. I quickly located today's date. It was almost one p.m. and penciled in for 12:30 was the character for "Yun" and the name of a restaurant: Silla Cho Siktang. Silla Cho, the Silla Dynasty. It ruled southern Korea thirteen hundred years ago, during and after the Three Kingdoms Period. *Siktang* means eatery. Next to that was an entry I couldn't understand, written in Japanese *hiragana* syllables interspersed with Chinese characters. The Chinese characters said "turtle mountain," although how you pronounced that in Japanese I had no idea.

I pointed at the entry and asked the flustered manager, "What's this mean?"

"Not your business," he said and tried once again to grab the appointment book.

The pit bosses were grumbling amongst themselves and glaring at us. One of them picked up a phone. I grabbed Bok by the lapels.

"Where's the Silla Cho Siktang?" I asked.

His eyes widened. "You must not bother Mr. Yun. His meeting very important."

"With some Japanese millionaire?" I said.

"How you know?"

I pointed at the Japanese writing. Turtle Mountain I figured was somebody's name.

"Where is Silla Cho Siktang?" I asked again.

Bok crossed his arms and snorted but Ernie had been rummaging in the side pocket of his jacket. Ernie plucked out a pamphlet printed in blazing color and handed it to me. It was a directory to the meeting halls and restaurants and other services located in and around the hotel and casino. The Silla Cho Siktang was located adjacent to the Olympos, on the other side of the parking lot, on a cliff overlooking the Yellow Sea.

I tossed the pamphlet back to Mr. Bok and thanked him for his cooperation. As we hurried to the front door, Bok was already on the phone.

There was only one bodyguard, standing off to the side beneath the brightly painted archway that was the entry to the Silla Cho Siktang. He was still talking on the phone, to Mr. Bok, I imagined, and he kept saying, "Nugu?" Who?

The guy wasn't too bright. Ernie poked the business end of his pistol into the ear of the young bodyguard. "Relax, Tiger," Ernie said. "We just want to talk." He grabbed the phone from the man's grasp and hung it up.

I frisked him, found his gun, and relieved him of it. I told him to keep his hands raised, and nothing would happen to either him or his employer. Together, the three of us walked into the banquet hall of the Silla Cho Siktang.

The entire expanse of the main floor was covered with immaculately clean tatami mats. A dozen low tables were arranged in the middle of the hall in a horseshoe shape. Some thirty men sat on silk cushions on the outsides of the tables. They picked with silver chopsticks at tender morsels on porcelain plates. In the center of the mats, a young woman, wearing the traditional embroidered silk dress of Korea, plucked on a *kayagum*, a straight-backed zither, and warbled songs of love in an ancient dialect.

The men were Japanese. How did I know? Their bodies were more slight than that of the average Korean, the bone structure of their faces less like granite. But mostly, I knew from the buzz of conversation, which I could not understand, and from their clothes. They were dressed casually in woolen socks, pressed slacks and cotton shirts, some with expensive-looking cashmere sweaters pulled over for warmth. Everything about them, from their neatly coifed haircuts to their glittering wristwatches and bracelets, reeked of wealth.

One man wore a suit jacket with a white shirt and tie, and he sat at the center of the head table: Yun Guang-min. I recognized him not only from the family registers we'd just seen, but also from our first visit to the Olympos Casino shortly after Han Ok-hi had been shot, when he'd walked out briefly onto the casino floor surrounded by his bodyguards and glared at me.

Beside him, dressed more casually than any of his countrymen, but with a casualness that bespoke wealth, sat a white-haired man who seemed as at home in this elaborate banquet as if he were having a bowl of noodles in his wife's kitchen. The way the other men smiled and bowed toward him convinced me that he was "Turtle Mountain," the boss of these Japanese businessmen, probably here on a sex-and-gambling tour of their former colony—now known as the Republic of Korea.

Young women, also dressed in elaborate *chima-chogori*, scurried back and forth to the kitchen, replacing dishware laden with mint leaves marinated in soya, boiled quail eggs, and pulverized seaweed flattened into paper-thin sheets, salted and toasted in sesame oil.

Other young women—with even more elaborate make-up, hairdos, and dresses of silk—sat amongst the men, pouring heated rice liquor into tiny cups from celadon jugs.

"Sort of like the Eighth Army chow hall," Ernie told me.

"Right." I slipped my shoes off and stepped up onto the raised wooden floor covered with tatami. "Watch him," I said, indicating the red-faced bodyguard, "and watch my back."

"What are you going to do?"

"Parley," I said.

I ambled over. The serving girls stopped what they were doing and gawked. The men gradually ceased their chatter. The player of the *kayagum* stopped plucking on her zither and slid unobtrusively back, until she was out of the way.

Yun Guang-min and his white-haired Japanese guest were deep in conversation. I stood at the center of the U-shaped array of tables, and waited.

Finally, they stopped talking and turned to look at me.

The white-haired businessman seemed amazed to see a foreigner so close. He frowned, but regained his composure and stared impassively. Clearly, it was up to his host, Yun Guang-min, to handle the situation.

Yun was a small man, neatly contained in an expensive wool suit, immaculately tailored. Gold-rimmed spectacles sat across the bridge of his flat nose and what with his high cheekbones and stern facial features, his expression was about as readable as a carving on the side of a mountain. At the moment, I was angry enough not to be too concerned about what he was thinking. I pulled the photograph Jimmy had given me out of my coat pocket and tossed it on the table in front of Yun.

"Your little sister," I said. "And her daughter and her son when they were kids."

He stared at the photo, but didn't reach for it.

"When they needed your help, why did you refuse?"

Short, manicured fingers crawled toward the photo, but stopped an inch away. Yun studied the photo for a moment longer, his expression as blank as it had been when I walked in, but the blood rushed up his neck and into his face, and even years of training in Confucian self-control couldn't stop it. Finally, Yun tipped his head back and stared into my eyes.

In English, he said, "What do you want?" His voice was like a lizard zapping a fly.

A chill radiated up my spine. Owning a casino on the edge of the Yellow Sea doesn't require just money, but nerve, ruthlessness, connections—with politicians, gangsters, those who tap into power. If he really wanted to, Yun Guang-min could snap Ernie and me. Still, I knew Ernie and I were probably safe. Too much heat would come if they started killing Americans. We weren't worth the expense, losses due to interruptions in business. Money talks. Big fat piles of U.S. taxpayer dollars. Yun Guang-min wouldn't touch us. We were safe, unless I pushed him too hard.

At the moment, with people dead from my .45, I didn't mind pushing him.

"What I want," I said, "is information on the whereabouts of the boy—now a man—in that photograph."

I pointed to the photo, the boy clinging to his mother's skirts.

"Your nephew," I said.

Yun Guang-min didn't look down.

"Why?" he asked.

"Because he's the one," I said, "who robbed your casino and shot Han Ok-hi."

Yun shook his head slowly. "He's not my nephew."

"He is," I said.

Yun shook his head. "No! He's nothing to me."

"Maybe that's what you want these customers of yours to believe," I said. "But you know the truth and so do I."

"You know nothing of the truth!" Yun's fists were clenched in rage. He paid no attention to the Japanese men who gawked nervously, not understanding the Korean. "You don't know what it's like," he said, "to have a sister who turns to foreigners. Who has the village whisper behind our backs, as if we're unclean. My children were ashamed to go to school, ashamed to stand in front of their own teachers!"

Yun stood, quivering, glaring at me as if he wished me dead. Yun Guang-min, the most powerful man in Inchon, for that moment could do nothing.

"Only one of your bodyguards is here," I said. "Where are the rest? Out looking for your nephew?"

"You're talking nonsense."

"Where's your nephew, Yun?"

"I *don't* know where he is." His face again flushed, his cheeks as red as the snarling dragons carved into the ceiling.

Were they in this together? Could Yun Guang-min have commissioned his nephew to commit the robbery of his own casino so they could split the profits? Maybe he had partners he was trying to steal money from. Was it possible? I didn't think so. The amount stolen, one or two days' take, was a drop in the ocean compared to the amount they took from the high-rollers from Japan and Hong Kong. Those guys bet fortunes, sometimes wiping out the entire accumulated wealth of themselves and their families and their corporations. The Olympos was pulling down more money per gambler than any Las Vegas casino could ever hope for. That's why GIs weren't welcome. We upset the high-rollers, and the money soldiers could lose was a pittance compared to what most of the Asians dropped before they even started tapping their lines of credit.

No, it wasn't an inside job. Everything I'd learned so far pointed to the smiling woman and her brother setting out on a quest for revenge against the world. Starting at the logical place. With the uncle who had left their mother to die on the streets.

I was about to ask another question when Ernie lost his temper. He fired a round into the ceiling.

All of us jumped and plaster, and bits of paint rained down onto Yun's table.

Now he'd done it. Up until this point, all our rude behavior could be explained by saying that we were gathering information for a murder investigation. Ernie's unauthorized use of a firearm changed that. He'd taken us over the line.

Yun's exalted Japanese guest, Turtle Mountain, jumped back in alarm. The bodyguard started to make a move, but Ernie pointed the .45 at him and shoved the young man back down and forced him face down onto the tatami on the floor.

The Japanese looked bewildered and pale. Concerned. Were they being robbed? A few rose to their feet. Ernie boomed another round into the ceiling.

"*Don't move!*" he shouted.

Everyone understood that.

His face twisted in anger, Erin pointed his .45 at Yun Guang-min. "You let your sister cough her guts up on the streets of Seoul. You don't lift a finger to help her son or daughter. And now you go dumb on us when your own nephew robs your casino and kills your employee. What kind of shithead are you?"

I'm not sure if Yun Guang-min understood all of what Ernie was spouting, but he must've gotten the idea. Yun was a tough guy. He stared right at Ernie, giving him the evil eye, daring him to squeeze the trigger and pop a cap through his forehead.

From the look on his face, I thought Ernie was going to do it. I sidled toward him, hoping to get close enough to deflect his aim if need be. I continued firing questions at Yun Guang-min. The casino owner answered angrily, telling me nothing, claiming he had no knowledge of why this man we called his nephew had robbed him. He had no idea where that man might be now.

In disgust, I backed off. No telling when reinforcements might arrive. Ernie sensed it too. He swiveled his head, and I knew he was anxious to un-ass the area. Yun Guang-min, however, called me over.

I returned to the table, expecting him to relay something useful, finally. Instead, he glanced down at the photo of his late sister and her two children.

"You forgot your photograph," he said.

I snatched it up. The son of a bitch had pointedly not touched it. His cold eyes seethed with humiliation. He'd pay us back, I thought. The free pass Americans received in Korea had just been revoked.

We took off.

As Ernie and I emerged from under the red arch at the entrance of the Silla Cho Siktang, a group of young men hurried up the main driveway. I recognized two. Young men in dark suits, straight hair slicked back. Yun Guang-min's bodyguards.

When they saw us, one pointed and shouted: "*Yah!*"

Ernie reached for his weapon.

I grabbed his arm. "No good, pal. We're outnumbered." Three of the bodyguards had already pulled out pistols. "Come on! Let's go!"

For once, Ernie saw the wisdom of what I was saying. He followed as I ran toward the lobby and the front entrance. Uniformed bell hops stepped backward. We shoved past and raced into the hotel lobby. Ahead, carpeted steps led to the casino. Elevator doors sat open. Clattering plates and flatware in the Olympos Hotel Restaurant and Coffee Shop raised a din.

Yun's armed bodyguards were only a few yards behind.

"Smooth move," Ernie said, clanging back the charging handle of his .45. "Now we're trapped."

"No. Not trapped," I said. "Come on."

I sprinted into the coffee shop, Ernie right behind me. Fashionably dressed Korean men and women gawked as we darted through the small sea of tables. I bumped into a waitress carrying a tray full of snacks and beverages but Ernie, right behind me, caught the tray in time and handed it back to the surprised woman.

Yun's bodyguards burst into the restaurant, guns drawn, shouting.

I darted through the swinging doors of the kitchen, sprinted toward the back, and halted at a tiled wall. Ernie bumped into me.

"So now we're trapped in here," he said, "rather than out there."

He crouched behind a big iron stove and aimed at the double doors. Outside men shouted, and a woman screamed.

"There's a way out ," I said. "I found it when we were here before, when I went to that office."

"But that was upstairs, on the other side of the casino," Ernie said.

"I heard pots and pans clanging," I said.

A cook emerged from a large storeroom, carrying a huge glass jar with something slimy inside.

"There," I said.

We dashed into the storeroom. Behind us, the bodyguards crashed through the kitchen doors, shouting, shoving a couple of cooks out of the way.

Wooden shelving lined the storeroom's four walls.

"Shit," Ernie said. He turned and said, "Take cover. I'll blast them when they come in."

I tugged on his arm. "Over here."

Hidden behind the last shelf was a door. Before I had a chance to turn the knob, the cook, who had been carrying the big jar, crashed back through the doors of the storeroom. He reeled backward, still clutching the jar, lost his footing, twisted, and fell to the tile floor a few feet in front of us. Bodyguards crashed in after him. The glass jar smashed, and oil and tentacles and squid flesh splashed along the slippery floor. The bodyguards hit the slime and slid, waving arms like pinwheels. Then they crashed onto the floor atop the supine cook. More bodyguards plowed in after, grabbing wooden shelving to maintain their footing, tipping over neat rows of tin cans and glassware.

I pulled open the door, grabbed Ernie by the back of his jacket, and pulled him through, out into a narrow hallway.

"Come on!"

We turned and ran up a stairway, into a parquet-floored hall that was familiar. We were behind the cashier's cage of the casino. I sprinted up the wooden stairwell leading to Yun Guang-min's office. Ernie was right behind. As we climbed to the top of the steps, we heard shouting. The bodyguards were in the hallway now.

Would they shoot us on sight? It was dangerous to murder U.S. Army CID agents. But only if someone knew. If you controlled the local police, and if the bodies of the two Americans disappeared into the Yellow Sea—well, how much risk was there in that?

I ran faster.

We crashed into Yun Guang-min's office, ran behind his teak desk. I knelt and pulled open the fire-escape door, and was hit in the face with a blast of wind and salt spray from the Yellow Sea.

Ernie leaned next to me and poked his head outside, gazing at the narrow rock ledge that wound around the corner of the building.

"We're going out there?"

"Watch your footing," I said. "And hang onto the rocks along the wall."

We heard voices and the pounding of footsteps behind us. Ernie glanced down at his .45, and then out at the ledge again. "Okay," he said. "You go first. I want a clear shot at those bastards if they come after us."

"Right."

I stepped through. The ledge was about two feet wide but seemed narrower once I was on it. Below, wild surf crashed into jagged rock, launching leaps of white foam that slapped onto my trousers and kept the ledge moist and slippery. Along the cliff wall, jagged outcroppings of rock were also slippery, but they provided reassuring handholds. I stepped along gingerly until there was enough space for Ernie to emerge from the door and close it behind him. Together, we sidled along the wall. The corner of the building was about twenty yards away. We were halfway there, when the door behind us popped open.

A man stuck his head out. One of the bodyguards. Ernie popped a round off at him, and started to teeter away from the cliff face. Holding onto a slippery chunk of granite, I grabbed the back of Ernie's coat. He regained his balance and leaned against the rock wall.

The bodyguard peered cautiously at us.

"Move it!" Ernie shouted.

I did, stepping as quickly as I dared toward the corner which would shield us. We were nearly there when I heard grunting ahead.

I froze.

"What's wrong, dammit?" Ernie yelled.

He looked past me and saw what I saw—another bodyguard. This one held a pistol pointed at us.

I crouched.

Ernie leaned around me and popped off a round at the man's hand. He missed. The gunman pulled back behind the cover of the rock ledge.

Behind us, another thug stuck his head out of the fire escape door. Ernie leveled his pistol at him, and the man ducked back.

"We're screwed," Ernie said. "We can't go forward, we can't go back."

"Yeah. You might be right.

"Does anybody know we're here?" Ernie said.

"I didn't call Riley. You?"

"No," Ernie said. "So there probably won't even be an investigation."

"Probably not. They'll just figure we deserted."

"Maybe we should have. It would've been a lot more fun."

I glanced down at the churning sea. When the waves rolled in, the water rose. It covered the jagged rocks. Ten yards out, the water was fairly deep.

"There's one way," I said.

"You've got to be kidding."

"I'm not."

The arm with the pistol stuck out around the edge of the building again. I leaned back and Ernie fired across my chest. The hand retreated hastily.

"How many more rounds?" I said.

"Six," Ernie panted.

"Save 'em."

"What for?"

"For later."

With that, I took a deep breath, waited for a wave to crash into the rocks, and leapt off the edge of the Olympos Hotel and Casino into the waters of the Yellow Sea.

Ernie splashed in behind me. When I'd recovered from the initial shock of the cold, I swam straight out to sea. Past the surf, in waters that were relatively calm, we floated for what seemed like an hour but might've been only ten or fifteen minutes. On the ledge above, Yun Guang-min's hoods shouted and pointed, but none of them had the nerve to dive in after us.

Fog rolled in, cutting off all sight of land. Ernie and I stuck together, but after a while, we thought we weren't going to make it. Our body temperatures were lowering rapidly, and we were no longer sure of the way to shore. When a dark shape appeared out of the mist, we swam toward it, shouting.

A grizzled old Korean fisherman stood with his son in the stern of their small wooden craft. Handling a single oar, they pulled us aboard. After resting a few minutes and offering the old fisherman much thanks, he obligingly freighted us north, a mile beyond the sparkling lights of the City of Inchon. Still past the breakers, we thanked the fisherman and his son once again. Then we tied our soggy shoes around our necks and swam in. We waded onto a gravelly beach behind a line of warehouses and sloshed our way to a city street, where we waved down a cab driver who proved willing to accept extra money to take us to Seoul.

Still wet but glad to be back in Itaewon's precincts, we went straight to the police station. I was anxious to relay my newfound information to Captain Kim. Inside the station, we were ushered quickly into his office.

The place reeked of fermented kimchee and stale cigarette smoke. Korean cigarettes have a peculiar odor, pungent and dis-agreeable, as if someone had let the tobacco leaves rot before bothering to pulverize them. Still, the odor cleansed my nostrils of crusted salt.

Wearing an immaculately pressed khaki uniform, the Commander of the Itaewon station first insisted that we take off all our clothes and ordered towels brought in. We dried and cov-ered ourselves with the towels. Captain Kim further ordered our clothing taken to a nearby laundry to be dried and pressed. Meanwhile, Ernie and I sat on folding metal chairs, teeth chatter-ing, trying to warm up.

I began to talk.

Kim listened patiently as I told him that the owner of the Olympos Casino had tried to have us killed. We had no jurisdic-tion in a Korean casino—we knew that. But when Captain Kim discovered that we'd been trespassing, and that no grievous harm had been done, he discounted the whole affair.

"Next time, tell me first," he said.

There were no grounds to press charges. And Captain Kim wasn't about to make accusations against a man as powerful as the owner without evidence any less convincing than two American bodies.

"Too bad we weren't shot dead," Ernie said.

I went on to the next subject. I explained to Captain Kim that Yun Guang-min and our killer-on-a-rampage were related, and that I expected Uncle Yun to be the next hit on the killer's list.

When I was finished, I braced for follow-up questions, maybe some attempt to shoot holes in my conjectures. After all, Korean cops, like cops anywhere in the world, are reluctant to accuse the rich of wrongdoing of any kind. Instead of responding, positively or negatively, Captain Kim said only, "I show you."

Ernie and I glanced at one another. When our clothes came back, we dressed and followed Captain Kim out of the station. He headed away from the nightclub district and trudged up clean walkways that led toward the fancy apartment buildings in an area of Seoul known as Hannam-dong.

We climbed higher and higher. Soggy leather squished beneath my feet.

Ernie leaned over and asked, "Where the hell's he taking us?"

"I don't know." I wasn't liking this one bit. A cold chill began to grow in the pit of my stomach.

Captain Kim hadn't been impressed with my brilliant detective work, and he sure hadn't been impressed with my theories about the Family Yun.

18

Dumplings.

Not the fried *yakimandu* I'd eaten with Ernie in the Seven Club, but a soft kind, kneaded from rice flour and steamed in a large pot. A kind that Captain Kim told me Koreans call *songpyun*.

"For Chusok," Captain Kim explained—the autumn moon festival.

"When is it?" I said.

"Tomorrow." He looked at me with disdain, as if I should've known.

He was right: I should've known. Chusok is celebrated on the fifteenth day of the eighth month by the lunar calendar. Therefore, it falls on a different day every year on the Western calendar. Still, I should've realized. But with all the goings on, I'd lost track. And besides, who could think with what was laid out in front of me?

She was so young. So beautiful in her hand-embroidered silk

dress. Blue cranes rising from green reeds adorned a background of pure white. A purity that had been splashed with blood.

Dumplings, the *songpyun*, had been stuffed in her mouth. And then, or maybe before that, her throat had been cut.

She lay on the tiled floor, in the kitchen of an opulent Western-style apartment in a modern building in Hannam-dong. It was a ritzy neighborhood on the side of Namsan Mountain, overlooking the squalor of Itaewon. From the open door of the balcony, a panoramic view of the main drag of the nightclub district spread before us. In the dusk, I could make out the unlit neon signs above the 007 Club and the King Club and the Grand Old Opry Club. Jumbled brick and wood and cement buildings stretched downhill toward the banks of the River Han.

"How'd he get in?" I said.

"Delivery," Captain Kim pointed toward the kitchen area, "of the *songpyun*. In old days everyone make at home, to honor ancestors. Now people buy from store."

On Chusok, the steamed *songpyun* dumplings were offered before shrines to a family's ancestors. Kim pointed to the sliding glass door that led onto the balcony. Ernie and I examined it.

"The lock was broken outwards," Ernie said. "As if it had been shoved from inside."

We peered over the edge of the concrete rail. Vines wound through a wooden trellis, many branches broken and hanging. Then we stepped back inside and turned our attention to the corpse.

She'd been a beautiful round-faced Korean woman, maybe in her late teens or early twenties. She'd been killed so young. And I knew her. At first I couldn't place her, but when Captain Kim said the name Haggler Lee, I suddenly remembered who she was. His serving girl. Usually, she worked at the warehouse, serving Haggler Lee and his guests coffee or tea. I remembered the American-made instant coffee I had been so graciously offered there a few nights ago. This penthouse, according to Captain

Kim, belonged to Haggler Lee. The serving girl had been left here to keep an eye on things while he spent the last day or two holed up in his warehouse.

We heard voices at the open door of the apartment, and Captain Kim and Ernie and I walked into the living room. It was modern, probably designed by some avant-garde interior decorator, so modern that there was no place to sit down. A group of Korean cops entered with a man held between them: Haggler Lee.

His face was wrinkled with worry.

"I didn't think he would do this," Lee said.

"Who?" I asked.

"The son of Miss Yun. He killed Jo Kyong-ah. Now he wants to kill me too. Why? Because I black market for his mother."

"Did you cheat his mother?" I asked.

"Never!" Lee shrugged off the cops surrounding him. "I'm a business man. I no cheat nobody."

His usually precise English grammar was deteriorating rapidly.

"She borrow money from me. I give. Then she come back, again and again. Always promise that some GI boyfriend was going to buy something out of PX for her and she would pay me back. She had GI boyfriend all right, plenty, but they never buy her nothing out of PX. She never pay me back."

"So you stopped loaning her money?"

"Of course," Lee said.

"Then why," I asked, pointing toward the kitchen, "would the son of Miss Yun murder your housemaid?"

Lee stared at a trickle of blood that had overflowed the tile and was now soaking into his wall-to-wall carpet.

"He couldn't reach me," Haggler Lee said. "I was at my warehouse, with my guards. So he come here."

Suddenly, Haggler Lee grabbed his face and fell to his knees. Then he was sobbing like a little boy.

Captain Kim's usually impassive face twisted in disgust, as if he'd like nothing better than to put his boot up Haggler Lee's rear. But he resisted the urge. Instead, Captain Kim turned his back on Haggler Lee and barked an order to his officers. Unceremoniously, they dragged Haggler Lee out of his apartment.

I stepped back into the kitchen and studied the moon-faced young woman who lay on the blood-smeared floor. The fat dumplings between her lips looked obscene. The gash in her neck even more so. Beneath her silk sleeve I spotted something, and I knelt down and pulled the sleeve up above her elbow. Cigarette burns. New. She'd been tortured before she was killed.

I stood up.

I was embarrassed, but relieved about one thing. There were no bullet holes in her body or anywhere in the apartment. This unfortunate young woman had been brutally murdered, but not with my gun.

Ernie and I spent the next couple of hours at the crime scene, and later that evening returned to the deserted CID detachment to catch up on our written reports. Ernie left after an hour. I'd told him I'd finish up. He had a date, I think, with Sergeant Whitworth, the medic at the 121, but he was being cagey and didn't tell me for sure. About midnight, I returned to the barracks and collapsed exhausted into my bunk.

19

It was Chusok. The 8th United States Army Yongsan Compound was pretty much closed down. All the Korean employees at the snack bar had the day off, so the American manager was working the cash register, selling nothing but coffee and donuts and pre-made sandwiches wrapped in plastic. Ernie joined me there, bleary-eyed. He wolfed down a couple of egg and bacon sandwiches, cold, and we walked out the main gate of the compound, down the MSR three-quarters of a mile to the Hamilton Hotel.

Already Suk-ja was waiting for us in the coffee shop.

"They no come," she said.

She, of course, had memorized the faces in the sketches of the smiling woman and her brother and had promised, as her contribution to the investigation, to spend as much time as she could in the Hamilton Hotel Coffee Shop, seeing if they showed up. Private Boltworks had said they loved this place, and I could see why. There were GIs here and foreign tourists, Korean business girls and bright-eyed college students, hanging out for the excitement of being near the notorious international red-light district of Itaewon.

Suk-ja was happy in her work, but I was worried as to what she was up to. Why had she left the Yellow House? Did she owe the mama-san money? Why had she decided to glom onto me? I was enjoying the attention, of that there was no doubt. If it hadn't been for this murder investigation, I would've enjoyed Suk-ja's company even more. But I wasn't fool enough to believe that she didn't want anything out of this. Yesterday morning, when I offered her money, she'd taken it, but with the proviso that it was merely reimbursement to cover expenses while she was on duty at the coffee shop. She wasn't taking any money from me in return for sex. Soon, she told me, she would receive her first paycheck as a stripper, and it would be her turn to treat me.

I wasn't holding my breath.

Suk-ja snuggled closer to me. Ernie sat across from us.

"Today," she said, "you go with me, Geogi. My older brother, he live in Mia-dong. We start Chusok at noon time. He want me come. I tell him about you and he say he want you come too."

I studied her face, wondering why in the hell she wanted me to meet her family. Ernie smirked at my discomfort.

"We'll be working on the case," I said.

"Doing what?" she asked. "We only know Miss Yun's son sometime come here. If he no come, how you find? Anyway, KNPs look for him. They find."

She was right. The KNPs would find him eventually. But how many people would be dead before they did? At least, in the most recent murder, he hadn't used my piece. As relieved as I was about that, it still troubled me. Why hadn't he used the automatic?

"Go!" Ernie told me. "You need a break. Go somewhere and clear your mind."

Maybe he was right. Everything I'd seen and heard the last

few days had jumbled into a knotted ball of grief. How to unravel it? How to stop the killing? No matter how hard I pressed, the answer was not forthcoming.

Suk-ja clutched my arm tightly.

"How about you?" I asked Ernie. "What do you plan to do?"

He shrugged. "Wendy has duty today. I'll probably run the ville."

"'Wendy?'"

Ever so slightly, Ernie's pale cheeks colored. "Sergeant Whitworth. The WAC at the 121."

"They don't call them WACs anymore," I told Ernie. The Women's Auxiliary Corps had been disbanded a few years ago, and female soldiers were integrated into regular Army units.

"Whatever you call them," Ernie said. "And anyway, I received a note from an old friend."

He pulled a piece of lined notepaper out of his pocket. It was folded elaborately into the shape of a swan.

Suk-ja grabbed it and, without asking permission, unfolded it. Quickly, she read the note.

"Who's this?" she said.

"An old girlfriend."

Written in broken English, the note said that she missed him and she wanted to be with him, and she had no place to go on Chusok. She asked him to meet her at the Seven Dragon *mokkolli* house. It was signed Miss Na.

I knew the Seven Dragon *mokkolli* house. It was a little dive in a back alley. It served warm rice beer. The type of place cab drivers and fledgling Korean gangsters hung out. Exactly the type of place Ernie loved.

"Who is she?" I asked.

"What are you, my mother?" Ernie sipped on his ginseng tea. "One of the Seven Club waitresses slipped the note in my pocket while we were in there drinking the other night. I met Miss Na when I first arrived in country. Sexy lady. I was with her for a while, but she went to the States on a *yobo* visa."

Invited to immigrate to the United States for the purpose of matrimony.

"If she's back in country, why didn't she talk to you herself?"

"The waitress said she'd been in there three or four times looking for me, but we've been busy on this case. So she asked the waitress to hand me this note if she saw me."

"Why Chusok?" I asked.

"Don't know. Maybe she figured I'd have that day off."

Suk-ja tugged on my arm. "We go to my brother's house, okay Geogi?"

"Okay," I said. "Okay."

Her face beamed with joy.

Burnt pine needles.

I had smelled them before and now I was smelling them again. Suk-ja and I had taken a cab to the northern district of Seoul known as Mia-dong. The cabby let us off on the main road, and we hiked through winding pathways up the side of a hill. I lugged a basket of Asian pears that Suk-ja made me buy, because it would be impolite to enter her brother's house with "empty hands."

It was a rickety hovel made of splintery wood, like all the others in the neighborhood. Her brother was a construction worker, she said, trying to become a carpenter, working secretly for a union that the government had declared illegal, like all the other unions in Korea. His wife was a stout woman with a ruddy smiling face, and they had three kids; one infant, two toddlers. When I shook hands with Suk-ja's brother, his brown eyes were moist, earnest. This meeting meant a lot to him. And somehow, in that brief moment, I read the anguish he felt at not being able to properly take care of his younger sister. Of being poor and seeing her go with foreigners in order to survive.

Suk-ja and I slipped off our shoes and stepped up onto the raised wooden floor. The main room of the small home had been cleared of furniture, and against the far wall were two large photographs, lined in black, of a wrinkled-looking man and a plain-faced woman.

"My parents," Suk-ja said. "They die long time ago."

"What's that smell?" I asked.

"Pine needles," Suk-ja answered. "We roast them at Chusok time. Makes house smell good. How you say? Cozy."

The brother lined up the children first. The infant in his small crib. The two toddlers knelt on the floor, bowing their heads three times to the photographs of their grandparents in front of them. Then it was our turn. Suk-ja moved the crib, and we four adults knelt. She motioned for me to watch her. She placed her slender hands—thumb and forefinger touching—flat on the floor in front of her. Her brother chanted something I couldn't quite catch, and then they bowed, touching their foreheads to the floor. Quickly, I mimicked their movement. The brother chanted again and we bowed. In all, we repeated this three times.

Then Suk-ja's brother brought in a rectangular table. I helped him unfold the legs, while his wife carried in the food: cabbage kimchee, steamed rice, tofu stew, roast mackerel, strips of dried turnip. Before we ate, a plate of *songpyun* was placed in front of the photographs.

Suk-ja's brother motioned for us to dig in. I picked up my chopsticks and inhaled deeply of the clean scent of roasted pine needles. How wonderful it was to be welcomed by such a warm family. They were poor, they suffered through much, but they had each other.

I set down a slice of kimchee. Suddenly my hunger left me. Everything rushed together in my brain: Chusok, the warm family setting, the scent of pine needles, the dumplings, the photograph of ancestors.

I turned to Suk-ja. "What's next?" I asked.

She stared at me blankly.

"At Chusok," I said. "You first roast pine needles, then you bow to your ancestors, then you serve them *songpyun*. What's the next step?"

"Oh. Understand. Next step is we take food for us and dumplings for the dead up to Happy Mountain."

"Happy Mountain?"

"Yeah. You know, place where dead people live."

"The cemetery," I said. Then I corrected myself. "The burial mounds."

In Korea, people are buried in mounds, six-foot-high round hills. Not flat graves. The idea is the dead can sit there and gaze out upon pleasant surroundings.

"Yes. Place where ancestors live. We have picnic there, perform ceremony again."

"Will you go today?"

"No. Too far. My parents' home in Taejon. Many people go daytime. All train, bus, too crowded."

"How about going at night?"

Suk-ja's eyes widened. "At night? Too many ghosts. Anyway, my parents, how you say, burned?"

"Cremated," I said.

"Yeah. Cremated. We keep ashes before, but I think my oldest sister in Taejon, she take them."

"So does anybody go to the grave mounds at night?"

"No, no. Nobody go. But today, during daytime, many people will be at all the cemeteries around Korea. On Chusok, bury places very crowded."

I rose from the table, apologizing to Suk-ja's older brother and his wife and then to Suk-ja.

"Where you go?"

"This case we've been working on, it has to do with Chusok. Everything about it has to do with Chusok. I was just too dumb to see it."

Each crime scene ran through my mind, like a movie film fast-forwarding through the projector. And now, when I compared those scenes to what I had learned here with Suk-ja's family, they all made a weird sort of sense.

First, Captain Noh, the Korean cop in the village of Songtan, didn't want to explain to me the significance of the roasted pine needles at the murder site of Jo Kyong-ah. He thought someone was mocking Korean custom, and he didn't want to admit such a loss of face to foreigners like me and Ernie. Second, both Jo Kyong-ah, and later Specialist Five Arthur Q. Fairbanks, had been forced to kneel face-down in an awkward position, as if they were performing the *seibei* bowing ceremony. Third, Haggler Lee's young serving girl was found with *songpyun* dumplings shoved in her mouth—the next step in the Chusok ceremonies.

The final step? Grave mounds.

"I have to go," I said.

"I go with you."

I didn't argue.

20

I had to find Ernie. Even if that meant interrupting his tryst with his old girlfriend, Miss Na.

The proprietor of the Silver Dragon *mokkolli* house was a rotund man with a bushy black mustache and a white apron tied around his waist. As soon as I walked in the door, he looked perplexed. Then he pulled out a sheet of lined notebook paper and handed it to me.

This one folded in the shape of a turtle.

I unfolded it. It was written in *hanmun*, Chinese characters, and said only: *Hyodo*. Filial piety.

I remembered the words because they were the first two Chinese characters my Korean language teacher had written on the chalkboard. The basis, she'd told us, upon which Confucian society is built.

In Korean, I asked, "Who gave this to you?"

"She said American man come. Tall American man. Dark hair. Like you."

"What did she look like?"

"Korean, but not Korean. Light-colored hair."

"Half-American?"

"I think so."

"Smiling strangely?"

His eyes widened. "How you know?"

I asked him if he'd seen Ernie or any other American GIs. He said no. GIs seldom found their way into this dirt-floored *mokkolli* house and when they did, it was late at night and they were too drunk to know where they were.

Suk-ja and I thanked him and walked out the door.

Next door to the Seven Dragon *mokkolli* house was a noodle shop with a parking area for cabs. *Unchon Siktang* the sign said: Driver's eatery. The cabbies could catch a quick bowl of steaming noodles while one of the young men out front hosed down their cabs and washed them off. There were three of these young men, all wearing rubber boots that reached almost to their knees. I asked each of them if they'd seen any GIs in the area today. None had.

We entered the noodle shop.

A stout woman with a bandana over her hair said she'd seen a GI approaching through the back alley. Maybe he was heading for the *mokkolli* house next door but she couldn't be sure. I described Ernie to her, and she said yes, that was what he looked like.

"What happened to him?" I asked.

"Back there." She pointed. "He stop for a few minutes. Waiting. Then black car pull up. Window open. He lean in. Talk. Then he raise both hands to sky, like praying."

"Praying?"

"Yes. I think so."

"Then what did he do?"

"He get in car. They go."

"Did you report this to anybody?"

"Report? No. Why report? I no want trouble here at *Unchon Siktang*."

I asked her a few more questions, and then jotted down her name and told her we'd be talking to her again soon.

"Abduct?" Captain Kim pronounced the word awkwardly. "You mean somebody take go?"

"Yes. In a black Hyundai sedan. Ernie's hands were raised, as if somebody inside the car was holding a gun on him."

Captain Kim studied my face. "Maybe your gun."

I nodded.

"That's why you feel so bad."

I nodded again.

"This woman, Miss Na, you know her full name?"

I didn't. And that made it impossible for us to check to see if she'd actually returned to Korea as Ernie had been told in the note. Was this a setup? Had somebody known about Ernie's old flame, and then used her name to induce him to meet them at a certain place and time? Captain Kim told Suk-ja and me to sit down and try to relax while he made a few phone calls.

I used the phone at the other desk and finally got through to the Charge of Quarters at the barracks where Ernie and I lived. I waited as he wandered down the hallway and checked with the houseboy. No, Ernie wasn't in, and nobody'd seen him since this morning. I called the CID Detachment. Riley was in catching up on paperwork. I told him what I suspected.

"Ernie's been abducted?"

"Maybe. Don't say anything yet. I can't be sure."

"Sure you're sure. It's this case you been working on. That nutty broad is smarter than you and Bascom put together."

I told Riley where I was and told him, if Ernie showed up, to have him find me immediately. And I made him promise not to tell anybody. Not yet. Not until I was sure.

When I hung up the phone, Captain Kim was staring at me. Then he told me about the news from Yoju.

If Ernie thought there was any way to escape without being shot, he would've tried it."

"Maybe not," Suk-ja said. "Maybe he want go."

This was possible, although I didn't want to admit it out loud. Ernie was crazy enough to think he could turn the tables on whoever had the nerve to try to take him captive.

Captain Kim said that near the outskirts of Yoju, at the burial mounds, a huge crowd had gathered for the traditional Chusok ceremonies. Mr. Yun Guang-min, the owner of the Olympos, had gone there this morning in his chauffer driven Hyundai sedan. That made sense, because his ancestral home was Yoju and he, like everyone else, was visiting the burial sites of his parents in order to pay his respects. Only one guard traveled with him and the chauffeur.

Along the route, Mr. Yun saw a warm chestnut stand on the side of the road, and he made his driver stop. He loved chestnuts and bought enough to feed a small army. He explained to anyone listening that, when he was young, his family had been too poor to afford them, no matter how much he craved them. He laughed and said that all his relatives teased him about how crazy he was for warm chestnuts.

The chestnut vendor shot the bodyguard in the chest. The vendor was a woman, her hair covered with a bandana. While her partner waved his automatic pistol around, she ordered the driver out of the car, took his keys. Her male accomplice forced Mr. Yun into the driver's seat, and she and the accomplice climbed in back.

The vehicle made a U-turn and headed northwest, in the general direction of Seoul.

The KNPs had the sedan's license plate: a bulletin had been issued. With the roads jammed on Chusok, it was unlikely the sedan would be spotted.

Had the black Hyundai been the same car that Ernie climbed into?

I thought so. The smiling woman and her brother were going for two victims. They were going to make sure that this would be a Chusok to be remembered.

Would it do any good to notify 8th Army? No. They had no way of doing a better job than the Korean cops. In fact, if a pack of cowboy MPs barged in while I was trying to save Ernie, they'd only get somebody killed.

I was on my own on this. And I had to find him.

"Where would they have taken Mr. Yun?" I asked Captain Kim.

"I don't know," he said.

"It's Chusok," I said, trying to think it through. "Like all Koreans, they want to visit their ancestors. Their ancestors are in Yoju, the same as their uncle, Mr. Yun."

Suk-ja crinkled her nose. "They no like them."

She was right. She was exactly right. The smiling woman and her brother had been ostracized by their own family. They wouldn't want to worship ancestors who had turned their backs on them. So who would they worship? The one ancestor who hadn't turned away. Who had stood by them always. Their mother.

Where was she buried?

Probably, she hadn't been. The Uichon mama-san had told me the smiling woman carried with her a white box wrapped with black ribbon. That almost certainly contained the ashes of her deceased mother. To worship her, all they had to do was set the box on a table and bow.

At the murder site of Jo Kyong-ah, the black marketeer, she'd been forced to bow in front of a table partially cleared. Had the smiling woman and her brother forced Miss Jo to bow to the box containing their deceased mother's ashes?

When Specialist 5 Arthur Q. Fairbanks was executed, the killer had set a cardboard-like paper against the pump handle and forced Fairbanks to bow three times. A photograph of Miss Yun, the mother? And then another person had entered the courtyard. His sister carrying the white box containing their mother's ashes? Then Fairbanks was killed.

I pulled out the photo Jimmy had given me. Miss Yun Yong-min, her daughter, and her son. Such a pathetic little family. Three people, all alone in the world. If I was correct, there was no set site for the smiling woman and her brother to pay homage at the shrine of their deceased mom. They could've taken Ernie and Mr. Yun anywhere.

21

It was late afternoon. The sun would go down soon and the lights of Itaewon would blink to life as they had for so many years since the end of the Korean War. But tonight, they'd blink on without Ernie Bascom.

Suk-ja and I stood out on the street, waiting. A motor bike putt-putted up the street. A red helmet flashed by. I watched as Jimmy the photographer parked his bike in front of the King Club, his boxy camera with flash slung over his shoulder, ready for another night's work.

Then I knew.

I grabbed Suk-ja's hand. "Come on."

I dragged Suk-ja across and stopped Jimmy before he could enter the swinging doors of the King Club. I pulled out the photo he had given me and asked him some questions. Jimmy's memory was excellent, and he pointed to the big wooden arch under which Miss Yun and her two children had posed, all three smiling bravely. Together, we recited the name of the Buddhist temple where he'd flashed the photo: *Hei-un Sa*. The Temple of Sea and Cloud. Jimmy gave us directions.

Suk-ja and I thanked him and waved down a cab.

Before we left Itaewon, Suk-ja insisted on stopping at a pay phone to place a call. To her brother, she said. While I waited in the cab, I watched her chatting away, unable to hear what she was saying. It didn't matter. I figured I already knew who she was calling and what she'd be saying. Still, I worked on finding a way to believe that I was wrong about her and that she really was talking to her brother.

With the passenger door ajar so the inside light would stay on, Suk-ja and the cab driver studied a map of Kyongi Province.

"Over there," she said, pointing.

We had already traveled many miles east of the outskirts of Seoul, and I knew from driving these areas during daylight that we weren't far from the Han River Estuary. The map indicated we were close to the temple, and the driver agreed with her. I closed the door as he restarted the engine. He drove down the bumpy, unpaved country road.

Litter lined the sides, and muddy tire tracks were everywhere. It had been a busy day out here, but with the crowds of Chusok worshipers back in the city, the area was desolate and barren. Wind swirled inland from the cold sea.

Why did I believe that the smiling woman and her brother would come out here for their Chusok ceremony? Because they'd been happy here. They'd visited with their mother when she was alive, many times, according to Jimmy. It was the logical place to finally bury her ashes. But as Jimmy had warned me, land—even a small burial mound—could be expensive. Hundreds of dollars. Even thousands, if the mound had an unobstructed view of the sea.

The terrain started to rise. According to the map, the cemetery tended by the Buddhist monks was located on the bluffs along the River Han, at a spot where the Han meets the Imjin River and they flood out into the Yellow Sea. During the day, the view must've been beautiful beyond compare.

Maybe that's what all this was about. Maybe the robbery of the Olympos Casino, in the minds of the smiling woman and her brother, hadn't been a robbery at all. Maybe they had just decided to claim their inheritance. An inheritance from an uncle who should've, by Korean custom, taken care of them from the day they were born. And maybe their desire for money was not so they could splurge on the finer things in life, but to buy their mother a burial plot that would give her the respect in death that she was never afforded in life.

Maybe, if you looked at it their way, this entire crime spree—starting with bopping me over the head and proceeding to murder after murder—could be seen as an act of filial piety of unparalleled proportions. I might be wrong. But if I was right, the smiling woman and her brother would be here tonight.

The cab's shock absorbers groaned as we bounced over a muddy ridge. We were north of Kimpo International Airport, even farther north of the port city of Inchon. In churning waters beyond rocky cliffs, the theoretical demarcation line between North and South Korea ran through the center of the Han River Estuary. A few of the small islands on the northern side, I knew, were patrolled and heavily fortified by the northern Communist regime.

The wind was whipping up. A few splats of rain fell onto dirt.

"*Andei,*" said the driver. No good.

He was right. If the wind blew in rain clouds off the Yellow Sea, these dirt roads would turn to mud in a matter of minutes.

The driver slowed, wanting to turn back.

"*Jokum to,*" I said. A little farther.

He sighed and kept driving.

The road started to rise more steeply. Lightning flashed over the Yellow Sea. I spotted the outline of grave mounds dotting the hills.

The driver stopped, backed up, and started to turn around.

"All right," I said. "All right."

I climbed out. Suk-ja too.

"You go back," I said. "I have to find Ernie and I have to move fast."

I paid the cab driver. More rain spattered his windshield. He wanted to get out before the roads turned to mud. I told Suk-ja to climb inside.

"No. I go with you."

"No!" This time I shouted. "I have to go quickly and quietly. I can't slow down and worry about you."

In the reflected glow from the headlights, I saw her face fall. She lowered her eyes.

"Okay, Geogi. Sorry I bother you."

"No bother." I patted her on the shoulder. "I'll see you tomorrow night."

She glanced at me, eyes flashing with anger. Then she climbed back in the cab, and the driver rolled forward. I stood watching them until the headlights reached the main road. The cab turned and sped off around a bend out of sight.

The roiling clouds came fast, pushed inland by a stiff breeze. All about me was becoming darker. The only light came from the swirling beam of a distant lighthouse, and the occasional flash of lightning over the water.

I walked uphill, toward the grave mounds.

The cloud cover broke for a few seconds and, as if to light my way, a Chusok moon, as full as the calm face of a Buddhist saint, shone.

* * *

When I was a kid in East L.A., the worst part was not having parents. Poverty, hunger, all those things you can stand—but without parents, you're nothing.

Some of my foster parents were all right, some not so right. But I always knew that I lacked something fundamental that other kids had. A place to belong. A person to love you. A spot that was all yours and yours alone in this vast empty universe.

That's what ancestor worship was all about. Why the Koreans made such a big deal about it. It told them who they were, where they belonged, how they fit into this gigantic puzzle we call human life. I envied them their dedication, and although I usually didn't admit it to myself, I longed to join them.

But I had no place in it. Before I was old enough to start school, my mother died in childbirth, along with the sibling she was laboring to bear. Shortly afterwards, I'm told, my father ran off to Mexico, never to return.

At Suk-ja's brother's house, they'd set up two photographs of the ancestors of her nephews and nieces. I envied those kids. At least they knew who their parents were.

I would never know mine. Not personally. But somehow, whenever I was in trouble, I felt that my mother was near.

Walking beside me.

The grave mounds rolled like an undulating sea to the cliffs overlooking the confluence of the Han and the Imjin Rivers. There was movement behind one of the mounds, of that I was sure. My eyes had adjusted to the darkness, and I could differentiate one shadow from another. Occasionally, I could even hear the sound of murmuring voices, floating out to me on the salt-tanged wind.

I was freezing—cold and damp. The rain had fallen intermittently, coming in squalls of sudden pellets, but I'd been out here long enough to be soaked. My teeth chattered.

How I wished I had a weapon. If I hadn't been so stubborn, I could've checked out a replacement pistol from the CID arms room. But that would've entailed filling out paperwork, and walking it from Staff Sergeant Riley's office to the First Sergeant's office and then the Provost Marshal's Office, facing smirking clerks all the way. I not only didn't have the time, I didn't have the stomach to run such a humiliating gauntlet without punching somebody square in the nose. So I lived without. A decision I now regretted.

Crouch-walking through the mud, I edged closer to the high mound near the edge of the cliff.

Someone screamed. A male. Anguished. And I recognized the voice: Ernie.

I was at the side of the mound now. A human figure lay against it. The head bobbed forward occasionally. Ernie? Tied up?

Standing in front of him was a man. Standing still. Waiting. Kong, the son. Brother of the smiling woman.

Almost certainly he was armed. There were twenty yards between us. How to cover that without being spotted and gunned down? Only one way. Lightning.

When it flashed again, I would be blinded. But so would the man standing over Ernie. Before he could spot me or take aim, I'd be on him. That was my only chance.

The tall shadow stepped forward and once again Ernie screamed.

I crouched, flexing my knees, waiting to spring. No lightning. The wind picked up. More rain, but no flash.

All around me loomed burial mounds. Some had stone urns on top for burning incense. Others supported statuettes, likenesses of the dead in the cold ground below. Their stone eyes seemed to be watching. Smiling. Amused at my puny efforts.

The wind howled. More droplets of rain. It dribbled down the back of my neck. I worked my way forward.

A flash and lightening filled the world. I was on my feet, moving, trying to pick up traction in the sloshing mud. I ran. In the flash, I'd seen someone near Ernie, lying face down, unmoving, looking for all the world like a corpse. Was it Uncle Yun Guang-min?

And then my vision cleared, and I saw him: Brother Kong, in all his glory. His arm at his side, holding something long and heavy. He turned his startled eyes toward me. His hand came up, the barrel of the .45 still not pointing directly at me. With a great leap, I was on him. Punching, ripping, kneeing, screaming.

Ernie shouted. What, I didn't know. The gun lay in the mud now and the wide-eyed man beneath me stared up into a fist plunging toward his mouth. I punched him again and again. Blood ran, out of his nose, and mouth, and ear. He stopped struggling. His head lolled to the side. I could now hear what Ernie was saying.

"Untie me, goddamn it! Untie me!"

I grabbed my .45, shoved it in my pocket and stood, legs wobbly. The man didn't move. He was out cold. I turned, staggered forward, and knelt beside Ernie.

The red light of the Chusok moon peeked out from behind storm clouds. I could see that my assumptions had been correct. Lying next to Ernie in the mud, the back of his head blown open in a bloody pulp, was Mr. Yun Guang-min, former owner of the Olympos Hotel and Casino.

"Wires," Ernie said. "In knots. He kept pulling on them, tightening them around my wrists and ankles. Hurt like a mother. Untie them, will ya?"

"Okay, okay."

I studied the knots as best I could in the dark, going mainly by feel, listening for any movement behind me. Finally, I twisted the tightly wrapped wire but, as Ernie groaned, I realized that I was twisting the wrong way. I reversed the torque and the wires popped free. Ernie reached across and unknotted his other hand.

"Untie my feet," he said.

I did. Ernie ripped all the wires off of his torso and hopped upright. He strode toward the supine man in front of us, knelt, and lifted the back of his head.

The moon had risen higher. *Borum*, the Koreans call it. The full moon. It was only a third of the way above the horizon but with this temporary break in the fast moving clouds I had enough light to see clearly the unconscious face before us. Kong. The brother of the smiling woman. He was an Asian man, or an American, depending on your point of view. His nose was broad but slightly pointed, his eyes were Oriental, but deeply recessed in his skull, and his lips were full. The hair was brown, almost as dark as a Korean's, but the tips of each strand curled.

"Half-*Miguk*," Ernie said.

I thought of the photographs I'd seen of Miss Yun. He looked like her. She had been a beautiful woman, and he wasn't a bad-looking man. He looked like the little boy he'd been in those photographs: frightened, worried, clinging to his mother's skirts.

"Who else is up here?" I said.

"That's it." Ernie wheezed. "The sister left. Couldn't stand the rain."

Ernie grabbed a few strands of broken wire. Together, we rolled the brother over and tied his hands behind his back.

I was exhausted. Ready to crash right there. But I knew we had to transport this guy to the nearest Korean police station, turn him in, and then convince somebody to police up the dead body of Mr. Yun Guang-min. After that, we'd spend the next couple of hours giving our report. A long night but it had to be done. I had just started to twist wire around his wrists, when I heard the footsteps behind us.

Ernie and I both turned.

With the full moon framing her head, a blonde woman stood

with her shoulders thrust back, pointing the barrel of a pistol at my nose.

She was smiling.

Ernie and I rose slowly to our feet, holding our hands out to the sides.

With her free hand, she motioned for me to pull the .45 out of my coat pocket. I did as I was told, holding the weapon butt first.

She pointed at the ground in front of her, and I tossed the weapon down. She bent at the knees, careful to keep her pistol pointed at us, and picked up the .45. She stuck in her belt, behind her back.

All the while she was doing this, she kept smiling gleefully, the madness in her eyes flaming.

"You know nothing," she said, still smiling. "You don't know how many times they beat up my brother. He come home from school, every night, bleeding, cut up, bruised. One time they break his arm. Another time they break his, how you say?" She pointed at her side.

"Ribs," I said.

"Yes. Hurt every time he breathe. No can go doctor. No have money. Me? I'm okay. Kids make fun of me, other girls laugh at my hair, but nobody beat me. Just boys all time touch, pinch me, say my mother *yang kalbo*. You understand?"

"Foreigner's whore."

"Even teacher one time say why I don't go back my own country. My father country. I no say anything. Too ashame. I don't know my father. Where he go? Who he? What his name? I don't know. I ask my mother, she slap me. Later, I ask my mother if my brother's daddy same same my daddy. She slap me again. Then she cry. How I know who my father is? And then my mom get sick. Can't work in nightclub no more. Can't earn big money from GI. GIs who come to our house every night, sleep in bed with my mother, make a lot of noise."

She inhaled and exhaled, heavily, as if asthmatic. Smiling all the while.

"And me and my brother, we lay on floor next to bed, hold each other, try to sleep but we no can sleep. Drunk GI wake up, tell my mother to do things she don't want do. And then they fight and GI try take money back, but my mother won't let GI have money, and they fight more, and finally my mother do what he want her do. And before finished, my brother, he already sleep. Me? I no can sleep. I listen my mother. After finish, after GI sleep, she cry. Once I go to her, touch her arm, ask she not cry. She slap me. Tell me go back to sleep. But Ai-ja . . . " With her free hand, she pointed at her own nose. "Ai-ja no can sleep. Ai-ja never sleep. Ai-ja always watch out for GI. Watch out for woman who no help my mother. Woman who always take things my mother get from GI boyfriend, things out of PX, sell to this woman. Later, when money gone, does she help my mother? No way, José. *Karra chogi*, she say. Get lost. So we leave and my mother every day she more sick. Every day she catch GI, but sometimes they no pay her and what you gonna do? We stay in *yoguan* at first during winter time, sleep outside during summer. But next winter money all gone. Snow come, we sleep outside. Sometimes, my brother he get angry. *Taaksan* angry. He punch GI. But GI punch him back and brother fall down, no can get up. When he's older, he get up, punch GI. Sometimes, he win and GI run away. Is my mother happy? No way. She slap my brother, tell him go away, she no can feed him no more. So he stay away all day, but at night he find us and he sleep with us on sidewalk."

Her brother started to rouse himself.

"Pretty soon he wake up," the smiling woman said. "He all the time wake up. Even big GI knock him down, my brother he tough. He all time wake up."

The moon hovered behind her head, and her smile was as bright and broad as the red face of the lunar orb. But the storm clouds off the sea were on the move again. They rolled inland and started to blot out the moonlight. The darkness deepened, and more drops of rain splattered the mud.

"And then VD honcho come," the smiling woman said. "What's his name?"

"Fairbanks," I said.

Ernie's eyes darted, looking for escape, but even Ernie knew he couldn't outrun a bullet.

"Yes, Fairbanks," the smiling woman said. "He come. Say my mother have TB. She say 'bullshit.' We cry, we scream, we punch but they take her anyway. Where? We don't know. Me and brother, we don't know."

Her smile was broader than ever now. So broad that I honestly believed the flesh on her face might rip open.

"So me and my brother," she said, "we run away from, how you say? *Koai-won?*"

"Orphanage," I said.

"Yeah. We live on streets of Seoul. My brother, he run fast. Sometimes he see old people with money, he grab money and run. Or he grab food and run away, but sometimes KNP catch, lock him up, but next day let him go. I wait outside, then we together again. Later," she said, "I start make money again the way my mother's boyfriend teach me."

At her feet, her brother groaned. He raised his head from the mud, shook it, looked around, and sprang to his feet, flinging loose wire from his wrist. Without speaking, his sister gave him the pistol. He grabbed it and aimed it at me and then Ernie.

"*Kei sikkya,*" he spat. Born of dogs.

The smiling woman said something to him in rapid Korean. He backed up a step.

"Here," she said, pointing at the burial mound. "Me and

brother get money and we pay at temple for this place to put my mother." That explained why she no longer had the white box wrapped in black ribbon. "Bald men come and say a lot of thing I no can understand and they light fire and wave, what you call?"

"Incense," I said.

"Yes. Incense. And they do lot of pray and we put mother in ground."

Then she stepped away and I could see what rested against the side of the burial mound. A photograph. I strained to make it out. The rain came down harder.

"My mother," the woman said. "She was beautiful, right? All GI likey." Her smile was a mad leer.

Her brother growled. She turned to him. "Anyway, we do now."

"Do what?" Ernie said.

"You," she pointed at Ernie with the barrel of the .45. "You lie down here. In mud."

She pointed at the side of the burial mound, near her brother, just a few feet from the dead body of Mr. Yun. The brother waved his .45 also, and Ernie complied, lying down face first at the edge of the mound.

"You," she said. "You Sueño, you face my mother."

She knew my name. I was surprised at that. I shouldn't have been. These two had done their homework. Why did they want me and Ernie? Maybe because Ernie was fair, like the smiling woman, and I was dark, like her brother. We were stand-ins in this ceremony we were about to perform for the fathers they'd never known. That was what she'd meant in the back alleys of Itaewon when she told me she had a job for me.

I shuffled sideways until I was standing before the photograph.

"Now," she snarled. "You do *seibei*."

She wanted me to lower myself to my knees and bow to her mother. I hesitated, thinking about it.

"Now!" she screamed, her face angry, but smiling. When I still didn't move, her brother jacked a round into the chamber, moving a bullet inches closer to Ernie's head.

"Okay," I said. "Okay."

She chanted some singsong Korean. Not the ancient ritualistic incantations I had heard earlier at Suk-ja's brother's house. Simpler words. Words I could understand.

"This man, this GI, pays homage to you, Mother, for all the bad things he did to you."

I knelt, but didn't bow my head to the ground.

"He looks like my brother's father," she said. "That's why we have chosen him to take his place in sacrificing to you."

I glanced at Ernie. His eyes were wide with fear. I nodded my head slightly.

"Bow!" the woman shouted.

"The hell he will," Ernie said.

"*Sikkya*," the brother hissed, and stepped closer to him.

"You're both nuts," Ernie continued. "You understand? Dingy dingy."

It was luck, nothing more. I rose to a kneeling position and moved at the brother, preoccupied with Ernie. I knew Ernie would lunge at the woman. Not a move we'd rehearsed. But in general, if you make a play for someone who has the drop on you, go for the opposite person. Counter block, as they say in football. You go for the one guarding your partner, your partner goes for the one guarding you.

We had to try something. When she'd said sacrifice, both Ernie and I knew it was all over. These two were crazy beyond redemption. And they were desperate. They knew the KNPs would catch them soon enough, so there was no bargaining with them.

They'd be executed for their crimes. Hanged. Their fate was beyond doubt and they knew it, but if they could take revenge on all the GIs who'd abused them and their mom over the years, now was their opportunity.

On Chusok, no less.

Kong swiveled. I was dead. Just as that reality was sinking in, Ernie lunged toward the woman.

But as he did so, the world exploded into light. Lightning.

I dove to my right, landed on my knees, leapt back to my feet. I plowed into the brother and he was on the ground again. He went down easy; he'd been hurt the first time. I had the .45.

Ernie clutched the woman from behind, a forearm around her neck.

At the bottom of the hill, gears churned. Around a bend, headlights flashed. The lights turned toward us, a line of them. As the beam from one pair of headlights flashed on the vehicle in front of them, I could read the stenciled *hangul*.

Kyongchal, it said. Korean National Police.

The vehicles formed a line at the bottom of the hill, and uniformed officers climbed out. Behind them, leaping out of a taxi was Suk-ja. My relief at seeing her was quickly overcome by the men who climbed out of the cab with her. The two missing bodyguards of the late Mr. Yun.

Suk-ja had been working for them all along. She'd been sent to follow my investigation, hoping to get a line on the whereabouts of the smiling woman and her brother, so Mr. Yun's thugs could put an end to them.

Where else would she have found the money to buy her freedom from the Yellow House? Only from the casino owner, Mr. Yun. And the phone call she'd made earlier this evening from Itaewon. To Yun's thugs.

While Ernie and I searched for the smiling woman and her brother, what else had Yun's minions done? They'd murdered Haggler Lee's serving girl. She hadn't been shot with my .45. Her throat had been cut. Nothing like the other killings. Probably the brother had bought the dumplings, delivered them to Haggler Lee's apartment, and, pretending to be a delivery boy, gained entry. Why kill the serving girl? He hadn't. He'd waited there with her, holding her hostage. Hoping for Haggler Lee's return so he could have Lee perform his ceremony. And then he would have been ritualistically murdered like all the others. But he'd been interrupted. Suk-ja had earlier tipped off Mr. Yun's thugs that Ernie and I thought Haggler Lee would be the next victim. Yun's thugs barged in. But the brother ran to the balcony and escaped down the vine-covered trellis. That's why the window was broken outwards and the vines had been pulled down to the ground. The man they sought had vanished. Yun's bodyguards hoped the serving girl knew something. They tortured her with burning cigarettes. Nothing. So they killed her.

Could I prove all this? Probably not. I'd report my suspicions to the Korean police, but what was the chance of justice being done?

Ai-ja gazed down at the police cars below.

"So," she said. "They will hang us."

She was smiling when she said it. Her smile seemed saintly.

I glanced at her, then at her brother. He was dazed, kneeling. A few feet from him lay the bloody corpse of Yun Guang-min, his uncle. I knew what I had to do.

"We have a few minutes," I said.

"For what?" Ernie asked.

"I'll show you."

I fired a shot downhill. The policemen crouched.

"What?" Ernie said. "Are you nuts?"

"Stay back, you bastards!" I fired again.

This time the KNPs scurried back to the cover of their vehicles and began radioing headquarters.

"What the hell's wrong with you?" Ernie screamed.

"Just a few minutes," I said. "That's all I need."

"For what?"

Ernie's mouth fell open, but he didn't try to stop me as I sloshed in the mud back toward the burial mound.

I grabbed Ai-ja by her thin arms and dragged her over to her brother. Together, we helped him up and walked him over to the mound with the photograph of their deceased mother. In the ruckus, the photo had been knocked over. I set it upright and stood the smiling woman and her brother on either side. The KNP radio squawked below. I resumed my position in front of the photo. They both faced me.

"They're coming up the hill again," Ernie said.

"Hold them back!" I shouted.

Ernie's eyes widened. "You're nuts!"

"Keep them back!"

"Okay, okay."

Ernie turned and fired a wild shot over their heads. Police shouted and sloshed in the mud.

"They gone?" I asked.

"Not gone. But they won't move out from behind their vehicles for a while."

I turned back to Ai-ja.

"Go ahead," I said. "Say the words."

She was confused at first, but then she seemed to understand. Haltingly, she started to speak.

She chanted the words of contrition. I fell to my knees in the mud. She continued to smile, speaking of all the sacrifices her mother had made and how the entire world had turned its back on her. When she finished, I performed the *seibei* as it was supposed to be performed—bowing solemnly again and again, taking my time.

When I was done, I stared up at her and her brother. She was crying, but still smiling. Her brother's face was twisted, as if he couldn't believe what he was witnessing. I looked away and stared at the photograph of their mother held between them.

"I'm sorry," I said to it. "On behalf of my countrymen, I apologize. We were wrong, very wrong, to treat you and your son and your daughter as badly as we did. We should've taken care of you. It was our responsibility, but we didn't live up to our responsibility. For that, I shall always be ashamed. And I humbly apologize."

I bowed again.

I rose to my feet, and waited. Their heads were bowed.

"You don't have to hang," I said.

She looked at me, a quizzical expression on her face.

In answer, I pointed toward the cliffs behind us.

"The Yellow Sea," I said.

For the first time since I had seen her that night in the King Club when she drugged my drink, the taut flesh of her face relaxed. The smiling woman dropped her smile. She looked at me, face calm, lips straight. She was radiantly beautiful.

Her brother looked back and forth between us, more confused than ever.

Facing me, she lowered herself to her knees and bowed her forehead three times into the mud. When she rose, she said, "Thank you."

She smiled again. A real smile. Not one of madness. I savored it, like the beautiful face of the autumn moon.

She grabbed her brother's hand, pulled him toward her, and hugged him. He embraced her.

Below us, doors slammed. Men shouted to one another. A half dozen sloshed through mud, heading uphill.

Ernie stood awkwardly, holding his .45, glancing back and forth between me and the smiling woman. "What are you going to do?" he asked.

"They'll decide," I said.

Ai-ja nodded to Ernie and whispered a little thank you. Holding her brother's hand, she stepped toward me and put her hand on my shoulder, stretched to her full height and kissed me gently on the cheek. I felt the lingering softness of her lips. She and her brother walked away from us. Away from the KNPs.

Hand in hand, sister and brother walked toward the cliffs overlooking the rocks below. The storm clouds had cleared once again, and the Chusok moon shone brightly in the starry sky.

They paused. Yun Ai-ja and her brother gazed off into the distance. They seemed to take a deep breath. Hands joined, they stepped over the edge.

22

"Are you Sueño, George, no middle initial, on temporary assignment to the Criminal Investigation Detachment under the provisions of Eighth Army Supplement to Army Regulation 250-17, paragraph five?"

"Yes, sir."

"And are you aware of your rights under the Uniform Code of Military Justice while being charged with misappropriation of government property in conjunction with a Report of Survey?"

"Yes, sir. I am."

"And was the weapon in question lost in the line of duty?"

"No, sir."

"And has the weapon been recovered?"

"Yes, sir."

"Intact and in serviceable condition?"

"Yes, sir."

"Therefore we can waive replacement charges."

His name was Major Wardman, a quartermaster officer
assigned as the disinterested party to conduct a Report of Survey
concerning my lost .45. He had broad shoulders and a big square
head, and the collar of his dress green shirt was one size too
small. As he leaned over the paperwork, he licked his lips and
squinted, filling in each block of the carbon-copied forms with
meticulously printed block letters.

"However," Major Wardman continued, "you are responsible
for the misappropriation of the government property and its sub-
sequent use in multiple felonies. How do you plead?"

"Guilty."

"Do you waive court-martial jurisdiction?"

"Yes, sir."

"And you accept punishment as outlined under the provisions of Article 15 of the Uniform Code of Military Justice? To
wit: Thirty days confinement to quarters, loss of one month's pay,
and extra duty for thirty days to run concurrently with previous-
ly mentioned confinement."

"I do, sir."

"Sign here."

I scribbled my name.

"In the future," he said, "watch the drinking."